URBANE

Stonehouse Publishing Inc. is an independent
publishing house, incorporated in 2014.

Cover painting by Samantha Walrod.
Cover design and layout by Elizabeth Friesen.
Printed in Canada

Stonehouse Publishing would like to thank and acknowledge
the support of the Alberta Government funding for the arts,
through the Alberta Media Fund.

Alberta
Government

National Library of Canada Cataloguing in Publication Data
Anna Marie Sewell
URBANE
Novel
ISBN 978-1-988754-44-4
First edition

URBANE

A NOVEL BY
ANNA MARIE SEWELL

HAZEL: FIST-FIRST

If only I had just punched her in the face.

I really wanted to, had balled up my fist as soon as the light dawned. The trouble is I was shocked by the state of her. And it stopped me.

HAZEL: BEARS

The thing is, sometimes I wake up and I just want to see bears. I just want to be where I look out the window and there might be deer, or moose, or an elk. Not junkies. Not Kevin the idiot with the lawn-mower and nothing better to do than roam the boulevards mowing city grass for nothing, like a relict teenager who never graduated from driving up and down the neighbourhood streets.

Not the City crews haphazardly watering this tree or that, all of the trees desperate for water, not because of climate change, but because public good demanded that the streets and sidewalks be torn out and rebuilt, and all the elms got their roots smashed and bashed and trashed. I don't want to hear Jenny down the street hollering at her sister or her neighbours, her voice hoarse and familiar as a crow.

I tell myself it is okay. I enumerate who lives here with me. Crows, for one. And ravens, not that you can tell a crow from a raven unless they stand together, ours not being those huge Northern ravens. But we have merlins. And pigeons. And blue jays. And the magpies, those loud and entitled devils. Sparrows, too. Chickadees. Geese live here, ducks, pelicans up in the Hermitage. But no bears.

I miss bears.

I tell myself not to forget coyotes and rabbits. Bucketloads of them. There was a cougar spotted on a golf course a couple summers back. I've seen poop in the woods that made me suspect a bear was near. So, why do I miss the bears some mornings? Why do I feel like I lost everything that matters when I moved into the city?

I shake my head.

This kind of land-sick moroseness is the sort of woo-woo shit Sandra lives. Not me. I have it firm in my mind and spirit–every place on Earth is on earth, you are always on the land. It just doesn't feel right some days, and some days I almost want to run back to the farm. But there is no farm to run back to, thanks to Sandra.

Okay, if I'm honest, thanks to me, too.

And that fucking George.

I mean, I promised Dad we'd never sell the land. And Frank and Sandra agreed, when I got married first, that George and I should live there. And I was not entirely unhappy at first.

I look back at that person and I feel like I don't even know her, and she is definitely not me.

How can she be me? Eighteen years old, too stupid to know better than to be dazzled by someone paying attention to me. Sure, it made sense that Sandra should live with us, too. After all, I was not a farmer. Not like her.

She was always the one who knew how to make things grow.

I can't say what I was good for.

I can't always remember clearly what happened in those years.

How it came to be that I ran away with my kids.

That I left Sandra there.

That I tried to make a family with George.

That I was relieved when he found The Embryo.

That he had the nerve to turn up at the farm, demanding his rights. *His dower rights*, he said.

And Sandra didn't fight him.

She made a deal, whereby she got to go out to the little cabin on the corner of the land whenever she wanted, and he and the Embryo got the farm.

I'll never understand it.

***

'It's simple, Hazel,' says Sandra. 'I was alone on the farm. Frank was so busy–'

'Being Super Indian of the Academy,' I nod. She flushes.

'Well… yeah, okay,' Sandra doesn't like it when I critique Frank.

'You and the girls, you were better off in the city.'

She waves her hand to stop my protest.

'No, really, Hazel,' she says. I know she's right. I just can't stand it when she's so fucking magnanimous about it. What does she know? She doesn't know I wake up missing bears.

DEVIN: BEAR AT SEA

Devin wakes up in a cold sweat. The morning light slowly dissolves the lingering fragments of the dream–again, *LeWayne shouting and running after Rabbit. His knife in the dream world is a scimitar, shining with its own light, pulling him away out of sight. The wind in the dream shrieks and shrills, many voices wordlessly taunting, mocking, mourning. LeWayne runs. Devin lumbers after him, out of breath, his legs useless logs, feet slipping in bloody grass–*

Devin tastes sulphur on his tongue as he lies blinking in his own room. He can't tell this to Sandra. He can't tell this to Father Efren.

He remembers the funeral, Father Efren presiding, LeWayne's brother pressing an envelope into the priest's hands after, the priest shaking his head, hooking his chin toward the straggling remnants of LeWayne's family. Devin doesn't need to hear what they're saying to know the gist of it–LeWayne's brother too proud to let his little brother go out unpaid, the priest telling him to use the money to take care of their ragged and broken mother, the messy-haired little sisters hunching around her bewildered and adrift.

Remembering that, Devin feels the rage again–*How useless both men!* The brother who was no fit stand-in for a real father; the priest who could bury people but not keep them from dying.

Devin considers Rabbit. He tries very hard, lying in the quiet early morning, to remember exactly what he saw: LeWayne had a knife–not a scimitar, just a stupid hunting knife he'd gotten from somewhere and had been showing off.

As if you know how to hunt.
As if he knows how to skin a deer.

Cody and Tomlin mocked LeWayne, but their eyes glittered with envy and a little bit of awe.

HAZEL: HOME TRUTHS

'Go out and talk to him,' she says, the soul of reason. When I frown, she adds, 'Do you want me to come along?'

'God, you are so fucking stupid, Sandra!'

Sandra's broad face darkens.

'You think I want to have to ask this–anything?!–of you?'

'Exactly. Too fucking good for me. What could I possibly know or have to give to you, Ms. Perfect?!'

'Jesus, Hazel, pull your head out of your ass for just a minute, will you!'

We're both yelling.

Sandra doesn't usually yell.

Too late.

She's gone.

And I'm the asshole, again.

I stand there in my kitchen and shake my head at myself. My sister came to me for help and I pissed her off so bad that she, madam peace and love and fucking harmony, slammed my door on the way out.

I put my boots on and clump morosely up the street. She doesn't live too far away, but it sure feels like a long walk. I don't go to her door when I get there though. I know where she'll be, round back in her garden. I don't know what to say, exactly, but I hope she'll give me a break, let me try to set it right. I'm not mad at her. Not exactly. Not exactly at her. Like I know she's not exactly mad at me. Or not only at me. Or not only mad.

It's a sister thing. We've both been through some stuff, and we've both got chips on our shoulders. *At least I don't have any illusions about mine*–I catch myself thinking. *Stop that now, Hazel*, I tell myself. *It does not help.*

And your sister, who never asks for help, is asking for your help.

So, I push through the gate, and find her sitting in a heap in the arbour thing way in the back, lit by fairy lights–fairy lights, for God's sake. If I'm honest, it's kind of awesome, especially since I know she built it all by hand, with some help from Devin and his reprobate friends. Speaking of whom.

I scuffle my feet, clear my throat, grunt out 'Sorry about that, Sis.'

She shrugs and grunts in return, just a sound.

'Look,' I say, 'the thing is, Devin is bound to go through a hard time. His friend was murdered and he witnessed it. He got questioned by the police–'

'I was there!' Fuck. Sandra is not just in a heap, she's crying. I pull myself together.

'Yeah. You were. Look. You did just fine. Right. Just like you did bringing him up. God. He's a good kid.'

'I always thought you figured you could do it better, being a *real* mother and all.' It's dark among the fairy lights, but I can tell she's pointedly not looking at me.

'Yeah, well. I always figured you thought there was no way I could handle one more. Anyhow, Frank and Evelyn named you as Devin's guardian, so that's that. And you did fine.'

She turns her head now.

'But he's not fine, Hazel.'

'I know.'

'And the garden…he's always come to the garden when he's got troubles, you know?'

'Come to you.'

'Yeah. Come to me. And now he just gets mad and storms off.'

I light up a smoke. She doesn't even complain, barely waves the smoke away. There are a few mosquitoes up late and beginning to snoop and whine around us.

'What's he got planned, now that he's done high school?'

'I don't know. He won't even talk about that anymore. Just gets mad and stomps off.'

At least we're talking, I think, and I try to keep my head.

'Look,' I say, 'part of this is just his age, you know that, right? Just the moment when he has to choose a path in life. That's not the easiest.'

'How was it for your girls?'

'Huh,' I say. 'Well…Frankie was easy. She enrolled herself in university. She applied for scholarships. She just walked on out the door and into her life as if she'd never had a question in her mind for one red minute. And now she's got this big research fellowship and she doesn't even tell me what it's all about, just that it's Ethnomusicology and she'll be traveling around for nine months, and she'll write.'

'Missy went to Korea, remember?' says Sandra.

Then she falls silent for a little too long. I have to do more than just brag about my girls. I have to 'fess up a little.

'It kind of scared me, you know, when she did that. I mean, what do I know from Korea? And Missy, well, she's always been a tough kid, but God, you know, that society? So chauvinist. I read all these stories about rape and–'

'Hazel,' Sandra interrupts me. I just boggle at her open hand.

'You got one to spare?' She says, as if she's never bitched me out for smoking, never thrown it in my face that it probably helped kill our dad, our brother…

I shake out a smoke, she lights it, takes one drag and then just holds the cigarette, letting the smoke rise.

'Yeah, but anyhow,' I continue, 'you know what Dad always said. The world is tough, but we're made for it.'

Sandra takes another drag, doesn't even wheeze.

'But were you really surprised when she said she wanted to go?'

I blow smoke, ease my shoulders. Sandra's unheaped herself and we're talking almost like we used to.

'Nah, suppose not,' I admit. 'Missy always liked a challenge, and Korea solo was that, for sure.'

'She had a pretty good example, after all. You never backed down from anything.'

'Pff,' I say, blowing smoke, at a loss for words. That's just not true, and she knows it. But we're talking, for the first time in a long time, and as the blue smoke curls up between us, we bumble along, taciturn and stiff.

We arrive at knowing that we'll have to figure out a job for the boy, to give him purpose and help shift him out of too much introspection. If, and only if, he says he wants to go away, I'll get my girls to help him figure that out. There are programs, internships, study things. Maybe he can go to Africa, and my old friend Minkah can find something for him to do.

Sandra doesn't return to the idea that brought her to my door, made me call her stupid, the notion of getting the farm back and him holing up there to heal. She's probably seen that that's unrealistic. I don't mention it again, either, because I'm starting to wonder if maybe it's Sandra who needs it. For all that she seems to be so involved in urban planning reform, in grassroots work with the Garden Network and so on, maybe she misses the land, and its certainty. Wasn't that what she'd said she thought it would give Devin, certainty?

And as I walk home that night, my boot heels clicking on the sidewalk, I look around the same old streets and wonder if maybe I could stand to get back to the land. I move off the sidewalk, let my feet fall as silently as possible in the grass. Tears well up. Yeah, I'm mourning, too–for my brother, my nephew, for every stupid one of us, and for the hulking dog who used to soft-foot by my side. Not that he was quiet. Nope, that asshole would probably say something stupid right now if he was here, so better that he's gone.

Spider who was also Jim, dog and man, a person battling against demons both internal and external, who'd come into my life through a vision and showed me some things. One thing to consider yourself the inheritor of a culture and worldview that means you comprehend the world as a living being, and All My Relations and all that. In my life before Jim, being Indigenous had mostly meant staying clear of the labels people 'round here seem almost desperate to stick on you, to make you other than simply human. Being half-Polish meant knowing those labels included a whole extra layer of labels used to exclude you.

I'd had to learn not to let people label me. I'm not a fucking piece of fruit, am I? I'd carried my inheritance on my own terms, and never thought too much about the magic of its mythology. And that's a fair way to get by. That worked for me until I came home and found the mythology sitting on my sofa, his feet up on my coffee table. When you actually live with a shapeshifter... I don't know. I shrug, walking alone in the dark, answering a question nobody has asked me: *What's it like to live with a werewolf?*

First off, I'd tell them he was a dog. I've thought about that some, since Jim. My dad and his cousins from the Rez had ruined my sleep as a kid with their stories of wicked people who turned, not into noble wolves, but into cunning dogs, and did all sorts of evil.

Jim was a dog.

And he knew those stories, too; and he understood he'd fucked up big time when he realized he was a dog, literally.

We cremated Jim's body, if you want to know, and Maengan and Missy drove his ashes back East to Ontario, put them to rest in his home territory.

About the inquest into his death, less said the better.

He was killed by officer Joshua Campeau, Amiskwaciy Police Service, who died in the altercation. Just another Indigenous mutt gone astray.

Huh. You could say that about both of them.

DEVIN: GROUNDING

Devin says less and less to Sandra. His mornings are too cloudy after nights of wild dreams he does not want to discuss with his Auntie, so he tries to avoid her in the mornings. She is so busy these days, running off to her big project, bubbling about it when she gets home.

'Sawitsky is great. Perfect for the job,' she says to Devin, describing the manager they hired today. 'She has a degree in horticulture from UBC, studied Japanese design in Kyoto, and she's farm-raised, from the Peace Country.'

She says *Peace Country* with respect bordering on awe, and Devin thinks of it like he has since his smallest childhood, as a mythic land where serenity grows. He knows that's foolish. He's met cousins from the Peace Country, and a harder-headed, more pragmatic bunch he's never seen. Plainspoken to the edge of crudity, loud laughers, quick to lash out at perceived foolishness, they charged the air around them just by striding into the room.

In their presence, Devin stayed quiet and listened while they'd played cribbage with his father. He'd never seen anyone else scoff openly at his father, dismiss his lofty pronouncements and laugh through the night with him, the cards clicking and flipping, ribald trash talk and silly jokes peppering the air as they traded wins and losses on the board, and delivered the news of the north.

Devin remembers one of the cousins, big like him, calling to him when he tried to slip away to bed.

'Hey. Get in here, kiddo.'

He'd hesitated.

His father said, 'Let him go. Boy should be in bed.'

'No,' said the cousin, fixing his black-brown eyes on Big Frankie. His father shut up, dropped his gaze. The big man turned his moon-face back toward Devin, and cracked a smile.

'Now, come on over here.' He lifted one mighty arm, still grinning, and his eyes reeled Devin in. The boy leaped and landed against the big man's broad body, and closed his eyes instinctively.

He knew. This man saw him. And he hugged back as hard as he could, because he'd seen something, too, in those big round eyes–a pain and gentleness underneath the gruff. Devin clung to the big cousin, who patted his back, holding on loosely until Devin let go first. Stepping back, Devin saw tiny pinprick holes in the man's t-shirt. The man noticed.

'That's from my work,' he said seriously, man to man. 'Welding.'

'Oh.'

'Man's work,' he said, jutting his chin a bit. And then he nodded at Devin's father. 'Your dad does man's work too. Just a different kind.'

And the man laughed, and tapped Devin's shoulder with a paw.

'Now,' he said, 'you got hugs for the other cousins?'

Devin had looked around the table, overcome again.

'It's okay,' said another cousin, winking one hazel eye at the boy, 'no pressure.'

And Devin had dithered a moment.

'How about a handshake?' said the hazel-eyed cousin, and Devin had shyly circled the table, his hand engulfed in broad, blunt hands. His father, with a glance flicked at the big man, opened his arms, and Devin quickly, shyly ducked inside, pressing his cheek to the ribbon shirt.

'Good night, my boy,' his father's voice had been oddly soft.

Devin had slept that night in dreams of broad vistas, fields and rivers and the far blue of mountains, at peace.

HAZEL: POST-APOCALYPSE

Sometimes, I wonder about astrology.

I mean, mostly I am clear that it is bullshit. My mom used to buy those fucking scandal sheets at the supermarket checkout–the ancestors of YouTube and Twitter and all that–full of 'Shocking!' things about people we didn't know and would never know, presented to us as if it were gospel truth that we cared about some plastic person's plastic surgery or twelfth marriage or whatever.

I liked to read them for the Alien Abductions, if I'm honest.

And now I wonder, was that as random as it seemed then? I mean, maybe it was a way to connect to the lost stories from both sides of my family, the campfire stories, the late-at-night stories, the kind we only heard when dad's cousins came out from the old Rez.

But my mom knew some stories, too; just as old, just as mysterious. When I was two years old–I know this through family story repeated into quasi-memory–I was having a tough time in some way–feverish, bad sleep–and she brought my grandmother to do a ceremony.

The first time she told me this story, I was hooked, and I'd bug her to tell me every so often.

'What kind of ceremony?'

'A wax ceremony.'

'What does it do?'

'It shows you what is bothering a person.'

'How does it work?'

'You pour wax over someone's head–no, no, not on your actual head! You lean them over a bowl of water, and pour the hot wax past the top of their head. When it hits the water, it cools into shapes. The shape of the wax shows you your tormenter.'

'What shape did it show for me?'

'It showed a dog.'

So then everyone knew that was the spirit that was bothering poor little me.

At first, I was satisfied with this mystical answer.

But later, I thought to ask her how seeing the dog spirit shape in wax in the water solved anything.

She shrugged, defensive.

'I don't know how it works. It just did. She came, she poured the wax, pointed out the dog spirit there, and you stopped being bothered.'

Boy, if she'd lived to know how wrong she was.

I'm standing in my living room, just kind of blank. Jim is everywhere I look. And Spider.

Spider Jim, the were-dog who until recently shared my home.

When you're in it, you just live the situation. You don't analyze. You pour the wax.

But now, I look at the place he habitually sat, as a man. The place where he liked to curl in dog form. I remember the first day I caught him shape-shifted, how natural it seemed to just find him some clothes and get on with life.

But that's not normal, is it?

What is normal, anyhow?

I shake my head. I don't have time for this, really. Because if I really start to try to analyze my life, I will go stark fucking mad.

It might be too late by far.

The thing is, Spider Jim is dead.

***

But Maengan is not.

Maengan, my little cousin, distantly related, somehow my responsibility.

I saved his life, he says.

Yeah, well. Not exactly. I found him in a state, cleaned him up and kept my mouth shut when he didn't want people to talk about what happened. I could figure, by the state of him, that he'd been beaten up, maybe even sexually assaulted.

I did not know he'd been turned into a werewolf.

So bite me. How could I have known?

When he showed up at my house, I confess I really didn't know what to do. It forms a bond, doesn't it, when you help someone in extremis? But it doesn't mean you know what to do with them in ordinary time. And in the clear light of Amiskwaciy's sun, there was something odd about the boy. But how odd I did not know.

So I didn't do anything but be approximately polite.

As I say, I didn't know he'd become a werewolf.

And I also didn't know he'd take up with my oldest daughter.

Believe me, if you knew Missy, you'd maybe make the same mistake. She's a war mare, that one, not the kind who dates easily. I'd been wondering, if I'm honest, if she were gay, and just keeping her sex life her own business.

Fine by me.

But she's apparently seriously involved with Maengan. And that's a problem.

Not for the blood relative thing–the relationship is distant enough not to cause genetic problems, but…what if they have puppies?

I'm an asshole, aren't I?

I can't keep worrying the mental bone of this.

I call Shanaya.

Lately, we talk a lot.

She doesn't think I'm weird.

She can't, because after all, Shanaya holds aces in the game of weird; the woman is a part-time tiger.

I shake my head, standing there in my living room. And, as if on cue, she calls.

'Hey. Road trip?'

I sigh.

'I guess I'm driving? Should I pick you up at your office?'

'Sure,' she purrs.

I wish she wouldn't let her voice do that, it kind of creeps me out when I'm in this mood. She thinks it's funny.

Maybe she needs me as much as I need her. Someone who knows. Someone who likes her anyway. Someone with whom she can be herself, stripes and all. Don't we all need that?

DEVIN: EVERY CHILD

On the day before he graduates, Sandra takes Devin down to the civic garden project site and introduces him to Sawitsky. Casually, Sawitsky shows him around, and just as casually, asks him about aspects of gardening. Devin finds himself disarmed by the broad-bodied blonde woman, her ice-green eyes both shrewd and kind. It's soothing to talk about plants and the ways they grow, to let flow the years of knowledge he's picked up without thinking, all those seasons in his auntie's garden.

Sawitsky invites Devin and Sandra to join her for tea on the makeshift patio outside the Atco trailer where she keeps her temporary office. She thumps the wooden decking with her heel. 'Pallet from the brick place,' she says with a decisive nod. 'Works good.'

'You, look,' she says when they've done their tea. 'I've got a summer crew the City foisted on me, but come September 1st, you've got a job here. Deal?'

His memory flashes back to the Peace Country cousins, their plainspoken ways.

'Deal,' he says, and grasps her calloused hand in a quick, decisive shake.

***

He graduates, and there is a little Indigenous part to the ceremony. The Cree language class sings an Honour Song, playing drums painted orange and emblazoned with the motto 'Every Child Matters.' The school board-sponsored Elder gives every student a round moose hide brooch, beaded with the school logo superimposed on a medicine wheel.

As he receives his diploma and gets pinned, Devin looks out, not surprised to see his Auntie Sandra crying. Aunt Hazel is scowling, arms wrapped tight around herself. Missy and Maengan grin and wave. Frankie lets out a little whoop and flashes one hand up to the sky.

Devin completes his traverse of the stage, overcome by the understanding in a flash of how much this simple act–finishing high school–means not just to them, but to their memories of generations blighted by the Residential Schools, and all the other ways Indians got sifted out of the sandbox of belonging. Devin descends the stairs very carefully, his vision blurred by tears.

Everywhere, there are tears that day. Of joy, of pride, of farewell. But nobody there to cry for LeWayne. Every child matters. But they still drop out. Still go wrong. Still die.

Devin finds Cody, who somehow made it through, and they look for Tomlin's people. Nobody there. So they go together and find the principal, pick up Tomlin's scroll and moose hide pin. They return to the reception in the gym, and Sandra catches his eyes right away. Frankie folds Cody in a quick hug, and spies his mom standing awkwardly nearby. Frankie hugs her too.

'You must be so proud,' she says to them both.

His Aunt Hazel–he's never called her 'Auntie,' he realizes with a start–brings a tray of food and pop and passes it around. Devin is distracted a moment by how odd it feels to see Hazel serving folks, acting the role he's accustomed to seeing his Auntie Sandra perform. Sandra, mind you, is sitting down, her broad face beaming an agony of joy and sorrow.

Devin sits down next to her, reaches over, puts his arms around her. She wraps her arms around him hard.

'Your parents would be so proud,' she says, a little shaky. 'I'm sure they're watching today. You've made them so proud. And me.'

She holds on until Devin lets go.

'Hey, everyone,' he says, standing up. He catches Cody's eye, and Cody comes over and stands beside him, his second-hand suit a little rumpled.

'Thanks.'

'Thanks,' repeats Cody.

No more needs to be said. They are held in a circle of belonging. Then Devin holds up his hand.

'Me and Cody're gonna go now, okay? We're gonna find Tomlin.'

'You want us to come?' asks Missy.

'No,' says Devin quietly. 'No, that's okay. Little thing we gotta do ourselves, together.' And he holds up Tomlin's scroll and moose hide pin.

They find Tomlin's brother at home.

'I ain't seen Tommy today,' he says, rubbing a hand across the side of his head where the hair is shaved close. 'Who knows where he goes?'

He looks the boys up and down, his eyes catching on the beaded moose hide emblem on Devin's lapel. He reaches out and flicks it with a finger.

'Huh,' he says. 'What next? Whiteman school got nothing to do with our ways.'

He shakes his head.

'You got a message for Tommy?'

'No, man, it's okay,' says Cody. 'Just tell him we said hey.' And he pivots, leads Devin away.

Devin hears Tomlin's brother behind them as they walk away.

'Huh. As if.' The door closes with a sad and empty click.

'Now what?' Says Cody as they walk slowly along. The sun is hot, blinding where it strikes down through the boulevard elms.

Devin shrugs.

'Guess it's just you and me,' he says, and heaves a big sigh. The backpack on his shoulder emits a dull clink, and Cody cocks an eyebrow at him questioningly. He has his own backpack. Devin shakes his head with a grim little smile.

'It's just ginger beer.' He says.

Cody shakes his head.

'Me, I brought the good stuff.'

Devin says nothing in reply, and they walk on, wending through the streets and alleys via places they know Tomlin might be hanging out in, adding miles to their journey.

They reach the graveyard after eight, with plenty of slanting golden daylight to spare.

And he's there.

Facedown on LeWayne's grave, Tomlin looks dead in the reddening sun. Devin grabs Cody's sleeve to hold him back from running to the grave.

Tomlin has heard their approach, and swept his hands up to cover the back of his head, reflexively hunching his thin shoulders.

'Hey man,' says Cody softly. 'It's us.'

'Go 'way,' snaps Tomlin, half-rolling into a fetal curl with his back to them.

'Come on, man,' says Cody. 'It's us. We're here for him, too. Get off that grave and come here, man.'

'Fuck off.'

They sigh. Devin lowers his pack to the ground, opens it, pulls out a cheap dollar store picnic blanket, plaid nylon over crinkly plastic.

'We got food,' says Cody, passing his pack to Devin.

'Fuck off.'

As Devin pulls out the bag of pastries scavenged from the grad reception, Cody stands with fists on his narrow hips, staring at Tomlin on the grave.

'Look man,' he says, stalking across to Tomlin's side. 'You ain't the only one lost LeWayne.'

'Fuck off. Wanna die.'

'Well you sure as fuck don't own this grave. Shove over.'

And he drops down and pushes Tomlin hard from behind.

'Fuck OFF!' Tomlin screams, sliding in the dirt. He rolls and grabs at Cody, and they scuffle and grunt and gasp until Tomlin slackens in Cody's grip and begins to sob. Cody holds him then, two bereft boys wailing in the ruddy light.

After a few minutes, they pull themselves together, help each other up, stagger over to where Devin has laid out an ad hoc picnic. Leftovers from the reception, a clamshell of strawberries, his large bottle of ginger beer, and beside it, Cody's mickey of vodka.

He's got four plastic Ikea glasses, and as they settle, Tomlin wipes his face and focuses on these.

'Orange one for LeWayne,' he says. 'I call green for me.'

They don't really know what to do, but they do it anyway. They fill their cups and lift them.

'To LeWayne,' they chorus, and drain their cups.

They pour vodka and ginger beer into the orange kid's cup, and each of them takes it in his hands in turn, and speaks to it.

'Fuck, LeWayne,' says Cody, going first, 'brother. Why'd you have to go and get killed?'

'Brother,' says Tomlin, His voice trembles and his hand shakes, but he takes a deep breath and lifts his eyes, 'I miss your stupid fucking face.'

Devin holds the orange cup for a long silent moment, then sighs.

'Me too, LeWayne. What they said.'

And he holds onto the cup while he clambers to his feet, somehow not spilling any. He flicks his chin toward the grave, and Tomlin crawls over, cup in one hand, and sits to one side. Cody comes over, refills Tomlin's cup, then moves around to the other side, sits down and pulls the other cups out from under his arm, pours a shot into each one. Devin sits back down at the foot of the grave. He lifts the orange cup, his hand shaky, so it splashes a little.

'This one's for you, LeWayne. For all the times.'

And he pours some drink into the dirt, and without thinking, passes the cup to Cody, who pours and passes to Tomlin, who empties the last of the drink. The sun chooses that moment to touch with one finger the tilted tin marker at the head of the grave, the little numbered sign that will be all that marks this grave until and unless LeWayne's family can afford something permanent.

Tomlin reaches over, tears streaking down his dirty face, and straightens the marker.

'Aw, brother,' he mutters, eyes red. And he suddenly throws back his head and howls, not like a wolf, but a purely human cry of despair and loss. Cody and Devin close their eyes and join in, a long wordless and wild wail that reverberates in the evening sun.

The sounds of the city seem a world away.

There is only them, a broken circle of brotherhood, wailing and pounding the earth with their fists. It becomes a heartbeat drum rhythm and they chant, and Cody's voice drags them toward the melody of the Honour Song from their school. Ragged and wordless, they sob and wail out their grief.

In the reverberating silence after the song, a crow calls. And another answers.

Tomlin wants to leave his moose hide pin at the grave, but Devin presses it into his hand.

'No, man,' he says, his eyes a little more owlish than usual, his voice unaccustomed to vodka, but his intent water clear.

'Tommy, you wear this. You earned it.'

'Wear it for him,' says Cody. 'Like a promise. Live for him.'

'And for you. And for us,' says Devin.

They shoulder their packs and put Tomlin between them.

'Yeah, you fucker,' says Cody, as he slings an arm around Tomlin's waist, 'Live for us.'

'Fuck you,' says Tomlin, staggering. He turns and rubs his teary, snotty face against Devin's shoulder, then turns and head butts Cody aside, pulls out of their embrace.

He looks back at the boy's grave behind them, then turns and stands up, a little bit a man among men.

'I'm living for me.'

He looses a tiny echo of song into the air, hiccups.

A crow calls.

They laugh in the falling darkness.

HAZEL: FARM FIRST

So Shan and I, we're going on a road trip today, out to look at the Farm. It used to be mine. And when I got divorced, I sold it to my sister, cheap. Only she fucked up, and didn't get the dower rights clause clear.

Okay, I fucked up there, too. Neither of us knew that George would be weasel enough to take it to court, to claim that I'd sold it against his will, to claim he had rights to the land as my husband, because he technically still was then, even though he'd shacked up with an embryonic waif called Édith… It's a long story and it makes me mad, and for some stupid reason, I told Shanaya about it, and now, she's got me thinking it may be possible to reclaim my land.

Did I mention she's a full-time lawyer, in addition to the tiger thing? And she figures it's worth at least going out and talking with George and his Embryo wife.

We get to the farm, and find nobody home. But nobody. It's totally quiet. We sit in the car in the yard until a pickup arrives, with some weasel-faced guy who struts over and stands there like he's about to take a piss on the car before Shan rolls down the window and asks, 'Is Mr. Jones home?'

'Who's asking?' he blusters.

'His ex-wife,' I say, opening my door and standing up out of the car. What is with this guy? He's barely taller than me, skinny as a teenage Banty rooster, but old enough to know better. I stride around the front of the car and stick out my hand to him. Startled, he responds in kind and I give him a wring-the-piss-out-of-it shake and drop his hand like it's a dirty dick.

'And you are?' I drawl.

'Anson. His land manager.' I try to hide my shock. 'Mr. Jones ain't here. He's on a business trip. Won't be back 'til probably next week. You should call ahead. Save yourself the gas.' And he turns to strut back to his truck, clearly trying for a power move of dismissal.

I don't answer, just go back round and get in the car.

'You heard the man,' say to Shanaya. 'Let's go.' And as we turn around and head out up the drive, I cut him a wave, casual as you like.

'You know that fellow?' Shanaya asks.

'Nope,' I say, 'never seen that ass-pimple before in my life.'

'Language!' Shan quips, but she's grinning evilly, too.

'I did phone,' I say. 'He didn't answer, but he also didn't reply to tell me he's away.'

She quirks a brow.

'I have his number because I got it in the settlement.' Shake my head. 'Actually, because Sandra had the stupid idea it might matter somehow sometime to be able to get in touch with him, if for any reason the girls needed me to. What reason would that be? They never even bring him up.'

Shanaya mms noncommittally.

'Say,' I say, 'turn left here, and follow this road.' We turn onto a little-used road that wanders toward some scrubby looking brush. The road dips, peters out and becomes a bumpy grass track, admittedly a little more in-use than I expected. We make a couple slaloms round little rolls of land, then we are there, in what passes for a yard, tall spindly grass with a few deer tracks through it, the mixed forest ringing this little slightly cupped clearing, and on one rim of the cup, the cabin. Sandra always said this site had good feng shui. I always said she was full of shit. But it can't be denied, looking at it, that this place has something.

'It's beautiful!' Shanaya cries softly, reverently.

I shrug.

'Yeah, I guess.'

She looks at me like I'm crazy. I hate that, how all my friends get that look sometimes, like I'm the one saying worshipful things about a cabin on the corner of some land on the buttock edge of the Gnarly Hills.

It's a nice cabin. My uncles built it, and then they helped me update it when I was a young married woman. I sigh. I genuinely loved this little bit of land, this cabin, this peace. I turn my face away. Far too late, far too much water under too many bridges, to get all sentimental about the could've beens, the dreams of some girl that I guess was actually me, though that sure doesn't seem likely as seen from this moment in time.

***

FYI, we didn't break in here. Sandra had a key George forgot she had. To be fair to Sandra, she just gives me her key. But does she have to talk in that gentling-the-wild-beast tone to me?

I had forgotten it, too. For a miracle, it still opened the little back door of the little cabin.

DEVIN: ALL APOLOGIES

LeWayne's death fades from the community mind swiftly; not least because of the big news out of the Vatican. The Pope himself is coming to Canada to apologize for damage done by the Residential Schools the Roman Catholic Church helped run. The Pope is coming, not just to Canada, but specifically to Amiskwaciy.

What is it about this grungy little prairie city that makes it important enough to be the first stop on what is being billed as a Pilgrimage of Penitence? For one thing, there is the mighty community of Maskwacis, whose leadership was key in making this happen, who went to the Vatican, (not the first delegation to do so, but the ones who somehow got through), somehow caused the Pope to decide to come and ask forgiveness.

Among the Catholic community, there is both a buzz of hope and a fizzing unease. Among Devin's family, scoffing and skepticism are the tone of the day.

'Is he going to repeal *Terra Nullius*?' Frankie asks rhetorically, as they sit around Missy's kitchen table.

'Pfft,' Maengan and Missy scoff in unison.

'Of course not,' adds Missy. 'This is just some sort of empty theatre, again.'

They are the TRC generation, who came of age during that remarkable journey of years when Residential School survivors and their descendants, and the relatives of those who died, came to meetings across the land and testified about their experiences.

Missy and Frankie had gone and volunteered at the Truth and Reconciliation Commission event in Edmonton, the last of the series; that meeting was the catalyst for the reclamation of the city's Indigenous name. The TRC put Amiskwaciy on the map, literally.

But still, there are bigger, more important cities.

'Father Efren says the Pope's going to Lac Ste. Anne,' offers Devin.

'Huh,' say Missy and Maengan in tandem.

'Did you know,' says Frankie, 'that lake was a spiritual gathering place long before the RCs laid claim to it?'

Devin nods owlishly. He hadn't known, but it makes sense.

'In fact,' Frankie continues, 'there used to be a pilgrimage trail that ran from Pigeon Lake up to Lac Ste. Anne. There's a sacred spring at Pigeon Lake. I got to see it with my friend Jess. She was looking to buy this really cool house there, and asked if I wanted to go see it. I don't know whether she ended up buying the house, but we took a walk with the woman selling it–an anthropology prof– who showed us the sacred spring, told us the Cree folks used to use that place for healing.'

'We should go see it,' says Missy.

'Well, the thing is,' says Frankie, 'there's a Christian retreat centre next to it, now; and also, a cemetery, built just uphill. So the water's not potable anymore.'

'Typical,' snaps Missy. 'Don't suppose the Pope's going to stop in there and bless the water, maybe apologize for letting his people fuck it up with their dead?'

They shake their heads. They know.

'I doubt the pontiff knows anything about that,' says Frankie.

The four of them fall to talking about possibilities, about what it would take to revive that trail; not to wait for any Popes or officialdom to grant leave to do so, but to simple go out and search, on foot, for the way–for any way–to reconnect the two lakes, to make again a trail on which people might journey, alone or in groups, seeking to reconnect to the living land.

'We'd have to be inclusive about it,' says Frankie. 'Because that's the only way it would work, is if we get a bunch of people from different backgrounds to buy in.'

'Like they do with the Camino,' says Devin. 'Auntie Sandra goes every year.'

'Camino?' says Maengan.

'Camino Edmonton, they called it when it started. This journalist, Graham Hicks, and his friend started it as a way to get people using the River Valley trail system. Now they call it Amiskamino, officially, but Auntie says the old timers still just say The Camino.'

'It's five days, right?' says Frankie.

'Five days,' nods Devin. 'Some people camp, most do it like a day trip. I went with Auntie once.'

'So did I,' says Frankie, and they all stare.

'What? She asked me this year, I went. It was great. The end.' She shrugs and chuckles. Devin looks out the window. His Auntie went without him, never even asked him? He excuses himself, crosses to the bathroom, and just stands there in front of the humble mirror. Why didn't she ask him, this year of all years? He stares at himself in the mirror, then looks down, remembering. It was one more morning when he had shut her out, stopped just short of rude, but given her no room to engage with him, had wrapped his inchoate hurt around him and left her kitchen as fast as he could.

Still, he's discomfited by the realization that his Auntie had just found another companion, had reached out to someone she felt would fit with her and the ad hoc group of walkers at the core of the Camino. Devin shakes his head, splashes his face with water, pulls himself together.

***

Another evening passes with the four young people chatting and dreaming, gambling on cribbage and poker, until the small hours send them each homeward.

Devin declines Frankie's offer of a ride–where did she get a car? She winks and doesn't say.

'You sure?'

'Yeah, I need to walk,' says Devin, all owlish seriousness. Frankie gives him a side-on hug and slides into the car, and Devin sets off on foot.

He frowns and mutters to himself. What he didn't find a way to tell them was that he was going to be volunteering to help when the Pope came to town, because the diocese had informed Father Efren that, for whatever the reasons, the Pope had put their little inner city parish on his itinerary, and planned to make a stop to Sacred Heart Church of the First Peoples.

Devin agrees readily when Father Efren asks him.

'I don't know,' said the priest, 'What all the Diocese and the higher ups will want us to do if–if!–this turns out to really be a thing, but I'm parish priest, and surely it is my discretion as to whom I want helping to prepare the church, who will serve as ushers and so on. I want you there with me, Devin.'

Devin bobs his head, slightly bemused at the priest's mood. Father Efren generally crackles a little with pent up energy, but in Devin's experience, it's usually a kind of frustrated love raging against injustice. This new mood is a bit unsettling.

Devin has acted as usher before, for funerals. He remembers standing in the park beside his friend's dead body, numbly wondering what would happen, how boys like LeWayne got buried.

He bore the pall for LeWayne, carried his friend's body in the cheap casket, in the event buried with a simple ceremony paid for by donations made anonymously.

He knows that some of those donations came from Father E; and he knows better than to ask. He remembers Father Efren pressing an envelope into the shaky hands of LeWayne's sniffling mother, knowing that the envelop contains grocery store gift cards and preloaded Visa cards and cash money. He'd stifled the thought that LeWayne's mother would drink most of that gift.

It didn't matter. *It's the thought that counts*, wasn't that the cliché? But it didn't matter what thoughts were there either, neither thought nor drinking could change LeWayne's death, such a point-less, ugly death. Such a shrug from the world at large.

So Devin says yes, and goes home.

Over dinner, his Auntie Sandra is bubbling too, about this impending papal visit.

Devin frowns, too aware that his cousins don't share her optimism. He's pretty sure his Aunt Hazel doesn't either. And what would his father have said? Devin pokes at a green bean.

Sandra unconsciously cradles her liver and sighs when she talks about it, about how profoundly awe-inspiring it is that a bunch of survivors got together in 2007 and fought to a win at the Supreme Court, proving the harm done to them.

'And in recompense they asked, not a bunch of money like people always accuse Indians of doing, but for the establishment of a Truth and Reconciliation Commission. Years later, tears later, the truth not yet fully told, still they are able to persuade the Pope to come to Amiskwaciy.'

Devin tries out his own rhetoric.

'Auntie, do you think it might have been a mistake to push through the renaming of the city before the papal visit?'

She cocks her head in inquiry.

'Well,' he continues, repeating something one of the cousins had said, 'on the upside, it means he has to say *Amiskwaciy*, even if he doesn't learn a single stitch of Cree or any other language to greet us in.'

'Oh,' says Sandra, 'I hope they will do that, will at least teach him 'tansi' or something.'

'But on the downside,' Devin continues, 'he could use the revival of the city's old name against the survivors–*see, it wasn't so bad, you got access to true religion, and modernization, and you got your city's name changed, too. You are doing okay.*'

His aunt gives him a measured look, helps herself to more green beans.

'We *are* doing okay, when you think about it,' says Sandra. 'We survived. And yes, now we have our name. We are the only Amiskwaciy Waskahikan in the world.' Then she thinks a minute. 'Well, there's that tiny town of Amisk, and there's Beaverlodge up in the Peace Country, which would be Amisk Waskahikan in Cree, but we are the only Amiskwaciy on the map, anywhere. I think those old people would feel proud.'

Sandra waves a green bean in the air for a moment.

'Though I wish,' she says, 'they'd have chosen to spell it like it's said–A-misk-wah-chee.'

She lowers the bean.

'But I guess that would've made the change too easy. This way, my boy, the White bigots have something to complain about–it's too hard to say–and the Indigi-bigots have something to gloat about–who's the uneducated savages now, can't say our name? '

Devin stares, surprised by this sudden flash of bitter sarcasm.

Sandra shrugs and eats the bean.

'You'll just have to go and see for yourself. Me, I've got a meeting with Sawitsky and some of the City Planning moguls that day.'

***

The day the Pope arrives in Canada, Father Efren calls Devin to come on by. The priest looks at the earnest young man, turns and begins to pace around his rectory office. He fetches up against his battered desk, turns again, clamps his lips together and scowls.

'Look, Devin, I don't know what to say,' he begins. 'This whole thing is turning into a circus.'

The priest scrubs at his newly-shorn hair, his face red and heavy.

Devin takes in the priest's haircut, his jeans replaced by black slacks, and feels himself go dark.

'The thing is,' the priest continues, 'they are flapping on about the Holy Father having his own personal team of handlers and his own special guards. They travel with him everywhere. Specially trained and all. And it turns out I don't have a say here.' The priest clenches his fists at his sides.

Devin draws a deep breath.

'It's okay, Father E,' he says. 'You gotta do what you gotta do, right?'

'I do, Devin,' says the priest, 'but I don't gotta like it.'

They are standing on the rectory verandah, and now the priest gives in to impulse and pulls out his tobacco pouch to roll a smoke.

'They figure, though,' he says as he rolls, 'that they're going to set up an overflow in the gym.' He nods his head toward the low profile of the Sacred Heart School, closed in the early 2000s and made into a site for various community groups. The little gymnasium boasts a large screen and plenty of folding chairs.

The priest clears his throat.

'I don't feel right asking you, Devin,' he says. 'I wanted you with me in the main church...'

Devin shrugs.

'If you need someone to usher in the gym, I can do that,' he says.

He walks away feeling uneasy and slightly melancholy, but committed to show up, for Father E's sake, but also out of curiosity. What manner of man is this Pope, who made waves on his ascension by driving a tiny car and insisting on humble lodgings?

And what will he say? Will he mention *Terra Nullius*? Does he come compelled by the hundreds of graves coming to light at Church-run schools across the land? Does he feel the angry weight of those uncounted bones, or of the graves doubtless littered all around the world as the cost of conversion?

HAZEL: STORM

Shanaya shakes her head at me. She knows I'm holding out on her. We've been sitting at the table by the wood stove in the cabin for hours, playing cribbage, talking, kibitzing.

'I know you're hiding something, Hazel,' she purrs.

I shake my head, lead with a seven.

'Fifteen two,' she says, laying an eight, 'and I know you are. I can smell it.'

'Twenty-three for two,' I snap down my eight. 'Smell that.'

She snaps down her own eight–of course I should have figured she had another one.

'Thirty-one for eight,' she snarls softly, 'Now dish.'

I stare at my cards accusingly. As if they can help. The thing is, I need to talk about Maengan and Missy. But how do you tell your dear friend, a shape-shifter, that you don't like your daughter's boyfriend, also a shape-shifter? But on the other hand, I really need to know more about…certain practicalities…and so I need to find a way to ask Shanaya some very touchy things, without offending her… I squirm a bit in my chair, pinned by her golden gaze and my sense of doom. I don't like talking about sex at the best of times, and maybe I should let that sleeping dog lie…

Suddenly the door rattles and shakes. Fiercely. Desperately. Not the wind, though the night is stormy. Someone is there, trying to get in.

We jump up.

I blow out breath I didn't know I was holding, and step toward the door; here's a nice change from the tiger stalking my prejudices.

I reach the door just as it opens.

In a theatrical flash of lightning, a wild-eyed spectre stands, key in one hand, crouched in absolute terror. I feel my fist ball up to punch her in the face.

And lightning flares again. My jaw drops and I just freeze. And Shanaya grabs me and pulls me aside, and the figure leaps inside and slams the door.

'Help me! Please.' It gasps. And collapses in a heap.

Shanaya springs into action, dropping down to feel a thin wrist.

'Get a blanket, Hazel' she snaps.

I get the blanket.

When I return from the bedroom, Shanaya has half-carried the little figure over to the stove. She hooks a chair leg in passing, pulls it with her foot nearer to the stove. The figure flinches at the scraping sound.

Shanaya eases her onto the chair, and then begins to strip the drenched clothing from her unprotesting form.

Dear God, what in the actual fuck?!

Her back, her arms, her torso, are all marked with bruises. She doesn't try to stop us, just feebly lifts her legs one by one so we can pull off her boots and bloody socks, shifts her bony butt so we can pull the ruined trousers off her, hips and legs also bruised in great hideous welts.

She's only half-conscious as we wrap her and transport her to the sofa. Then Shan stokes up the wood stove, and we haul the sofa closer, with her slightness barely registering as weight.

'Window,' she gasps, her head snapping up as lightning glares through at us. I don't question it. I just go to pull tight the gap in the curtains–black out drapes. All of them, I see now in the dim light, also have heavy new sash locks and bars. I seal us into a security cocoon, circle back to the kitchen, lean on the counter and just gape a moment at the creature by the fire.

She's shaking so pitifully.

Shanaya gets the fire roaring, and sits chafing the woman's unre-sisting hands and feet, gently, one by one, then tucking them back into the heavy quilt she's brought to supplement my blanket.

Then as I rummage around for sugar or honey or anything sweet to put in the tea I'm brewing, Shanaya finds a towel and starts scrubbing the woman's stringy hair dry.

She stirs, at that, her head lolling a little, and suddenly speaks.

'Cut it off.'

Shanaya stops, and the woman looks round at her, says it again, rough and plain.

'My hair. Cut it off.' Her stark eyes, her skin so pale, she pulls the quilt tighter around herself.

She looks Shanaya in the eye. Shan nods, looks around.

'There are shears in that drawer,' the woman juts her chin to in-dicate where, and I move like I'm underwater and get the shears and hand them to Shanaya. She looks a question at me. I shake my head, quickly. No way I am touching her hair.

So, I just make the tea, while Shanaya hacks the cold wet locks from the woman's head. They fall like snakes, like rat's tails, like wax or entrails. The woman looks at me. She knows I won't do any-thing until she says what to do with her hair. She knows that about me.

'Burn it,' she says. 'Please.'

It doesn't take long to shear her, and I grab the broom, sweep up the hair, dump it obediently into the roaring stove, close the lid against the stink of burning hair.

By the time Shanaya's done, the woman has pretty much stopped shaking, and made inroads into the sweet tea.

She hasn't said anything else, though. And I sure as hell don't know what to say to her.

She stares at nothing, her eyelids drooping, and keeps starting awake again every time the thunder cracks. She looks around wildly, and Shan pets her shoulder. She's wrapped the wreckage of the near bald head with her big pashmina scarf, and it droops like an over-weight peony. Shan grabs the near empty mug from the woman's unresisting hand, and our unexpected guest is asleep.

Out cold more like.

'Wonder who she is?'

'It's *her.*'

'Her who?'

'Édith.'

'*The Édith?!*'

I just nod. Shanaya stares at me, and I shrug. I have no earthly idea why The Embryo has suddenly burst back into our lives, out of the storm.

***

In the morning, she's no less there, no less astonishing, no less Édith. In fact, she's up before me, and it's her rattling at the stove that wakes me. Padding into the main room, I stare at her.

She's so thin, her hacked-off hair poking out in all directions, and she's dressed in a shapeless ensemble of sweat pants and woolly sweater. I think it's a sweater. Either that or a *Zabeh* died and she skinned it. And she's humming. Some tune that tickles the back of my mind, can't place it, but its jaunty melancholy insinuates that I really should.

Watching her build up the fire, it strikes me I have always held in my mind that she's some helpless and decorative thing, but she is not. Bruises notwithstanding, she moves with capable, practiced ease, stoking it up, adjusting the dampers, at home in this rough-hewn rusticity.

Of course she's at home, Hazel. Isn't this her cabin? On her land? Or what she must have been thinking is her land all these years. Is she singing? 'No...rien de rien...' In French?

As if she hears me thinking–or it could be because I'm staring–Édith turns.

'Good morning,' she says softly. 'Shanaya is outside. She said she wants to check and see if I was followed. I'm not sure–'

'Oh,' I say, 'don't doubt for a second. If there's sign out there, she'll find it.'

'She doesn't look like the type–' she stops, a bit embarrassed, but we both understand.

'You'd be surprised,' I say.

What else can I say? I know how Shanaya looks, with her flowing hair, her big golden eyes, her feline elegance and urbane air of polish. I've also seen her other side, but you don't out your friends. Besides, Édith is the one who owes some explanations here.

'So,' I say, not sure where to begin, and I cover my confusion by going to the icebox. 'Do you want some breakfast?'

This is so awkward.

'This is so awkward,' she says, as if reading my thoughts. And I turn, and we just look at each other. Neither of us knows quite what to say, both of us bursting with questions, wary of getting into it. I take a deep breath. She takes a deep breath.

'Why are you here?' We speak together.

'You first.'

She laughs then, a little weakly. I've got the eggs out, so I just start cracking, filling the enamelled bowl, looking at the yolks and whites as if they matter more than anything at this moment. I've never been good at doing this one simple thing, cracking eggs into a bowl without getting shell in there. And I'm on form, and bits of shell bob in the viscous pool, like fragments of a shipwreck.

'I–' we both say it, still weirdly in sync.

'Jinx' she says then, and I meet her gaze, and damn it, those big eyes are brimming over with tears. She's shaking. What do I say?

If this were a sitcom, Shanaya would burst through the door about now, and break the tension and help us past this into a new scene, but she is still out there somewhere and the door remains closed. Just the two of us in this little cabin, this scene from a kitchen sink drama.

I push the egg bowl aside, lean my butt against the cupboard, and cross my arms.

'First things first. Who's chasing you?'

Now the world takes my cue and there's a sound at the door, and

The Embryo, entirely unlike a helpless waif, picks up the fire poker, braces herself. Of course it's just Shanaya.

The two of them lock eyes, and Shanaya nods.

'All clear. For now.' She locks the door behind herself. Édith puts down the poker.

Shanaya glides across the room, grabs a mug and pours herself some coffee, then settles into a chair, seeming entirely unperturbed by the air thick as raw eggs with tension. *The eggs!*

I grab a fork, start whipping them.

'Scrambled eggs?' says Shanaya. 'I could kill for some scrambled eggs.'

Everyone's a comedian.

I notice then that Édith has already put the cast iron pan on the stove, and added butter, which is just getting to that bubbly tan state.

'Thanks,' I mutter, and pour in the eggs.

Salt. Pepper. Spatula. I scrape a little harder than necessary, scrambling them in the pan. Just to make it clear, I am not attempting any fancy fucking crepes, or omelettes, or anything except chunky, messy, scrambled. The eggs du jour.

DEVIN:...VS. OLD LADIES

Come the day of the papal visit, the weather seems to agree, there is cause for ambivalence, and bright sun alternates with gusty drifts of sudden cold rain.

Devin arrives to find armoured vehicles lining the little residential streets around the church, and dozens of police in full body armour standing around, straddle legged, talking amongst themselves. He overhears three of them muttering about the Swiss Militia, notes there are city police and federal police, and also some very heavily tattooed men in unspecified uniforms among the throng. He wonders what force those belong to.

They've barricade the church with tall metal fences enclosing the church and rectory, shutting off that entire block. There's what seems to be a viewing stand, as at a fair or other event, but nobody sits there.

A small crowd has gathered, like flotsam washed by some invisible tide up against the fence.

Devin sees one small banner about Indigenous Lives, and a couple of people are wearing orange t-shirts with Every Child Matters etched in white across them.

He's wearing one himself, but he's the only volunteer doing so.

An effusive little nun in a green turtleneck checks him off a volunteer list and assigns him the job of handing out tickets. She gives him an envelope and he looks inside, where the tickets prove to be two-inch paper squares, each hastily printed with the event and the word 'ticket'. Another volunteer has a clipboard check-list with names of those invited to attend in the gym.

As the time draws near, Devin watches bemused as the volunteer team adorns the first rows of folding chairs with little bags each holding bottled water, a little granola bar, an apple and some sort of pamphlet.

Outside, more volunteers, tag-identified as Indigenous Mental Health workers, organize a circle in the dingy grass beside the gym doors, and light and smudge and say a prayer.

As the smoke rises, two ladies arrive, a chunky dark haired woman in glasses and a white-haired woman with a timeless dignity in her face, her eyes a map of northern forests and the mysterious life therein, lines of sorrow in her body. She walks slow, the younger woman beside her keeps pace but seems to thrum with anger even before they enter. Devin knows this woman by sight as a local, recognizes her energy, like his Aunt Hazel, a woman made hard by her life.

'Four cops for every person,' she growls. 'Counting only those in uniform.'

Devin drops his gaze. He can't justify it for her. She smirks and bobs her head at Devin, quirking an eyebrow to mock the little paper tickets Devin helps hand out. He bobs his head, says nothing. The effusive little nun burbles and chirps a welcome, overcompensating.

Devin is just a doorman.

He walks at the back of the group when they are told it is time to watch the Pope arrive. He stands with every hair on end as the little flock settles between the metal fences, blocked into an alley now. A line of RCMP officers stand wide-legged across the front fence, faces set in grim lines. The group, mostly older women, start to cluck and chuckle, mutter in a blend of humour and horror about the ostentatious belligerence of it all.

The white-haired Cree woman climbs up on a chair, and the dark haired woman pops up beside her. He hears them quip about being better targets at this height. He remembers, the dark woman is a writer. Maybe on assignment for one of the community-run papers, old-fashioned relics that people still read.

Sirens and a motorcade of armoured vehicles and police on motorcycles rumbling by and circling back signal the arrival of the pontiff.

Sure enough, he's riding in a tiny white Fiat.

The humble effect is rather ruined by the big black guard vehicles that block him from view, and the camera man on the rectory roof. The writer and her friend point their chins at his shrouded tripod.

'Probably got a machine gun under there too,' they joke. 'In case any of us need shooting.'

The Pope, visible only as a bit of his white cap bobs intermittently above the line of vehicles, is evidently being greeted by a drum group. The sound seems very far away.

They bundle the Pope into the church through a side door. Devin knows that's the vestibule with the elevator, accessible for the old and infirm.

Out here, the old and infirm muster their walkers and canes and turn to go back to the gym. The white-haired woman, Devin notes, is using a jaunty leopard-print umbrella for a cane. The writer continues to crackle and mutter as they make their way back to the gym.

'Back to the Road Allowance,' the writer snipes as they pass by him.

Back in the gym, Devin finds himself watching them as much as the Pope on the big screen. They are seated along an aisle, about four rows back, and he can hear them murmuring all through the address. The pontiff all in white speaks slowly in Argentinian Spanish, while subtitles run below in English and French.

'Not an Indigenous word to be heard,' grumbles the writer.

The Pope sums up the sins for which he is here to apologize as 'making the Indigenous feel inferior' by 'disrespecting their culture,' and as the subtitles confirm this is really what he's saying, the writer calls out in the dark: 'What about the murders?'

'Show some respect,' chides a man in the back.

'Mah!' retorts the writer, 'him first.'

And the two women laugh low, angry growling laughs.

They kibitz all through the presentation, and Devin fights the urge to join them.

He is here to usher.

When the gathered flock are invited to go watch the Pope leave, the two woman chuckle scornfully and he hears them quip to the empty air:

'What would we see anyhow? More cops and guns? We're done.'

And they strut down the aisle toward the entrance, against the slow tide humbly stumping back toward the door to the fenced alley leading to the viewing of the Presence.

The chirpy nun spares them another smile, as if to win them back.

The writer's having none of it.

'Thanks for your hospitality,' she says, 'you're very sweet. But that? That was a pile of bullshit.'

They hand Devin back their little tickets as they pass him and he turns to watch them go, burning with contagious outrage.

As they step down onto the sidewalk, they come past a police SUV. Behind the black metal grill that fills the open back window, a K9 officer suddenly fires a volley of loud snarling barks at them. As one, the women turn.

'Aww, shut up!' They roar in unison.

And they walk away, laughing.

Devin stands there quietly, thrumming with the weight of their pent up anger released. These are his people. They seethe at the barricades erected between them and the supposedly penitent Pope, and yet the worst they do in retaliation for the generations of loss and abuse is to mock the hollowness of the barricaded ceremony, strut tall past the armed and shielded warriors of city, state and church, and they only lose it when the attack dog barks first.

Then they laugh, with an undertone of reassurance and fellowship. The dog can't help it, he's been held in the armoured car for hours, prepared for terrorists, not for this ambivalent smattering of upright old ladies.

His people.

But he has to finish his duty to Father Efren, who is also his people.

HAZEL: NICETIES

I serve the eggs and I sit down, and silence falls over the table. I hate not knowing what to say and I feel like they're expecting me to speak, the way their eyes are flashing here there and everywhere. I smack my coffee mug down, a little too firmly, and sit up straight.

'So.' I look from one to the other.

I hate that they seem so in sync. I hate that I am jealous of that when Édith is clearly in terrible trouble.

'I take it you've introduced yourselves already?' I try to keep my voice neutral.

'Not formally,' purrs Shanaya, winking at The Embryo. 'Shanaya Bhattacharya, at your service.'

I can't help it. I cut in and speak before the Embryo can.

'Édith Jones.' I introduce her, with a mocking flourish. Asshole.

'In the flesh,' she murmurs, and shoots me a look which shades between defiance, anguish and just a hint of awareness of the absurdity of this moment.

'But it's Pomeroy now.' She sips coffee, bobs her head at Shanaya. "Édith Serifa Pomeroy. At your service.'

Shanaya pushes back her burgeoning mane and purrs, 'Pleased to formally make your acquaintance, Édith.'

They raise their coffee cups as if in a toast.

I hate her. Skinny little plucked chicken sitting bantering with *my* friend.

'Now,' Shanaya continues, 'I think you'd better tell us what is going on. Are we, for instance, expecting a large party of attackers? An army? And armed with what armaments if so?'

Shanaya's utter self-possession baffles Édith, who cocks her head to one side, looks at me.

'Same questions here,' I say.

It all seems so absurd. Édith here, from a past so distant it seems another life, whom I didn't expect to see here. Why wouldn't I expect to see her here? After all, she and George own the place.

'Where's–?' And now she cuts me off.

'George? I don't know. I don't want to know. He might be with them. Might be dead.'

'Dead?' I say.

'Them?' says Shanaya.

'There are seven of them,' she says to Shanaya, 'that I know of. Seven men, with quads, looking for me and the kids.'

'Kids?!'

'The kids I stole from them.'

Her eyes are pools of horror now.

'I'm not crazy,' she says to me.

'No,' says Shanaya, holding herself very erect. 'But you need to tell us, as swiftly and clearly as possible, who are these men, where are these kids, and what you expect us to do about it all.'

Some embers in the stove box pop just then. We all jump.

I still don't know what in the hell is going on here, but I do know I'd better stifle what's left of that fire ASAP, and hope whoever has chased Édith back into my life hasn't already smelled the woodsmoke.

'They don't know which way I went. They don't know this area,' she says. 'I think they don't know. But the kids… they don't know the way either. I wanted to lead them here. I…' she shakes herself. 'I left them. They can't get here from there. And those men won't find us easily, they won't know this is where I…went.'

I'm staring. I know it. *How did she get here? And where are these kids, these men?* I looked outside for myself. I'm not a tiger, but even a human ought to be able to see footprints in the mud, or some kind of trail. But there is nothing besides our own tracks. And Shanaya found nothing. I want to shake her and demand that she explain how she dropped down on us out of the dark and stormy night. But at least I've got enough sense in the clarity of morning to sit tight and let her tell us what she will.

Tell us that George was much worse than I knew.

That she didn't know when it started, but that he was trafficking young agricultural workers, part of a network of truckers and grain handlers moving stolen girls–and boys–along with their legitimate cargoes.

'They call themselves The Harvestmen. I didn't know what they were, for so long.'

Every time she looks like she is going to sink into catatonia, Shanaya urges her on.

'Yes,' Shanaya says, just that. 'Yes.'

And I just sit there astonished, watching the spectre of the life I might have had sit there telling me about how she found the courage to leave, and how she just couldn't let it go.

So, did she go to the authorities? No, because she knew he'd kill her if she did.

Did she tell anyone?

No, the astonishingly daft Embryo just went and found where they were keeping a shipment of these youths in a train car, slipped in, and told them she was preparing a safe house, and that she would be back for them.

'I promised them.'

She says it low and firm. Not like some tragic heroine in a melodrama, but like a real woman, the kind I always told myself I am. Another irrelevant flash of jealousy stabs me. *This too, she will take from me, that I'm more woman than her?* I give my head a shake. *Fuck off,* I whisper to my lesser self.

They both stare at me. I guess I said it out loud.

'Not you.' I say. 'I just…can't believe I hated you for so long, and look at you. You're a fucking hero.'

And there we sit, locked in a cabin, drinking coffee, staring at each other–not the Maiden, the Mother and the Crone. Not Niña, Pinta, Santa Maria. The Embryo, The Tiger and The Asshole.

Holy Mother, I need a smoke.

DEVIN: NO APOLOGY

Devin goes home without seeing Father Efren. He simply finishes his allotted tasks and leaves, walking away with his skin slightly crawling as he passes the many armoured trucks, cars, vans. Nothing has happened with them.

He wants to shout at them as if they were snapping dogs.

He wants to cry for them. It all feels hideously wrong and out of place.

He tells himself that his father would have wanted him to be there.

It comes to mind that his father would have been in the main church, with all the other community notables, if he'd been alive.

He, Devin, would probably still have been assigned the gym.

Devin shakes his head to clear it, blinks back tears. He takes the long way home, wandering through small streets and pocket parks, trying to find peace by contemplating the yards full of flowers, fruit, vegetables, the old gardens started by the Italian and Portuguese immigrants who built these tidy houses, nested in this working class haven, shook their heads at the Indians skulking through the alleys and sleeping in the parks.

Devin walks for hours before he gets home.

He walks past Missy's but doesn't go in. What will she and Maengan say?

'What did you expect? This apology means nothing.'

It does not help LeWayne. It does not help Rabbit.

It does not help Devin's own father and mother, sickened by the world and dead too soon. He doesn't know all the mechanisms that Empire deployed, the precise details of the evils of the government programs to 'destroy the Indian in the child,' but he knows the cost.

LeWayne is part of the cost.

LeWayne is a mutt, a child of a mother already broken-minded. He never could focus in school. He could fixate, though. Too easily, he could fixate on violence and threat.

Devin thinks about LeWayne's survival, how much that depended on him fixating, and reacting quickly. He reacted, and the older he got, the more erratic his reactions, the more he struck before thinking.

Devin shakes his head. Not that LeWayne wanted violence. It seemed like that, but it wasn't. He wanted to stop the threat. He got hit until he got big enough to hit first.

Maybe he'd have grown out of that, if he hadn't been high, hadn't gotten excited about Cody and Tomlin mouthing off about this girl Rabbit being the one who killed those men. And where did Cody and Tomlin get that stupid idea? Devin can't remember whether or not it came from him, but his steps are leaden, and the possibility that he triggered his friend's last stupid move drags him down hard.

He walks, weary, up the sidewalk to his home. He knows where to look.

Sandra will be in the garden, picking out something fresh to add to dinner.

Devin steps through the gate and sees them, Sandra and Father Efren. Father Efren in the garden with Sandra, sitting too near her, his face all lit up, talking about how happy, how light, how suddenly unburdened he feels.

'I don't have the words to say exactly why, but I just know this changes everything. If the Pontiff himself can come all the way here from Rome, and humbly beg forgiveness, if after all the suffering of the people, a way has opened for healing...such great wrongs...and the most powerful man in the Church kneels before us to atone-?'

Devin can't hear any more.

'*Atone?!*' He bellows.

They jump, but he doesn't bother with their reaction, just whips around regalvanized and runs shoulder-bowling down the street, away. He doesn't know where he's going. He gasps as he runs. He slows to a walk, his more natural speed. He thinks as his heart quietens. He turns up certain streets, keeps walking.

He finds Missy's building, climbs the fire escape and trudges along the wide metal balcony to her door, which is already open, she's spied him coming.

'I don't know what to do, Cousin,' he says.

'How about you come in first of all,' says Missy, and Maengan takes his arm just lightly, pulls him in and closes the door.

HAZEL: EXIT STAGE LEFT, WITH EMBRYO

So, what else is there to do? We clean up the cabin. We empty the ashes from the stove, pour them down the outhouse hole. We sweep the floors. We wipe down surfaces where fingerprints are too easily noticed.

'Not too clean,' says Shanaya, out of the blue. 'We're not expecting a forensic expedition on our heels?'

Édith shakes her tufty blonde head at that, sweeps some fine dust into the dustpan and throws it up like some ancient thresher of grain, high and away into the main room.

Shanaya coughs, laughs, shakes her head.

'Come on, ladies.'

Édith, last out, produces the correct keys to lock up. Where did she get those? I wonder, and why didn't she just use a key when she arrived?

But Édith has pulled her hoodie over her head and she scurries across the yard. I can see her shaking. She's running on nerves. I can't forget those horrible bruises. I give my head a shake. Who can say what you think when you're hurt and running? When you get to a place you've come for sanctuary, and see a strange car there, and you have to crouch and wait and figure out the risk of staying out in the storm against the risk that whoever is inside is part of what you're running from…that does leave me with a question, but now's not the time to ask her how and why she gambled on us. She was right, what else matters?

We bundle her into the jeep, in the backseat with the tinted windows, and we go.

And we're driving and it's morning and where are we going? We're arguing down the highway. What do we do now?

'We go to the police,' I say. Me. Someone has to say it.

Shanaya, my lawyer friend, should be the one to say, *Let's get to the authorities,* but she is in the thrall of Édith, and keeps throwing her conspiratorial glances in the rearview mirror. She throws one now.

'Do you think that's wise, Édith?'

Wise?! Édith? The Embryo?

I look out the window, growling under my breath. And then things get a bit blurry, because I can't help remembering Jim, when he was just Spider, just the strange dog I sprung from the Humane Society because I'd had a vision. Remember Spider sitting in my front seat as I drove him home that first morning, and me wondering what the hell was coming next?

I'd really had no inkling.

Now Spider–aka Jim, part-time human, part hero part schmuck– is dead. Dead stepping in front of a bullet. Dead in a surreal gunfight in an alley in UpTop, the terraformed geothermal heatsink that powers our city, dead in a moment I've seen a thousand times in my head since, but still don't understand. Jim is dead. His daughter–the daughter he hid from me while we risked our lives stalking perverts through the streets of Amiskwaciy, the daughter he was hunting the whole time–his daughter is vanished. Disappeared. Not like the MMIW, not a case anyone who was there would report to any authorities. They have no category for 'stepped into a glowing light, hand in hand with a Sasquatch' in their files for the disappeared.

It's all incredibly–

'Hazel.'

Shanaya's voice brings me back.

'What?' I blurt.

'Are you in?'

'Am I in what?'

She skewers me with a glance of those big golden eyes. Not unkind. Not fooled. She knows in an instant that I've missed all they've been talking about, that I've been back in that night.

'Ady and I–'

Ady!? Fuck sakes.

Shan and I lock eyes. She gives her head the tiniest shake. I can feel blood surging into my face, and I can feel Shanaya's not at all intimidated. I back down. It's my car, but it sure feels like she's driving.

She clears her throat, throws another glance in the rearview at the Embryo lurking behind my seat. That's another thing. I hate her sitting right behind me. If this were a sitcom, she'd be sitting improbably in the middle of the backseat, framed for the camera shooting from the front. But this is life, and she's buckled in, behind me, so I can't even see her. But oh, I know she's there. The little…

'Hazel,' Shan says again. 'Édith and I are going after them. The Harvestmen. We're going to get those kids free from them. Are you in?'

'Are you crazy?'

'That's a different question,' purrs Shanaya, the lawyer, her fingernails tapping a quick rimshot on the dashboard.

'Let me get this straight,' I say. 'You want to go, not to the authorities, but back to whoever beat the shit out of th-Édith, and play superhero?'

'You don't have to come,' says Shanaya. 'I can take you home first.'

I sigh.

"The fuck you can, woman.'

I turn back to the window, away from her tigerish grin. Because really, what choice do I have? If the bruises on The Embryo's back and legs and arms are any indication, those kids don't have time for us to 'go to the authorities' and explain, and risk tipping off whoever did that to Édith.

And I know who did it. My ex-husband.

The one she stole from me. The one, to put it more correctly, who moved on from me to a more vulnerable person, a more likely victim. In some way, if I'm honest, I'm grateful to the wretched little woman behind me in the backseat, for distracting George enough so that my girls and I could get away. But I don't owe her anything, do I?

And Shanaya should know better. She's a lawyer, for fuck's sake.

'You're a lawyer, for fuck's sakes.'

Her fingernails drum across the dashboard again, triumphant. She's also a tiger.

There's a little thing that makes a difference, doesn't it?

My shapeshifting dog of a…whatever Jim was to me, I don't know how to say…anyway, he's dead. And because of him, one of the big changes in my life, is that I have a close friend who's a shape-shifter, too. Except she's a tiger.

I have so many questions.

How are we going to do this? How are we paying for this caper?

I sure as fuck don't have the money to drop everything and spend God knows how long on the road chasing dangerous criminals.

'So you're in, then?'

'Mm.' I flick my eyes, flex my lips toward The Embryo behind me.

'She's asleep' says Shanaya.

'Okay then, look,' I say. 'You realize this is crazy, right?'

She says nothing.

'That we should go to the authorities because we might be getting into something that is far bigger than we know.'

'Bigger than a Sasquatch and a gunfight?' Shan keeps her voice low and tight. I look at her, hard. She is practically thrumming with excitement.

'But you're a lawyer, shouldn't you want to–?'

'You know what I am. What I really am. And for once in my life, Hazel, so do I. And it's thanks to you and…all that stuff that happened…and now I can finally see the point of being what I am. I was born to do this, Hazel.' She locks eyes with me for an instant, then turns back fiercely toward the road.

I'm really hooped here. She is alight with the fire of justice. I am riding with a comic book.

'Hey,' I quip, 'steady there. Don't go getting all stripy on me now.'

She chuckles. It's not funny.

Except that it is. It's absurd. And I start laughing. And Shan starts laughing. And the Embryo wakes up screaming and we almost run off the road.

DEVIN: BREAK

Maengan and Missy listen as he lets it out.

'I mean, I just can't talk to him,' says Devin. 'And I...can't stand to see Auntie...I mean, I want her to be happy. I owe her everything. And Father E, too. And I. I don't know. I'm just...'

He hangs his big head miserably, 'I'm in the way.'

He looks around, looks out the window.

'I'm sorry.'

'No, it's okay,' says Maengan.

Devin falls silent. Missy passes him a tall glass of water.

'Drink. You want some tea?'

Devin shrugs, Missy nods at Maengan, who fills the kettle, sets it on.

Missy thinks a minute, then sighs, picks up a deck of cards.

'Three way crib?'

Devin shrugs and nods.

'Here,' Missy says, 'You and Maengan cut for deal, I'll be right back.'

She steps out of the bright yellow kitchen, comes back a few minutes later and clicks her cell-phone down on the counter.

'Frankie's on her way over.'

Missy scoops up her hand, discards, and leads with a seven.

'Fifteen two,' says Devin, and they settle into the rhythm of the game, sipping at the tea and kibitzing about the game as the pegs jog round the board.

They're in the second game when they hear footsteps on the fire escape, followed by a light knock at the door.

'Let me in. I've got sushi,' calls Frankie, and Maengan leaps up to usher her in.

'Hey you,' says Frankie, hugging Devin in his turn. She shoots a glance at Missy, who quirks an eyebrow back at her.

'Hungry?'

Maengan deftly claims the sushi.

Frankie slings her coat on a hook and drops into the unclaimed fourth kitchen chair.

Maengan's already got down plates. He tears off squares from the paper towel rack, passes them around. Missy doles out shabby chopsticks, sets a cup down in front of Frankie, who taps the table playfully.

'Hey, tapping for tea is Chinese, not Japanese,' quips Maengan, 'can you do that?'

'Indigenous people,' says Frankie, 'are the original globalists.'

They chuckle and chatter and pass round the sushi.

Missy shuffles, flips four cards.

'Looks like you and Devin vs me and Wolfie.'

So the evening descends in bonhomie and the click of cards, and they play and chat, easing past Devin's anguish.

'So, Frankie,' says Missy after they've traded partners, 'You still looking for a house sitter?'

***

After they've gone, Maengan takes Missy in his arms.

'Fucking Pope anyway,' growls Missy against his chest.

'We're not the ones who broke the world, Miss,' he replies, 'and maybe all we've got are little ways to mend it, but little things are big in their own context.'

HAZEL: NORMAL

So we get Édith calmed down, and she apologizes, standing on the roadside, shaking.

'It's okay,' I say. I'm not entirely an asshole. The woman is covered in bruises and her eyes look like the gates of Hell.

'Hey now,' says Shanaya, 'let's get you back inside. Can you do that?'

The Embryo regards the backseat for a moment, peering at it as if it might contain snakes. Then she looks around at the empty road.

I follow her gaze, see a car in the distance.

That decides her. She climbs back in, huddles into Shanaya's dry robe, curls herself into a ball on the back seat. And we drive on, exchanging meaningful glances.

No more talk of charging off to rescue anyone. We have our hands full with the terrified little creature in the back seat.

***

Okay, so we've driven all the way to Big Bend, and we don't have a plan. We have a bedraggled, horrifically abused woman in the back seat, looking worse now that the bruises have started turning brown and green and that lurid yellow.

Édith wakes up again as we slow down to town speed, and this time, she sits up and stretches and looks around.

'Big Bend?' she asks.

'Mmhmm,' says Shanaya softly. She pulls into a strip mall parking lot, finds a spot and glances around at both of us.

'What should we do now?'

'You know what I want–'

Shanaya shakes a finger at Édith in the mirror.

'You're in no shape to go charging around saving anyone just now.'

'But–'

'But nothing,' I chip in. 'You need medical attention.'

'No,' she grates.

'Yes,' says Shanaya. 'And about a week's worth of sleep someplace safe.'

I expect Édith to keep arguing, but she just heaves a sigh, and I turn to look. She's slumped back against the seat.

'I am tired,' she murmurs quietly. 'So tired. Need to sleep, without dreams.'

Without screams, I think, biting my tongue. She looks like the bottom of a barrel of hurt.

'Anyone got a sedative?' Édith asks.

We shake our heads.

'Well,' she says, 'no matter. I think I do.'

Shanaya and I exchange alarmed looks.

'Where's my hoodie?'

'In the back.'

She starts to turn, groans to herself. I flash Shan another look of alarm, and get out, go round and open the door behind her, lean in and rummage behind the back seat. The hoodie stinks, I notice.

'Here you go,' I mutter, holding it out gingerly, my lip curling.

'Thanks,' says The Embryo and turns the hideous thing inside out. I just go back around and climb back in, and watch her pull open a little hidden pocket sewn into the inside of the hoodie along a side seam. She squeezes out a plastic bag, shakily extracts a pill, looks up at our horrified faces.

'Don't worry,' she says, 'it's prescription. Got some water?' Shanaya passes her a water bottle from the front console and The Embryo gulps down the pill, then sighs.

'Now look,' she says, 'I'll be out in about twenty minutes, probably sleep for a couple hours. Can't promise I won't wake up screaming. But at least I will sleep here peacefully for a couple hours.' She yawns. 'More than enough time for you two to get some lunch.'

'What?' we chorus.

'We're not leaving you here by yourself,' Shanaya protests.

'Yes you are,' says The Embryo, her eyelids drooping already.

'Look at it this way. Nobody followed us from the cabin, right?'

'Not that I could see,' Shanaya admits.

'Nobody knows I was there. Nobody knows I'm here. Ergo, I'm safe.'

She curls down and pulls the dry robe over her, the hood up around her face.

'You sure you'll be okay?' Asks Shanaya softly, watching The Embryo in the rearview mirror as she makes herself more comfortable back there.

Édith nods.'You guys just go ahead and act like I'm not here… ' her voice trails off, and we sit there a moment more, dithering.

It seems unnecessarily risky to me, but in some way it makes sense. If anyone was watching us leave the cabin, surely they'd have followed us? But we'd sent Shanaya out–she'd sent herself out, who am I kidding?–in her furry version, and she'd prowled and sniffed and declared that someone may have passed by, but that our precaution of keeping Édith out of sight may have kept them from coming too close. Why would they want to arouse suspicion by asking us what we were doing there?

My skin crawls a little, thinking that someone might have photographed Shan and I pottering about the place, might have shown those photos to George, he might have ID'ed me…

But nothing had happened, and we'd bundled Édith out before dawn and, at her own suggestion, left her curled in the car for a couple hours while we conspicuously tidied up–broke camp, so to speak–and left mid-morning.

'I don't like it,' I note to Shanaya. She shrugs.

'What else is there to do? I'm hungry, now that I think of it. But let's not leave her here.'

She starts the car, finds us a spot to park on Big Bend's schmaltzy main street, and we walk along to a little restaurant open early to serve the farmers and truckers and assorted other early birds of Big Bend. We take a booth by the window and order coffee and juice, and Shan lets drop casually to the waitress that I'd used to live out in these parts as a kid and we were just visiting.

I shake my head once, quick, alarmed, but Shan has judged correctly. Anyone listening in the half-full cafe would have caught enough to allay suspicion. The skinny waitress has no further interest in what two women might be doing here anyway, her attention centred on the three young men at the table in the back corner, clumsily flirting a little too loudly with her.

We have to wave her down to place our order.

'Hamburger steak and eggs,' purrs Shanaya. I settle for the eggs benny. These small town restaurants tend to make a surprisingly tasty Benedict, if you ask me. Mind you, nobody's ever asked me about my gastronomical preferences.

We sit there and eat a second breakfast of eggs and I'm a little surprised at how normal it feels.

Maybe the problem is the word 'normal.' A thing can be normal and healthy, or normal and unhealthy, or normal without that tying in anyway toward a judgement of its health or lack thereof. And a thing can be normal or abnormal without it being necessarily correlated to good or bad. So, you can be outside the norm, but still perfectly normal.

The Benny is okay.

Shanaya refrains from commenting on her meal, but clears her plate.

'Don't lick it clean,' I tease. She growls a little in response.

'You laugh,' she says, 'but I want to find some snacks for the road.'

'Where do you think we should go?' I ask as we step out onto the street.

'Not sure,' says Shanaya, 'but I will think better if I have a little more fuel to go on.'

So we stroll on down to the local market, an old 'Super A' –a brand from the darkest 20th century, practically extinct.

This store looks to be on its final legs, tottering like the last dinosaur.

Anemic tomatoes, over-wrapped potatoes and rusty iceberg lettuce; a strong selection of canned and frozen readymade meals. The meat section looks positively dangerous.

'Why do people eat worse in the country?' asks Shanaya, gently prodding a jaded looking pork chop, turning it so the light glimmered iridescently off the sheen on the surface.

'I know, right?' I say, pulling her away from the cooler. 'It's economics. Stores like this are mostly dead, because they couldn't compete with the big box stores in the big centres.'

'But don't they grow the beef and pork and such just outside town?'

'Yup. And the commercial producers still sell to the big companies who make more shipping it to the higher populations areas. Who sell it back to small-town distributors at a mark-up. Come on. Let me show you something.'

We leave the sagging little grocery without buying anything. I stifle a little pang of guilt. There was a time this store was hopping.

But we walk on, and I look for the sign. There.

We go into the little butcher shop, and Shanaya looks around, practically sniffing the air like a tiger.

I buy some cooked sausage.

'This is the good stuff,' I say, smiling at the clerk/proprietor like a regular.

'That it is,' she replies.

'Where's the Freson's?'

'Fifth Street, past the rec centre,' she replies, using her head to indication the general direction.

In the Freson's, they have local produce, pre-made salads, sushi even. I settle for a couple bottles of made-in-store green smoothies, a loaf of local sourdough and a store-logo cloth bag to carry it and we head back to the car. The Embryo hasn't moved, and though we brace for screams as I tuck the bag of groceries down behind my seat and incidentally check that she's breathing, she sleeps on peacefully.

DEVIN: PARAMETERS

'So,' says Frankie, 'I leave August 23rd. Rent will be paid up for nine months, you'd just have to take care of the monthly bills, feed yourself, and you know, make sure things don't completely fester and fall apart around here.'

She runs a hand along the books in the shelf that fills one living room wall.

Devin nods owlishly. Frankie gazes around the room, not crowding him, letting him sort his feelings.

'You want a hand bringing over any personal stuff? I'm free the day before I leave.'

He shakes his head.

'I'll bring it.'

'Yeah, but,' says Frankie, turning her caramel gaze on him, 'if I come along, I can let Auntie Sandra know what a really big favour you're doing me, looking after my place while I'm gone.'

She grins.

'And also, I bet you five bucks she gets all wound up about my research trip 'to parts undisclosed' and forgets to give you a hard time about moving out.'

Devin gives back the smallest of smiles.

'Not taking that bet.'

'Smart boy. Give me a minute, and I'll give you the lay of the land around here–laundry, neighbours, et cetera.'

***

When Frankie emerges from the bathroom, Devin is absorbed in admiring the way Frankie has decorated, transforming a plain off-white walk-up into a haven of turquoise, jade green and soft mauve; painted shelves, textured cushions, soft throws, the kitchen wares and linens too, accented with golds and tans. He startles when she speaks.

'Always have to have one black thing,' she says, and he notes a square vase in a corner. 'It grounds the colour palette, they say.'

'Where'd you learn all this?' asks Devin off-handedly.

'Books. Internet. But mostly,' she replies, 'just noticing what I like, and bringing it into my space.' She gestures.

'Feel free to adjust for your own comfort.'

'No,' says Devin, 'I like it like this.'

'It's okay,' says Frankie, 'nine months is a long time. If you want it different, go ahead. Just, you know, make sure you put it back like this for when I get home.'

She points at the candle holder set on top of a low diagonal corner shelf.

'And don't burn the place down, right?'

She laughs, laying a palm on his arm, the way she does. He smiles. What is it about Frankie?

'So where,' Devin hazards, 'are you going on this research trip?'

Still laughing, Frankie shakes her head and her long hair shimmers, the colour of dark November grass.

'Cousin, believe me, I'd tell you if I actually knew.'

She grows still and serious.

'Devin, can I tell you what I do know?'

She stares at him, and her caramel eyes burn with both excitement and a spark of deep fear.

He nods.

'Let's sit down,' she says, sinking onto the sofa and patting the seat cushions beside her.

She heaves a huge sigh and falls silent, her shoulders uncharacteristically curling forward. She stares at nothing for a while, her head bent to one side as if listening to an internal voice. Then she lifts her head and touches Devin's hand for a moment, before placing both her hands firmly on her own thighs and straightening up.

'I need someone to know.'

'Okay,' he says quietly, holding stillness beside her.

'Devin, remember that night?'

'Yes,' he says.

She doesn't have to say which night. Of course he remembers.

LeWayne runs into the alley. A scream. Voices sobbing Mama! Mama! Mama!

He clamps his own hands together.

'Three people died that night.' Her voice is low. 'At least three...'

Her voice trails off. Devin glances at her under his brows, startled. She clears her throat.

'Tell me,' he says. 'It's okay.'

'We–Missy and Maengan and me, and Mom and her friend Shanaya–we went out to UpTop, chasing Mom's friend Jim. He was up there hunting Josh...'

Devin nods, 'Yes, your mom's policeman boyfriend.'

'Ex-boyfriend. Really ex.'

'Right. So Jim was her–'

'No.' She shakes her head. 'At least, I don't know. I mean, they lived together. And actually, they had been working together. Mom and her vigilante werewolf–'

'Her *what?*' He sits utterly still. She stays silent.

He glances under his brows at her. She's shaking a little. He settles himself.

'Werewolf,' she murmurs. The blue and pastel sanctuary darkens like a twilight sky as Frankie sits quietly, her hands clasped over her belly, willing herself to breathe deeply.

'Jim was a shape shifter. Were-*dog*, actually.'

'Mmhmm,' Devin says, speaking from some ancient place inside. 'So, Jim was a shape shifter.' He thinks a moment more. 'He was that dog Spider?'

Frankie nods.

'He was also the father of that girl Rabbit,' she says.

Rabbit. A high thin scream. Mama! Mama! Mama!

Devin stands, paces the room while Frankie watches him in the blue gloom. He stops in front of her, rocking slightly, his owlish eyes holding hers in the deepening gloom.

'She killed LeWayne.'

Frankie nods, her head drooping.

'He ran after her. He had a knife.' Devin says it flatly, simply, and slumps back down beside Frankie.

They sit in silence for a few more moments, then Frankie continues.

'She was Spider/Jim's daughter. Joshua...Jim thought Joshua was responsible for killing her–Rabbit's mother. There were these two guys, I guess, that Josh was using as informants or something–'

'Three lightning strikes on the wall,' says Devin. She looks at him quizzically. He tells her about finding the slashes carved into a brick wall, figuring out that they correlated with the deaths of three men, all of them with ties to Amiskwaciy. He nods.

'Jim...Spider/Jim was right. They were all involved. They were feeding her drugs, using her as an informant.' He shakes his head. 'I don't know all the details. I didn't know, that night, that she was Rabbit's mother. I mean, I barely noticed that girl Rabbit. She was a couple years younger. Kept to herself.'

Mama! Mama! Mama! Devin feels tears sting his eyes. He shakes his head.

'She's a shapeshifter, too,' he says.

'Oh,' says Frankie, and lets go her shoulders a bit. *He knows.*

And they talk on all night long, sharing pieces of what they each know about the tragic life and death of Nell August, her daughter Rabbit, Spider Jim and Hazel. About a *Zabeh*–a Sasquatch–in an alley up in UpTop town, on a strange spring night.

As the night outside begins to recede, Frankie tells him of her own quest.

'The research side of it is me looking into ancient pre-European city sites across Turtle Island.'

He nods.

'What nobody else knows is, who I'm traveling with…' she stops. A faint acridity rolls through the room then, and a presence arrives, steps out of the blue air into the room, settles awkwardly on the floor and shyly greets him. Devin nods, owlish and surprised, sitting in stillness in the face of mystery.

He remembers, before settling to catch a couple hours sleep on the sofa, to text his Auntie Sandra, let her know he's stayed over at Frankie's, that they got to talking and, so sorry, he forgot to tell her earlier. *So sorry to worry you.*

He remembers.

Mama! Mama! Mama!

HAZEL: WHIFF

Shanaya drives. Édith sleeps. I consider how things smelled when Frankie left us.

The morning Frankie leaves, we all meet for breakfast over at Uncle Albert's. Best sausage anywhere, brought in from Mundare.

I'm dying to ask her more about this trip, if you want the truth; but she's not offering, and I don't know how to get information out of her that she doesn't want to offer, not without starting a fight. And I look at my sister sitting there, trying not to cluck over her boy Devin, and I guess I'm trying to grow or something. I realize I don't have to know.

Sandra and me, we both have to practice what we preach now, and let our kids be grown ups.

So we don't pry into what Frankie's research is, exactly. And not a one of us mentions the occasional acrid whiff of smell that curls past the table.

Maybe they've got a toilet backed up in the back or something, but my hair prickles up every time I get a whiff of that.

Still, why would that *Zabeh*, that Sasquatch, be hovering around a pancake house peeking at us and our breakfast?

Just as I'm thinking that, Frankie excuses herself, comes back with her toffee-gold hair shimmering.

'Sorry guys,' she says, 'this table isn't the best.' She flicks a hand in front of her nose, a small gesture just for us.

'I guess they're getting a plumber in after lunch; something broken in the men's room.'

Too much information, I think. But the kids exchange side-eye glances, little flickers of unspoken agreement.

I bite my tongue. *You're jealous, Hazel.* I tell myself sternly that I should be proud that my girls are close, can talk without words, and seem to be drawing Devin into that. Also Maengan Nolan, but I keep my reflexive sneer to myself. Missy seems to really care for him, and he seems almost…solicitous of her. And she's letting him do little things for her. My warhorse daughter.

It makes my skin itch a bit, but Sandra catches my eye before I say something stupid. It's a little disused, but it's still there between us, that thing sisters do. *Shut up,* I hear clearly in my head.

Okay okay, I reply.

Nobody watching us would even know that we are sitting there avoiding asking if anybody else smells a Sasquatch.

DEVIN: GIFT

Sandra surprises him.

He has gathered himself painfully tight, and he bobs his head nervously as he blurts out his carefully marshalled reasons why he is going to go housesit for Frankie.

'…if th-th-that is okay?'

She just quietly nods and *mmhmms* and agrees, and passes him a bowl of casserole. Then she excuses herself and leaves him at the table for a few minutes. When she comes back, she's smiling and calm, but he can see the tightness around her eyes.

'You've got a job come September, you can pay your own bills.' She nods, reaches over and squeezes his hand.

'It will be good for both of us, eh?'

When the day comes, Sandra is up early, picking beans and raspberries. She harvests two hills of potatoes as well, pulls an onion, and busies herself packing them into a box.

'Okay then,' she says, and carries the box out to the front step. She sits down beside the box, just sits with a cup of tea quietly watching the street until Frankie arrives in a little blue car.

'Okay then,' Sandra says, over and over, as they gather his things and carry them out to the little car. She's too preoccupied to ask Frankie whose car this is. But she stands there staring at it for a few moments when they've finished loading, then turns back toward the house.

'Just a minute, okay?'

The cousins exchange glances, but they don't have too long to wonder.

'Devin,' Sandra says, handing him the black case, 'maybe it's time you take this with you.'

'Dad's guitar?'

'Your guitar. He wanted you to have it. I just… didn't know when to give it to you. 'Til now.'

She wraps the boy in a big swift hug and then spins on her heel and goes back inside.

'Well come on,' says Frankie, 'let's get both of you home.'

***

'So do you play?' Frankie asks as they stand gazing at the guitar, lying in its open case on the coffee table in her living room.

Devin shakes his head.

'I-I-' he shrugs, 'I guess Mom showed me a couple chords.'

'Well there you go,' says Frankie softly, 'that's all they say you need, a couple chords and the truth.' She smiles gently, but Devin looks down, closes and locks the case, stands swinging his head like a trapped bear.

Frankie picks up the case.

'There's space for it here, see?'

She slides the case on its side along the wall behind the long sofa where it's tufted, rolled back leaves a triangular space.

Devin shakes his head, says nothing.

'Well, hey, ' Frankie says, 'Welcome home. I'm leaving in the morning, better hit the hay. You get the sofa for tonight.'

It's already dressed with sheets and blanket and a pillow in a smooth blue pillowcase.

'You need the bathroom?'

He shakes his head.

'Me first then,' she chirps, and leaves him standing there.

'Night night,' she calls blandly from behind the bathroom door.

He sits down on the sofa, thinking he'll just wait there a minute.

Gradually, he tips to the side and reflexively brings his legs up onto the sofa. He's out cold and doesn't budge when Frankie glides back into the room to check on him and flip the blanket over his side. It's a warm enough night, but she remembers her mother always saying *keep your kidneys warm,* and she smiles in the dark, for once at ease with thoughts of her thorny mother.

Frankie's caramel eyes gleam in the dim street light filtering in from the window, and she paces over to gaze out at the familiar view. She turns slowly and takes in her home, the nest she's made for herself, the sanctuary she's about to leave. Not abandon, but leave with a careful, deep-thinking young man at a turning point of his own. This is why we make sanctuaries, she thinks, smiling in the dark.

No knowing what her chosen path may bring, but she listens to her cousin's slight snore and knows that whatever happens for her, this is the right thing for him.

HAZEL: FOR WHAT IT'S WORTH

I am an asshole. I say it often enough. But I never tell the truth about why I'm such an asshole. I went to a counsellor once, who tried to tell me it's low self esteem. But it's not. I reckon it's accurate self esteem. I know what I am, what I've done, what I have failed to do.

I got my kids away from George when I began to wonder if he was seeing someone else. I didn't get them out when Missy hit puberty, I waited for Frankie. I say that was for a variety of reasons but the truth is, I was glad the Embryo came along, so I could dump George and run away and never have to confront the awful truth that I hadn't slept for years, one ear cocked to catch him if he dared to creep toward Missy and Frankie's room.

And I gave up my birthright because I just wanted to be free, free of the bad decision I made when I married George, against my mother's advice. I disregarded my mother, because I considered her sick. I judged her. And I defied her.

And I married that man and had two daughters with him.

But the truth is, I had three kids. I had a son. My son died at birth. At least, that's what everyone knows about it. But I'll never know. George was hitting me and I went to hit him back, smashed against the table belly-first trying to get at him and I knocked that baby sideways. What if I hurt him and that's why he died?

And I ran away from the land I loved because I was seeking safety and a road forward, and everybody knew then that cities eat

Indians (and also dirty half breeds like me) but the city welcomed me, and I was free of all the voices supposing they knew who I was or what I was worth.

Here, I was heroic, exotic, and a single mom. Okay, no lie, being a single mom was not great, not seen as heroic, got me a few more chips for my shoulder-wear collection, shall we say.

We pick up coffee in a Tim Horton's on the edge of Big Bend.

'Where to?' I ask Shanaya.

She blows out air through her lips.

'Don't know just yet, let's just head East a while, like we know where we're going.'

So we do.

'I should've punched her, you know,' I say quietly.

Édith snores in the back seat, and we drive, not talking.

Shanaya scoffs.

'We both know that was never an option.'

Okay the truth is, I fucking hate Tim Horton's coffee. It used to be good, but now? Forget it. If I'm spilling truths, the truth is I buy big bags of Lavazza Organic Light Roast from the Italian Centre. Grind it myself. Little Frankie gave me a grinder for my last birthday. Some days, mind you, I could grind it with my bare hands… I swallow the dark sour brew and snort.

'Nope. I should have punched her. Decked her and locked the door. Saved us a whole lot of trouble if I had.'

Shanaya frowns and I keep driving.

She's silently disappointed in me.

But in my defence, I should also note that I've started dreaming again.

I can't tell Shanaya. She gets me, but she'd think I was just making an excuse for wanting to thump The Embryo and be done with all this. It's not just an excuse. It's more like this: I feel like I missed the warning those sorts of dreams can bring. Feel like I missed a moment when I could have stayed clear of this mess.

It messes with your head, dreaming like that. Undermines the clarity of rage, if you want to put it that way–some might hold that this is a good thing, but it slows you down and then if you don't act, things get complicated.

I know. It happened to me before.

I dreamed, and I woke up convinced the dream was a message from the spirit realm, and I let myself think of that as romantic or important or true or something, and I stole a dog from the Humane shelter. But he wasn't just a dog, and things got complicated.

And without meaning to, I found myself living with a Werewolf –a were-*dog* to be more accurate–with a shapeshifting absentee father on a mission to avenge his dead but abandoned wife and find their daughter and maybe just maybe salvage enough of his dignity to begin to hope for a reconciliation. Only it turns out his daughter is a shapeshifter, too, and plenty capable of exacting her own vengeance, even if she didn't turn out to have the help and sisterhood of a *Zabeh*-Sasquatch, as most folks know them–*that* kind of complicated. The kind that ends in bloody murder in the dark in an alley up in UpTop town where nobody goes–nobody sane–at certain hours.

Anyhow…it's a long story, full of shapeshifters, murderers, and the struggle to figure out how to be Humane, if not human, and after it all came to a head that night, three people were dead: Joshua, who'd been a policeman, and also for a while my lover; LeWayne, one of my nephew's loser pals who hadn't the brains he'd been born with and went after Jim's daughter…and Jim. AKA Spider the Dog. Jim died taking a bullet to save his daughter, Rabbit–*who the fuck names their kid Rabbit, by the way?* I should note that her name, as Jim explained it, was actually beautiful in Mi'gmaq language–*Abeligumuj*–and carried all sorts of lucky connotations, but that kid had no luck ever that I could see…and then she just…vanished.

Swear to Fill-in-Your-Blank-Deity, just walked into a crack of light hanging in the air, hand in hand with that Sasquatch, the Sasquatch calling her *Sister*, and they walked into the air and were gone.

Stuff like that happens to you, you don't want or need any more

of dreaming. I didn't. Did I mention that I come from hardhead-
ed people on both sides? Polish peasants and Uppity Indians, you
can't tell us anything, because our survival has too often come down
to not being willing to be told by anyone...because they'd tell us
wrong, they'd tell us small, they'd tell us failure, they'd tell us dead.

We are dumb fuckers in some ways. We are assholes, not going
to lie. But we survive. Because we fucking choose to, every single
God-given day.

I look over at Shanaya. I don't think I can explain. But I do have
a story, and the road unfurls relentlessly open before us.

'My grandfather and grandmother made a pact, after they nursed
his parents through to their death during that old Spanish Flu epi-
demic–they swore they'd never go that sort of way, sick and suffering and dragging it out and making everyone around them suffer
taking care of them. That's what my mom told me. And it lines up
with history. Grandpa, aged, 88, called one of his sons and said,
Hey, take me to the hospital. Two of his boys came in and got him
admitted. He slept through the night, waiting to be tested. Woke up
in the morning, got out of bed, looked around and fell down dead.'

'Why are you telling me this?' Says Shanaya.

I shrug, grab a smoke, crack a window. Shanaya lights up, too,
glancing back at the sleeping bulk in the back seat. She cracks her
window too ever so slightly.

'Go on,' she says.

'Grandma lived a decade more, and spent a day or two more in
the hospital, lucid at 101, aware that she was getting ready to die,
and she just closed her wise hazel eyes and died.'

'Your Ojibway grandma?'

'No. My Polish one. At least, she was officially Polish, but you
know, maybe she was actually Ukrainian, not that anyone cares
about that here...'

'They sure did in the Ukraine war that nearly got us all killed,'
says Shanaya.

I huff out smoke and shake my head. We both smoke quietly.
Out there, the axis of power keeps shifting, global affairs keep push-

ing tides of people here and there.

'Anyhow…'

'You were talking about your grandparents?'

'My Polish side. They swore they'd never hang around being sick, and they didn't. I have no idea whether my dad's side had any such pact, but they weren't much for lingering either.'

'Mmhmm,' says Shanaya.

I blow out a cloud of blue, a slipstream curling away behind the jeep.

'My brother Frank, he suffered. And he made us all suffer with him. I hate him for that. And I love him more than I hate him. He was bull-headed and brave, but also superstitious and afraid, and he took on his own mortality and wrestled with it, and in the end, drowned in a way, thrashing at us all, angry…but you don't want to say he was angry or afraid. I don't tell the kids that. I tell them the good parts, the parts where he was brave, where he was brash and bullheaded and determined to beat the disease…but refused Western treatments. And discovered too late that he hadn't studied on the Traditional medicines, and hadn't accounted for his own fear of them, fear of the judgement that he didn't deserve for them to work for him, because he was half-White. Nobody tells you about that fucking sick thing, that internalized racism…such a bland and useless euphemism for a thing that eats people unless they grab it by the throat and beat its head in with the rock of pure truth–we are human. That is what we are born. The rest of it is bullshit.'

Shanaya coughs, grinds out her cigarette. I can feel her bristling. I put a hand on her arm.

'And yet,' I say, keeping my voice low, 'you know better. I know better. And I'm just trying to figure out what fucking use it is to know all this–'

I wave my hand stupidly, then whisper, 'knowing you are a tiger, and Jim was a dog, and there was a *Zabeh* on the hill in the night, and Maengan is a wolf–'

To my surprise, Shanaya laughs.

'Hey, Hazel,' she says softly, 'it's a lot. Give yourself a break.'

I look over at her, startled. She's got this awful sad gentle look on her like I've never seen.

'Tell me, friend, what in this world prepares you for discovering this?' And she flicks a hand toward me, letting it show a flash of fur, a flash of claw. I nearly drive off the road.

'Fuck!' I hiss, goggling in the mirror. The Embryo snores on, unaware. Shanaya giggles.

'Relax,' she says, 'she will be out for a while more.'

'I just, just didn't know you could do that,' I say.

'Well,' she purrs, 'I couldn't, at first. It took years to get comfortable in my own skin, so to speak.'

'Look,' I say, 'I've lost the thread here. I was trying to say that I'm...'

'Feeling a little overwhelmed, yes?' says Shanaya. She's still got that sad and gentle look, that tone in her voice that makes me want to cry. Damn it.

'Don't think this is the time to talk about it, but yes,' I hiss, flicking another glance at the lumpen shape in the back seat.

Shanaya lights me a new smoke.

'It's okay, okay?' she says. 'One thing I've learned is, when it gets too weird to think about head on, it's okay, in fact it's healthy, to put it out of your mind, think about anything else at all.'

'I'm no good at small talk,' I mutter.

She turns on the radio, finds an oldies station, and we let Fleetwood Mac console us with their songs of heartbreak and ordinary human love.

And yet, I can't deny what I've seen. Hell, I met Jim when he was being his dog self, Spider. He may not have been that wise, but he was smart enough to follow the coaching he got, to come to me in that form that I might more easily accept him. It worked.

Yeah, I've got my history with men, not always the best of choices, me–but a dog? Who doesn't love a good mutt? I'll never forget the day I came home and caught him being a man, naked no less, sleeping on my sofa...that was a shock, sure, but kind of funny.

My good friend Shanaya, now, she scared the everliving crap out of me the first time she shifted shapes.

That's the thing. There are any number of myths and legends from all around the world that feature shapeshifters–werewolves and vampires and bearwalkers oh my–but none of those really tell you how it works, or more importantly, why it happens. So it's scary as fuck. And in a way, that's what you expect, so it's easier to accept, in a way.

But seeing the mythological sleeping ball-ass naked on your sofa? That sure as hell brings to mind the How and Why–not to mention the *What the Actual Fuck…?*

I've had time since Jim died to consider those questions, and I haven't got any answers. But I do have a little bit of apprehension… and a little bit of rage…and a daughter who is now dating an actual werewolf. Fuck.

I sneak a glance over at Shanaya, who is singing sotto voce about *never break the chain*, her golden eyes fixed on the open land ahead. I try again.

'Jim, see, he was a were-dog, and that distinction accords with what I understand of those stories…my dad's cousins used to scare the ever-loving out of us when they'd come out from the Rez, with their late-night stories of bad people who turned into dogs. Not wolves. Wolves have a clan relationship with us, and they're considered to be teachers and frickin' paragons of virtue, wolves. But dogs. Dogs are symbiotic. They are part of us in a different way. They're the trouble right there in your own house, where you should feel safe.'

Shanaya looks stricken. I shut up. Steve Winwood comes on, singing about how there must be higher love. I don't know about that. But I know Shanaya came with me that night.

Know she's trusted me with her darkest, scariest secret.

'Wolves are cool, though. Natural. Like tigers. Tigers are cool,' I say, desperate to lighten the mood. I should not try to explain myself. 'Like in the Calvin & Hobbes books. Tigers. Cool.'

'Tigers could crush your head any time they wanted,' she purrs, and begins singing along with Steve... *I could light the night up with my soul on fire...*

I join in, and we let it pass, and I am not really okay, but my best friend is an awesome beast and that is, in fact, very cool.

Winwood's backup singers bring it home, wailing sweetly *Bring me a higher love,* and we rock on down the highway, me and my tiger friend and the bundle of trouble in the back seat. And I guess that is more than enough trouble, but my thoughts lope on wildly alongside.

My girl Frankie tells me that the dog thing is some sort of metaphor for colonial history... I don't know...

But however revered your wolves are among us? I do not like nor trust that Maengan boy my Missy has taken up with. Not going to lie, when I first saw him on my porch–my porch!–talking with her as if he belonged there? My blood ran cold. I don't know why.

Or maybe I do...

After all, he is the case in point that I thought of when Frankie started talking about trauma and history of trauma as triggers for shapeshifting... I met that Maengan out in Ontario. We were both at some conference.

A busy body old auntie from Dad's reserve introduced us and laid out the lines by which we are related–distant enough that I felt no need to embarrass him any more than he already seemed (teenagers!) and claim any kind of senior relative rights.

But when I stepped out for a smoke that night and found him hiding in the hotel courtyard, obviously beaten up–well, you don't have to be a relative to help a kid out, do you? He didn't want any authorities, didn't want to talk about what happened. He was mortified, and so I kept quiet, brought him in, made tea while he got himself cleaned up, and checked he wasn't concussed, then let him stand with his decision not to do anything else about it.

You want the truth? Maybe I feel guilty that I didn't insist that he tell me what happened.

Maybe it bugs me that it was so easy for me to decide I was honouring his dignity, instead of chickening out, by letting him–a skinny bashed up kid–tell me he was fine and would handle it himself.

But I did that.

And then he came and found me.

Moved to my city.

Neither of us still wanted to talk about it.

I still don't know if I believe what I think I believe about what happened.

And now he's seeing my daughter. And now there is not a damned thing I can do about that. Tell her about him? She's my daughter. You can't tell her anything she doesn't want to hear.

Besides, what can I tell her she doesn't already know? She already knew he was a werewolf that night that Jim died–and she's seeing him anyway.

Sometimes I think my family are crazy, every single one of us.

But then I think again–there are stories all over the world, in every culture, about shape-shifting. Why would this be an idea in literally every culture of humans in the known world, if it weren't based in truth?

We say things like *everyone used to believe the world was flat,* but there's no actual proof we all ever did believe that, is there? It's one story. Like werewolves are one story, among a world of stories about how some among us might be other than we appear, and might take other shapes for various reasons, from the grand to the grotesque.

The Holy Spirit, in Catholic Tradition, is that a shapeshifter?

I have these questions when I have time to think about things. And I thought about things through a whole season. Kept my head down, kept quiet. Worked from home. Acted normal and tried to think myself around to this all just being normal.

My girls just seemed to take it all in stride. Werewolves and tigers and *Zabeh*…they cried that night, then squared their shoulders and walked away from the alley and left Joshua's body there for the inevitable authorities to find.

I'm the asshole who looked around as we left the scene of the deadly confrontation, looked for surveillance cameras, but we are not New York City, we don't have cameras on every corner, let alone in the alleys up here. But the authorities would find him at some point.

Someone would anonymously call it in, for instance.

How were they going to deal with Joshua's death? A police officer killed violently, unprovoked, weren't they going to go after whoever did that?

There was a little talk about it, but to be honest, world events still blast into our local media 24/7 and in the face of major international crises, ubiquitous political scandals, and the doings of the rich and famous, most people lose interest in the death of an ordinary city cop, a single man, a man who after all turns out to be from a background not unlike my own.

I remember choking up reading Joshua's obituary, realizing I was actually going to go to the bastard's funeral. And I did, and I heard his eulogy, and I realized I'd never really known him, would never apprehend what drove him, what he was actually up to getting involved with me…getting close to Missy because she was posting information about some guys who died.

Joshua, it turns out, somehow being a mentor to all those dead guys. I remember their names being spoken in the service, remember the eulogist (some relative or other) talking about how he'd been like a big brother to those boys–*Boys!?* Sexual predators, addicts, petty criminals, those boys–I got pretty angry, listening. I guess I made a noise. I guess my neighbours in the sparsely populated pews heard that noise. People throwing dark glances my way… I wanted to stand up and shout, 'Those *boys* killed Nell August!' But I didn't.

I just slid out of my seat and left, as quietly as possible, because in fact I had no proof of that, despite months of looking into that stupid little pointless murder.

At the church sanctuary door, I turned back and surveyed the room. My moment of disruption had passed, and they were all turned back to the service.

There was Joshua's life's work, half a churchful of people, some of their faces familiar to me, not friends, just people I'd seen around for years. Some business owners. An official or two, jittering politely in their suits, and a handful of cops to bear the pall of own of their own.

One of those turned and looked right at me. He knew–not many had–that Josh and I had been a couple. I hunched my shoulders and dropped my head, uncomfortable feigning a surfeit of grief. Lifted my head, ashamed of myself. And then the tears stung my nose and that really pissed me off.

It's not like I cared deeply for the guy.

I slid out the doors, shaking it all off as I descended to the street. Walked along, listening to my shoes on the sidewalk, keeping my eyes to myself. The neighbourhood was quiet, sleepy under sun. This place had been his life and work.

I'd slept with him, but never really thought about the fact that Joshua Campeau was a boy here, grew up in this part of Amiskwaciy, survived its limited expectations and constant invitations to join the fallen and the failed, hung on instead to that other thread that binds this place, that sense of solidarity and mutual support. The old Italian gardeners would have been more plentiful in his childhood, those ones who tend their tomatoes and onions with one eye on the street, ready to nod and greet anyone passing, to give and receive the news of the day.

Joshua grew up here, and decided to become a policeman.

The man I knew so briefly was a nice man, in some ways. He spoke with a kind cadence, no need for tough-guy media cop pretences. He was handsome and he knew it, and he was vain about it, but I can admit now that I got it, that vanity. In fact, I found it endearing (until I didn't) that he seemed to regard his own physical beauty like a surprise, a gift he somehow hadn't expected. And he took pride in keeping fit, and keeping his taffy-brown hair well-groomed.

Isn't it strange, how much we can remember about someone we didn't really know? Someone we were glad to see die, when it happened? What are we, assholes? Guess I am.

DEVIN: SILENCE

At first, Devin mostly sleeps. Frankie and he share meals, but otherwise, she lets him be. So he sleeps, and contemplates Frankie's blue-toned apartment, and stays out of the little storage room, shooting dark looks at the door when he passes it. His bike is in there. Hers is hung from the ceiling on some sort of pulley system, out of the way. He'll ride to work, come the time.

For now, he doesn't need to open that door.

The morning Frankie leaves, they all meet for breakfast up at Uncle Albert's pancake house, Missy and Maengan, Hazel and Sandra, Devin and Frankie. Devin sweats through the whole meal, with no idea what to say to any of them. They all talk small talk, surface things, talk around the hovering presence of change.

Devin catches his Aunt Hazel shooting a glare at Maengan, realizes she does not approve. That shifts his attention. Not a surprise, really. Aunt Hazel is edgy like that. She's never been a warm and cuddly person. He wonders for an instant what his life might have been if she, not Auntie Sandra, had been his guardian after his parents' deaths. And he flashes a reflexive small smile at Sandra, then looks down, embarrassed when she smiles softly back.

They stand on the sidewalk waving as Frankie climbs into the little blue car. She pauses, gives them all one last smile with her arms raised high, her hands cupped together to form the shape of a heart.

'See you,' she says. 'Love you.'

And she closes the door on their responses, and drives away, heading south.

'You want a ride?' Maengan asks. Devin considers them all, then smiles softly.

'Thanks. But it's a nice day, think I'll walk.'

As soon as he gets back to Frankie's, he heaves a great sigh. Then he goes over and pulls the guitar case from behind the sofa and stows it in the little storage room, up high in the back.

He goes back to the living room, sits down in the silence, just breathing.

HAZEL: THE OBVIOUS MOVE

'Pull over,' I say.

'Mmm, no,' says Shanaya, glancing in her rearview.

'What?!'

'I'm not 100% sure we're not being followed,' says Shanaya.

'Shit,' says a tiny voice, succinctly, from the heap of blankets.

Shanaya shakes her head at me.

The car that's been following us speeds up and shoots by.

'Cop car,' I say. I recognize the shape, the extra burliness of it, that ugly colour that I think as 'plainclothes' that only non-cruiser police vehicles wear. We watch it accelerate away, nothing to do with us. All three of us heave a sigh, as if on cue.

'How you doing back there?' I ask.

'Alive,' says Édith. 'Where are we going, by the way?'

'Yes, Shan,' I chime in, 'where are we going?'

Shan quirks an eyebrow at me.

'I know a place,' she purrs, and as she turns South, I suspect I know. Central Alberta sweeps by, the heavy-headed grain in the fields, the hay, the cattle, all bucolic peace when viewed from a window. The Embryo is back under cover, missing the show.

Shanaya turns West, and we roll through the stupidly sunny afternoon, angling obliquely back toward Amiskwaciy.

'Do you think this is wise?' I ask.

Shan shakes her head, shushes me.

'It's fine, Hazel,' she says sotto voce. 'Don't wake her up.

Don't worry her.'

'She's awake,' says Édith groggily from the back seat. 'We'd better not be going to the police. I'll tell them you did this to me.'

'Trust me,' says Shanaya, 'and stay quiet back there.'

And sure enough, she brings us into the labyrinthine streets of Mill Woods and shortly, into a little strip mall parking lot.

'Wait here,' she says, and hops out of the car before we can respond. She goes into a little store, and she's not gone more than fifteen minutes, but it seems like a lifetime, sitting there awkwardly in the car. Every time I glance in the mirror, The Embryo is looking at me, and we both look away quick. It's almost absurd, and I'm close to cracking from the tension by the time Shan gets back. She opens the backdoor and puts a bag quickly on the seat, then hops in front again.

'What's that?' I ask.

'Édith, that's for you. Put it on, and you can sit up.'

'Uhh…'

'Over your head, Grandma,' says Shanaya, and Édith nods.

'Got it.' She pulls out a gauzy shawl and drapes it over her hair.

'Are you sure about this?' I ask, as we turn into Diya's street.

'Absolutely,' Shanaya says.

'But–' I begin, but Shanaya waves me off.

'I texted Diya when we were in Big Bend.'

'Seriously?!'

I gape just a little, wondering what that text would say– 'Hi Mom. Got room for a beat-up fugitive to hide for a while? We don't know if anyone's actively hunting her.'

'Trust me, it's fine.'

'But–'

'Shh shh shh,' says Shanaya, grinning like a fiend, 'Trust me.'

***

Shanaya parks on the street, steps out of the car, and stretches her back, shaking out her long hair. At that, I notice a curtain twitching on the second floor, and by the time Shan has helped the shrouded little woman out of the car, Diya has descended and is out the door, shouting hammily.

'Oh Auntie-Ji! How wonderful that you came to visit us!'

Diya barges past Shanaya and wraps the very startled Embryo in her embrace, slickly pulling her headscarf slightly forward as she does, and taking up position on Édith's right, arm around her waist, Shanaya at her left, they scoop the old lady form up the sidewalk.

Diya calls gaily back, 'Hazel, come come. Did Auntie-Ji bring a bag? Bring it. Come come.'

Chattering and burbling, Diya noisily conducts us into her house. Inside, she locks the door and leads the rather dazed and confused Édith to an armchair. The Embryo drops into it gratefully, loosing the scarf so it drops into a shawl collar–utterly gracefully so, as if it has been made for her, made to fit just like that and to show off her pallor and outsized eyes; the way her hair contrives to look like the newest edgy style instead of what it is, a mess hacked into baby-bird tufts by Shanaya in the cabin in the shocking night.

Diya reaches down and takes both of Édith's hands in hers.

'My dear, you must be exhausted.'

Never mind that she's spent the whole of the day so far curled up in Shanaya's backseat, sleeping. The Embryo does in fact look done in, and she just nods and in fact, a few tears drop down her pale face. I turn away.

Diya waves in annoyance at Shanaya, who passes her a box of Kleenex.

'La la, Miss,' says Diya, 'You need a drink. Stay here.'

Édith makes a little 'buh' noise blown out her lips.

I turn away to laugh at the world of feeling in that tiny breathy syllable. *Where would I go? I am so scared. So glad to be here. Thank you thank you. Who the hell are you? Are you for real?* All of that in a little puff of sound.

Diya sweeps out of the room and back in a flash, bearing a beautiful lidded mug. She pushes it into Édith's bewildered hands, removes the ornate lid and helps/forces Édith to lift it toward her lips.

The smell wafts throughout the room, warm, pungent, sweet.

'Wh-?' breathes Édith.

'Chai,' says Diya. 'Drink. It will warm you.'

It's not a cold day, but of course that's not what she means. I find myself wanting a little chai my own self, and as if reading my thoughts, Shanaya comes back (I hadn't seen her leave) into the room with a tray bearing three cups, a tea pot and several tiny dishes full of dainty things to eat.

'La, la, Hazel, sit. Beti, sit,' says Diya, as she stands, hands on hips, in front of Édith until The Embryo takes a sip. Then, beaming, Shanaya's mother sits herself down, proprietarily closest to the fugitive stranger she's already bullying into wellness.

I step outside for a smoke and Shan comes after me, bums one off me and holds it in her elegant fingers like she wants to stab somebody.

'God,' she says, 'I hate it when my mother pulls out that phony-Hindu Auntie act–*La la la, Beti*–like she's not entirely part of modern Canadian society, like she is drawing from some deeper well of tradition or something.'

I light her smoke. It doesn't bother me. I wouldn't know phony from real Hindu Auntie. Nothing I can say.

DEVIN: PICK A PATH

'So,' says Missy, 'what did you want to ask me about?'

'When did you know you'd found your path?'

Missy almost laughs. But he is so serious, always.

'My path?'

'Yes,' he takes a tiny sip of hot tea.

She considers.

'Do you mean my work?'

His round eyes meet hers. 'That and the John TakeDown thing. They go together, right?'

'I suppose they do, when you come to think about it. I just never really have. I just—did what felt right at the time.'

Her hands unconsciously cradle her navel. She'd seen battered hookers, and set out to stop men abusing them.

He bobs his big head.

'But…which came first?'

Chicken or egg…what choice, what consequence… She places her hands on the table.

'Good question. Frankie and me, we were always interested in history, in culture, in being Indigenous—you know, it seemed to matter.'

Devin nods.

'It does. But it's not a job, let alone a career.' He looks so sad. She remembers her mother ranting about how his father Big Frankie had 'Gone Professional' with his embrace of their Indigenous ethnicity.

And then she'd gone to Seoul on a working holiday visa, and found herself wandering through streets where she was instantly identifiable as Canadian. And yet, she'd run into strange walls and incidents that drove home to her that she was not simply Canadian.

'I remember going to the consulate, to a talk they hosted with a Korean cultural expert. And I asked a question, afterwards, because I got excited about what they were saying about Korean culture, how it had survived centuries of incursion from the Chinese, from the Japanese, from the Americans... I asked them what did they think was the key to the survival and thriving of their Indigenous culture.'

Devin nods.

'And the little woman giving the talk snapped upright as if I'd slapped her, and in front of all those people, in a room hung with paintings by Dale Auger, she yelled at me—*We are not Indigenous people! And we do not HAVE Indigenous people!*'

Missy thumps the table. The waitress, in the corner of her eye, flinches and pretends not to.

'And everyone around me shrank away from me, and I just sat there stunned. You'd have thought I was accusing Koreans of being recidivist criminals. I'd meant it as a compliment.'

Missy shakes her head, a half smile meeting Devin's own vicariously offended expression.

'I was so mad. Nobody, in all the crowd of Canadians who'd come to this event, not a single person spoke up. I looked for our Consul in the crowd and he was doing that thing where he could not even see I existed. And then the moment passed. And the event went on. And I wanted to leave, but I didn't. And nobody would acknowledge me. I was like a stink in the room.'

Missy feels the waitress's attention, and it stokes her anger higher.

'And then one little Korean woman came over to me. I suppose she was connected to the consulate staff somehow, she'd been talking with them, and then she spied me, despite how I was invisible to everyone else. And she sidled over and started talking to me.

She told me she had been to Canada. To the north of Quebec, as a young missionary.'

'Seriously? Huh,' Devin says.

'I know, right? Like we didn't get enough missionaries from the old Europeans... but whatever. There she stood, telling me about her experience there, and it dawned on me that she had been sent to explain, more or less, why I'd caused so much offence by implying Koreans were Indigenous.'

'*Those people*, she said, '*they fed me rabbit soup!*'

Missy mimics a delicate shudder of polite horror.

'*I mean, they ate rabbits! Killed them and ate them, and I had to, too.*'

'What did you say?' prompts Devin.

Missy snorts.

'I looked around the room, you know. Dale Auger paintings on the walls, Inuit carvings in glass cases, little maple sugar leafs on the fucking table with the refreshments... and I just said, '*Two words for you. Dog soup.*' And I left. Nobody said anything to me. Fuck them all.'

***

The waitress has come gliding with hot water to check on Devin's tea, and she gives Missy a horrified glance before flitting away.

'The next day, one of my friends–well, you know, one of the other people in the program–says to me, *Why you gotta fly the flag so high? I mean, look at you. If you didn't keep pushing the Indigenous thing, nobody would know. You look normal–*'

Devin snorts with laughter.

'Almost human,' he quips.

'But seriously,' Missy continues.' It made me mad. That there's a whole world out there that doesn't have any clue who we are. Or worse, has this bizarre blend of images of us, and that's all. And nobody wants to see us as people, as full-spectrum real and–'

She shakes her head.

'And I thought about Uncle Frank–your Dad, and how much it cost him.'

Devin looks stricken for a moment, then recovers his bland face.

'Yeah, eh?' He says noncommittally, smoothing it over.

'Sorry.'

'It's okay. You're right. It ate him up, trying to be a Good Enough Indian.' His voice carries a slight growl. His father listening to the Elder telling him and the other people in the circle who were there to 'offer up' their sickness, *just believe*, like a priest ministering to the helpless.

'Just believe,' Devin mutters. 'Don't think. Just believe.'

'Like your dad could ever be told not to think.'

They fall silent for a little while, sipping their drinks.

'I feel,' says Missy, 'like we're getting off topic here. What was the question?'

'Why did you pick nursing? Why not, I don't know, politics or law or something like that? And how does it fit with the John Take Down website thing?'

'Nursing… I guess that's your dad and your mom, you know.'

'Oh.'

There's a world of understanding in the syllable. *His beautiful mother, skin and bone and sallow skin, shuffling toward him as he stood by the sink, peeling potatoes. He'd thought she'd pass by, but she walked right into him, bumping against his shoulder, breath huffing out in some caricature of sound,*

'Zsst zsst shrrrr'

He stands frozen as she bumps and hisses, until his father comes charging across the room and grabs her, urgently gently, pulls her away, scoops up her useless body and carries her to her bed.

When his father returns to the room, Devin turns to him, but his father, eyes red, throws a big hand toward him.

'Don't,' he says, and stomps out the door, letting it slam behind him. Devin looks around when Missy comes up the kitchen stairs.

'What happened?' She whispers. Devin shrugs and shakes his

head. Missy puts down the laundry basket, steps over and puts her arms around her little cousin.

'And Grandma. You probably don't remember her much, eh?'

'Not at all.'

'Well, you know,' she starts to look uncomfortable. 'It just made me mad, so many of us dying young like that, and I thought I could help, you know? Do something that really helps people.'

'But not going in for doctor?'

'Not yet.' She quirks an eyebrow. He nods.

'Nursing got me working faster, earning money to pay for med school. If I want to go.'

'You don't know?'

'No,' she says slowly. 'I…maybe. I don't know yet. So, when you ask me for advice? Sorry, cousin, this is the best I've got. I really don't know my own path.'

He nods, politely dropping his gaze. She finds her hands have closed over her belly.

'But what about you?' She says. 'What are you thinking to become?'

He flushes and frowns. 'Not a policeman, that's for sure.'

She looks startled.

'Somebody asked me, after the–that night–whether a big guy like me was interested.'

'And?'

'Not in this lifetime.'

'So, what are you considering?'

'That's just it. I don't know.'

'And?'

He swallows some tea. 'I feel kind of stupid asking now–'

'No. Don't. Never.'

'W-what–' his voice has a shadow of the stammer she remembers from his childhood.

'What do you think is a good thing for me to do?'

'You're asking me?'

He's flushed and tense and looks like he's going to bolt.

She puts out a hand, taps his arm tentatively. They're neither of them huggy sorts.

She blows out a breath.

'Frankie's the one who's good at these things. But…if you ask me… ' she tips her head on one side, considering. 'I'd say, what feels like it makes a real difference? When you imagine yourself finishing a day's work, how do you want to feel?'

'How do you feel?'

'Sometimes, Devin, I feel exhausted. Sometimes so frustrated by all the ways things go wrong for people, and then all the ways they make their own problems, or make them worse.'

Devin nods owlishly.

'But even on those days, I'll tell you this. There is always someone, somewhere in the day, that is just a bit better off for me having been part of their day. I look for that moment. I hold onto that moment. You know who taught me that?'

He shakes his head.

'Your father said it to me. About your mother. That he stood in awe of her because wherever they went, whatever they did, she somehow made things better for someone, every single day.'

Devin drops his head. *His mother, dressed in turquoise, her head lifted in song, a spotlight on her long soft hair. His mother, playing a fiddle tune for little old Bert down the street, smiling back when he grinned and tapped his cane in time. His mother, shouting at his father. His mother, bumping against him helplessly, hands fluttering, mouthing words that came out 'zssst, zsss, shrrr' her tongue discoloured, her eyes not recognizing him.*

HAZEL: WILD

We have a week of relative peace then.

I don't even think of protesting about leaving The Embryo with Diya. I really shouldn't call her that anymore, I'm thinking. Shanaya says so.

'You really shouldn't call her that anymore,' she says as we sit drying off in the sun.

'I know.'

Shan convinced me to drive back out to a little lake in the Gnarly Hills we found this spring, and we are sitting at our table in the late season sun. She also convinced me to get in the actual water with her. Not enough that she had Roy to go with her, I had to go too.

She laughed at me as I thrashed right back out again. She spun and dove and swam and turned her face up to the sky, laughing.

Suddenly–and I'll never tell her this–as she raised her arms and face out of the quiet green waters, a ray of light appeared around her, and I saw a woman of light and a tiger of light and a sceptre of light and then it vanished. She swam on.

Me, I stood rooted as it all ran through me like electricity–shock, awe, fear, joy, rage and utter calm. My toes in the grimy sand. My breath firing my heart. My mind, choosing how to respond to the Mystic.

That is a wonderful thing about being me. I choose.

It's like this: I was born into a mixed race family in Colonial Canada, my mother's family Slavic, my dad's Indigenous. My parents,

I used to grouse, were joined at the oppression. But the actual thing is, what they had in common on the surface–Roman Catholicism–was, at the next level, differently rooted in them. Mom was born into a Catholic family who brought the religion with them in the 1920s and practiced it in their own living room and that of the neighbours until the first churches were built up in the wild of The Peace country.

Dad was born on a Reservation; both his parents had experience of the Church-run schools, and he had little language left to lose when he went in his turn. He still left at 12, rather than go on from Day School to Residential. It's not an uncommon story, that defiance and escape, or we wouldn't have survived as people.

Nor is inter-cultural marriage that uncommon, or imperialists and other xenophobes down through the centuries wouldn't have made so many laws against it.

The thing is, mixed-race kids erase the easy lines. We rampage about in our hybrid vigour and bind enemies.

Not that we destroy enmity.

If I were in a pouting mood, I'd point out that we all too often just become lightning rods for that enmity. Not one thing nor the other? Both sides will hate you. But if you are smart and lucky and if you study on it, you find out you are actually just the basic human reality, for the most part.

We're made to breed outward. And the power of making entire humans who are not classifiable by lines of racial purity, well that causes a lot of uproar, but that uproar undermines damnable institutions like slavery, eventually.

Standing there on the shore I hear in my head Lzzy Hale singing, '*When kings fall to their knees, they sing a woman's song*' her pale face and shock of blonde hair shining among the dark-haired, dark-skinned Mongolians drumming and strumming and growling along. Lzzy (without an 'I') Hale and The Hü. Hybridity and the power of song.

As Shanaya frolics, I consider that my Polish relatives got Christianized nearly a millennium since, but I remember the little rituals, the folkways, the sense the Grandma belonged to the land, every land every where. My mom was like that, too. At her request, the flowers bloomed, the grain grew fat. Sandra's like her. Yeah, I'm jealous.

But I digress. The thing is, both sides of my family were uneasy Christians, their real beliefs running like mycelia, the legs of mushrooms, underneath the surface and breaking out in so many little unquenchable ways. Not that their listed spirituality was fake, that's not it.

It's just that, raised among them, I understood early on that a person can choose, to profess whatever creed they feel suits them on the surface, but not to let that creed stop their mind, heart, body and spirit from really encountering the world in its unquantifiable glory.

We were not of the stripe of RCs that ran the Inquisition. We could be, if we didn't choose to remember that what's real is real, and the first book is your own experience of life. I chose that book.

Call me an asshole, I am sometimes; but I'm also a realist. I believe my own eyes first. And if I see a tiger of light and a woman of light and a sceptre of light surround my lawyer friend as she capers in a too-cold lake, too late in the season? I might feel the pressure to react with fear. I might have flash through my head all the imagery mainstream North American society used for so long to try to turn the ungovernable meek; might in a flash recall that, in many times and places, that woman in the lake would be considered a demon, a monster, a witch not to be suffered to live.

But my eyes and my heart and my experience of her are what I choose.

My mind is my own.

My friend is a tiger.

I choose to be glad about that.

***

'Hey!' I call out. 'You going to be much longer? I'm getting hungry here. Going to start a fire.'

She waves, grinning and I swear her teeth shimmer. *Damn, but she's unfairly beautiful.*

I do not like fires. I don't like to start them, don't like to tend them, don't really like all that smoke. I'm a smoker, you wouldn't think it would bother me, but campfires are different than tobacco. They make me nervous, if you want to know. But we should have a fire. The cold water is invigorating, Shan was right about that, but now I am frickin' cold. I gather such little sticks and bits of kindling as I can scrounge around the grounds. This little park has one of those bins for pre-cut firewood, but when I mosey over for an armful, it's pretty much empty. I'm gazing at it, ambivalently shivering, when Shan bounds up to me, bundled in her dry robe.

'These things are great, aren't they!' She enthuses.

'Mmm,' I muster in agreement, thankful for my own dry-robe, a present from Shanaya who got her cousin in England to send them over.

'Like a modern take on Inuit parkas,' Diya had enthused when we unpacked them. 'One for me, one for you,' she passed a bundle to Shanaya, 'and one for you, Hazel.'

Before I'd been able to recover and find any words, Diya had opened hers out and put it on, swinging her arms and prancing about the living room like a much younger woman.

'Go on, put it on!' She'd urged, and we had, and there we'd been, three cowled women sporting the latest UK trend, the oldest of us crooning and coquetting like a runway model, Shan and I rather sheepishly turning our sleeves this way and that, examining the fluffy lining, the waterproof exterior.

'Now you must take up wild swimming,' Diya had declared. Neither of us dared correct that 'you' to a 'we.'

***

And here we are, Shan and I shivering in our long hooded robes all fresh and invigorated, and I spare a grumpy thought for Shanaya's British cousin who'd gotten all swept up in the notion that swimming in nature, in icy bodies of water, year round if possible, is a health panacea. Shan had gone over to visit, after all the madness with Jim. At the time, I'd thought it would do her good. And then she came back raving about swimming at dawn with Cousin Sophie and her friends in the Cherwell in darkest Oxford.

Shan peers into the wood bin.

'Huh,' she says. 'So if we want a fire we have to forage for wild wood, is it?'

'Yup,' I say glumly.

She claps me on the back.

'Good. That makes for an easy decision. Get in the car, we can warm up as we drive.'

'What about food?'

'What? Did you actually bring–?'

I reach into the car and extricate a bag, from which I draw a pack of wieners.

'All beef.' I say. 'It feels a bit wasteful to bring them all this way and then abandon them.'

A crow calls nearby.

I grin.

'Of course, in my tradition, it's good to leave offerings for our fellow-travellers, for those who keep the land.'

I flip open my switchblade, open the pack and lay out a couple wieners on the table.

'Hey, guardian of the forest,' I say to the crow, 'enjoy.'

The thing is, I mean it. And so I'm actually feeling extremely harmonious, even before Shanaya adds, 'Save some for the water guardians,' and points toward the lake where some sort of fish–trout, perch, jack, who knows–just broke the surface.

'I expect purist conservationists from the university might frown on us polluting the water like this,' I say, keeping things light.

'Yes,' purrs Shanaya, 'but they are not here.'

And she strides back to the water, wieners dangling from both hands, and sidearms the lot of them out into the lake. The light does that glowing mystic thing on her again, like she is some aspect of some Goddess. Only I don't know which one would turn back around and come flouncing back, her own mouth stuffed full of wiener.

I laugh.

She nearly chokes, laughing too.

And I scatter the bread as an offering too, and we head out, content to find our dinner somewhere where human hands have already decided its form and done the alchemical work of preparation.

***

'Where's Roy?' Asks Shanaya as we drive.

'Staying with Missy and Maengan. Why?'

'Tell you what then, let's really splash out.'

I text Missy to say we might be late.

'K,' she texts back. Good enough. I don't see that she has any reason to protest. It's kind of her fault I have a dog, suddenly, again.

The girls gave him to me.

Frankie claimed she was going to keep him for a friend of hers, and then she got this research trip and so now she can't keep him, and I work from home mostly, so could I just, could I please.

Of course I smelled a rat. Or a sasquatch. Something stinky and meddling.

But I took a look at the weird little mutt and of course I said yes.

The fuzzy little bastard is cute, and he knows it. Maybe I shouldn't swear so much. Sandra's always shaking her head and squishing her lips at me.

'You don't have to talk like that, Hazel,' she says one time, ill-advisedly, 'you've been to university.'

Fine, the fuzzy little son of a bitch, then. That's not swearing. That's just accurate.

Roy is mine for the interim, and he's a real dog, not just part-time, not a shapeshifter, at least as far as I can detect. If he is, he's a lot smarter than he looks, because he never says a peep telepathically, never seems to affect my thoughts. He's just good-natured and kind of easy to have around.

As an added bonus, he isn't rude about it, but Roy doesn't seem to like Maengan.

Well, he wouldn't would he? What dog is easy with a wolf around the house?

DEVIN: RAVINE

In the wake of Frankie's departure, Devin starts walking. From Frankie's place, Devin walks East through the residential streets, crossing 99th street by Our Lady Queen of Poland church.

He stops for a moment before stepping out onto the rainbow crosswalk.

His father was half-Polish.

Does a quarter of him belong to Our Lady Queen of Poland?

He shrugs, keeps on walking, trying not to think too much, just watching the pattern of light through leaves along the shady sidewalk.

He walks until the houses end and he reaches the edge of Mill Creek Ravine, then he finds a path down into the forested ravine. He hears dogs and bike bells and human voices. Somewhere a crow calls. Gravity makes it easy, that first time, to descend into the tiny wilderness. He wonders why he's never come here before, and marvels at this world enfolding him. Leaves are beginning to fall, here and there, and the canopy is lightly flecked with gold.

He encounters people, but they let him pass without comment. It's his size, his hood up. Some of them outright shrink away. Women walking ahead of him look over their shoulders and tense up, gripping keys or cell phones or walking sticks.

He wants to apologize.

He wants to scream.

He just wants to be left alone to quietly walk; but the Ravine is popular.

He tries different times of day. There's always somebody out there; families, lovers, friends and tourists, runners and bikers and dog walkers. So he takes to traveling in the twilight, ahead of dawn.

It still leaves the days. He can't wait for his job to start.

But by the time it does, he is hooked. He wakes, walks in the twilight ravine, eats his breakfast and bikes to work. At home in the evenings, he abides in silence, waiting to be tired enough to sleep.

HAZEL: DEUS EX ETCETERA

So, in the event, we just keep driving, laughing in our dry robes like a couple of loony she-wizards until we start overheating, then we pull over and shed them, right there on the side of the road, to stand naked and laughing for a moment. Fuck it. I'm middle-aged, let anyone say I can't. I may not get a mystical light shining around me, my stretch marks and scars and saggy bits, but it feels gloriously good to just stand there in my skin and nothing more, letting myself be one with the world.

Then Shanaya yells 'Car!' cupping her hand melodramatically to her ear (tigers have super-hearing I guess), and we dive for our clothes, whip them on and wait for the car to pass us. The driver slows down a bit in case we need him to stop and help, the way some people still do–it's getting rare in this age of cell phones–and we wave him cheerfully onward, then ease in his wake back onto the highway, kick it back up to highway speed.

'Where are we going?' I ask.

'Not home,' she says. No need to say more, really. Diya is foster-mothering Édith and neither of us are comfortable in that scene. And both of us can handle business via our phones–wonder of this modern age, that! –and I don't have anyone at home to worry about, not even a dog…

We bear South, then West, find ourselves bowling down Highway 22, through rolling farmland and the newly bustling small towns; Alder Flats, Rocky Mountain House, Chedderville,

Caroline, and a few names now that tell the story of change–Amalapuram, Whiskeyjack, New Baraka–until we pick up the old TransCanada and arrive in Banff in the dark.

Bad enough she brings me to a tourist town, but Shanaya, bold as you please, drives right up to the Fairmont Banff Springs and gets us a suite. Of course there's one available for the beautiful barrister and her guest. A little apartment, two beds hidden by useless decorative pillows, a kitchenette and a fridge stocked with overpriced luxuries.

'In the morning,' she says, claiming her bed, 'we will find swimsuits and hit the hot springs.'

So we do.

***

'Sitting here steaming, looking at this view, I could almost forget that we have to figure out what to do about what Édith told us. About agricultural workers being kidnapped and trafficked–where? How? To whom? Tale as old as time…but God…' Shanaya sighs. The sound echoes weirdly.

'Shouldn't we just go to the police, Shan?'

'As a lawyer, I am inclined of course to agree,' she says, raising her aquiline nose and gazing at the far mountains. 'But…'

'But what?' I need to keep my voice lower. There are only a handful of guests in the waters with us, but sound echoes funny around here. I see a young guy in the corner flick a glance at us when I speak, look back out the window.

'But I have worked with immigrants before,' she says quietly. 'And with those who seek to exploit legal immigrants who don't know their rights and are frightened that they will put a foot wrong and be sent back to things they gave all they had to escape.'

I nod. I've read the news. I've transcribed things in court, admittedly mostly for Indigenous cases when I get the choice, but still. Everybody these days knows a little about immigration, we've had so much of it since the Delhi Tech deal brought us planeloads of people–mostly single, mostly young, mostly men until someone figured out that that's a recipe for unrest and at least balanced out the genders–to repopulate the small towns and revitalize the land in ways we're all still getting used to.

And if I'm being honest, I'm not too good with the police right now. Always been a bit ambivalent, as a woman of the Indigenous persuasion. It's true my looks are ambiguous, if you don't know my lineage. I tan easily, my skin carries a golden undertone, and my hair blends. I could be anything in this globalized world.

Unlike these kids we are talking about, who will all be plainly new immigrants. It will show in everything about them, not just in their darker skin. And either way, I've heard enough stories about how things are different for brown folks, when it comes to official-dom.

I study Shanaya's face a moment in profile as she stares into space.

The high nose, Diya's way of holding her head, the glorious dark hair with its odd brindle.

She turns just then, catches me staring.

'My dad was an Indian,' she says.

I frown.

'Well, duh,' I blurt, not thinking.

'No,' she says, 'Your kind.'

'What?!' I shout and everyone's eyes swivel to us. I'm properly embarrassed.

'What?' I repeat, in a meek little voice.

Shanaya looks away again, lets her legs drift up 'til her toes peek out of the water.

'I'm starving,' she says. 'I'll tell you about it over brunch.'

'I'm going to have to go out for a smoke first,' I say.

***

'*Deus ex Machina*,' I say, coming into the restaurant to find her sipping coffee.

'Hmm?' She says, raising her eyebrows.

'Deus ex Machina, God from a Machine.'

'Yes, I'm familiar with the phrase. But what brings that to mind?'

I shrug. A young man excuses himself and brushes past me, moving like he was born to this kind of scene, and I'm aware of the space I occupy.

'I just…walked through the place to find somewhere to smoke in private, and wow. There is no way I could realistically visit this place. Not me. But you can just sweep on in and not even ask the price. So, I am gifted an unexpected visit to just the sort of luxury I didn't know I needed.'

'Sit down, Hazel,' she says, 'don't be dramatic.'

I sit. She sighs.

'I'm sorry,' she says, not very penitently,' but I am a lawyer. Good money. And Diya's family has bags of money, so I'm,' she shrugs elegantly, 'an heiress, to boot, I guess you'd say. So, don't feel guilty. It's just money.'

Well it's not just money to me, I've never had it to throw around. But I look at her now and for once in my stubborn life, the chip on my shoulder isn't top of mind. Her astonishing revelation has me a bit thrown.

'Sorry,' I said, 'it just seemed…funny?'

'I suppose it is.' She grins. 'Deus ex Machina. Should I add that to my CV, then?'

'Nope,' I retort, 'but you could serve me some of that posh coffee.'

'Serve yourself,' she laughs, holding out the carafe to me, but the waiter has arrived and deftly takes it from her, fills my cup, takes my order and glides away like a swan.

***

'Now,' I say, once we've gotten through an excellent breakfast and are sipping one last leisurely coffee, 'what's this about your father?'

She drinks her coffee, puts it down, stifles a burp.

I boggle.

'Sorry,' she grins, 'better out than in, right?'

She catches the waiter's eye, signs the chit, and sighs.

'Now that I've eaten, it seems like a story better told walking.'

'You deceitful–'

'Come on, Hazel,' she says, 'you're dying for a smoke, right?'

I've been cutting back since we took up this cold-water swimming, but I nod.

And once we're outside, I offer her one first. She says she's quit entirely, but of course she lights up, once we're clear of the millennials outside the door. I imagine one of them is the guy from the hot tub and the restaurant, looking us up and down. What, does he own the place? All of them frown at our cigarettes, even unlit apparently anathema. Their rolling eyes seem to ask *How are you even still alive?*

***

We stroll through the town in the fresh cool morning with its scent of early frost and suspiciously bright-eyed elk mooching about.

'So, my father,' she begins. 'My father was Canadian. My mother met him in India while she was doing her undergraduate work.'

'What was he doing there?'

'He was a soldier.'

I quirk an eyebrow.

'What war?'

She shakes her head. 'No war. Not officially.'

'Oh?'

'He was part of a multinational UN-sponsored special operation.'

'How cloak and dagger.'

'Well, yes,' she says, 'it was. Growing up, I never got any details. I used to get mad at Mummy, think she was holding out on me. But she wouldn't say, no matter how hard I'd badger her.'

Shanaya holds out her hand, I slip her another smoke.

'And then a few years ago, I came home for dinner one evening, and she put some papers on the table. *Look*, she said, *they just declassified your father's mission.* I remember I was shocked. She hadn't been hiding information from me. She just hadn't known, because he'd not been able to tell her.'

'So, what was the mission?' I asked.

She blows out smoke.

'I kept the write-up. I'll show it to you sometime.' She looks off into the distance. 'The thing that sticks is that he was a marksman, a champion sharpshooter. Mom showed me that day, the trophies he'd won, that he'd never displayed, and she'd never displayed.'

I think about classified missions for sharpshooters, nod my head. My dad had been a soldier, too.

'Why didn't they throw them away, those trophies?'

'I asked her, and she said she didn't know what they meant to him, thought he was just being humble keeping them in a box. Then, after...she couldn't part with them, didn't want to display them...'

'Huh,' I say, fascinated by this glimpse of a Diya so unlike the decisive and forthright woman I knew.

We walk on, gazing at the semi-precious stones and artsy-craftsy bits on display in various shop windows.

'So, how old were you when he died?'

'Two? Three? I don't remember him,' she says, 'not really. I have a vague impression that he had a hideous plaid blazer, you know those ones in the '70s, orange and brown plaid and the like?'

I nod.

'My dad had one, too. So, what happened?'

'He fell off a mountain,' she says.

'What, over there?'

'No. Here. Robson, they called that mountain then. Mom always told me it was an accident; but I heard her one time, talking to a friend, saying she couldn't help thinking about how he'd not been in his right mind. He'd gone to the mountains to find some peace. She'd begged him not to go. And she'd known he was dead because I woke up crying and screaming, *Daddy daddy!*'

She shakes her head, runs a hand through her brindled black hair.

'But I don't remember any of that.'

We walk on.

'But he was an Indian? –Indigenous?'

'Well,' she says, 'that's another thing that my mother never talked about, until recently. I guess that was classified, too.' She makes a noise something like a laugh.

I shake my head. Diya, hiding an Indigenous husband in the cupboard, so to speak?

I snort.

Shanaya sighs.

'Actually,' she says, 'I pressed her on that, and she says, the truth is, she doesn't really know. Just that he always said he was.'

'Where from?'

'Said he was Montagnais. Bragged about how the mountains were in his very blood. That's where they met, both of them up in Nepal. She was doing a mad Diya thing and checking out the latest craze, trekking.'

'Diya!? Diya was *trekking?*'

'She says so,' shrugs Shanaya. 'She says she went with a group of school chums, and they met this guy in a teahouse in Kathmandu, actually.'

'Wild,' I say. I don't know what else to say, other than the obvious.

'So, what was his name, your dad? Surely not Bhattacharya?'

She sighs, shakes her head.

'No, Diya took back her family name. And I...well, I never really knew him, you know, so I don't mind that we don't flaunt his name.'

I stop and just look at her.

'Which was?'

She heaves another sigh.

'Bacon.'

'Bacon?'

'Don't laugh.'

'I'm not laughing,' I protest, hiding my asshole grin. 'Bacon like Kevin.'

'Like pig.' She shakes her head. 'Yes, I am a Bacon. Like Sir Francis, like Kevin, like pig. Bacon. From the old Norman or English, and occurring transplanted among the Québecois, particularly the Métis and Montagnais.'

'Huh.' I say.

'Does it show?' she says, turning her head ostentatiously left and right, 'That we are distant cousins?'

***

On the car ride home, she says, 'By the way, I've spared you the whole long drama of Diya versus my grandparents. They did not approve of her choice of husband. They threatened to disinherit her. She took her trust fund and absconded to Canada, to relatives in Mill Woods. They sided with her parents. She told them all where to go–'

'Ah,' I say, 'that sounds more like the Diya I know.'

'And then she told them she'd never bring me to see them. And they fought until 1987, when her father relented, because he thought her mother was dying. So we went there. And while we were there, I was Shanaya Bacon. And we never told them that here, we have always gone by Bhattacharya.'

People, I tell you. We're all full of surprises.

SHANAYA: STRIPES

She remembers things striped. She remembers that she doesn't know what she sees. She remembers her father, safety and Old Spice after-shave. But she remembers his terrified eyes. One tiger. Two tigers. Some things you just can't explain. The smell of Old Spice trailing out the door, away.

What would it be like for a man who was taught that there are monsters in the world in the old ways, and that you are safe if you live a modern life? What would that man make of being a soldier sent to the high places of the world?

Imagine meeting a beautiful young woman with eyes both gold and shadow, with a glory of black hair, a proud nose, a voice both clipped and musical.

He fell off a mountain.

DEVIN: BASICS

One day, Devin picks up the guitar. He holds it a little gingerly, as if he's not supposed to, as if someone might come in and yell at him for this trespass.

Nothing happens, for long minutes.

So, he strums it, open stringed, and listens. He tunes the D string. Strums again. Adjusts the B. Strums a third time and nods.

And then he looks around again, reaches one finger and switches on the little built-in tuner. No light. He sighs, pops open the battery compartment to check the size. He looks around, considering, puts the dead battery on the coffee table and plucks the strings two by two, tuning them to each other.

'Close enough for jazz,' he murmurs, and starts to play, the chords coming back, tears tracking unnoticed down his round cheeks as he remembers his father's scornful voice, taunting his mother.

Why bother showing him anything? Kid's as thick as a plank. No ear. And slow. He'll never be any good.

Slowly, Devin's big fingers reach the shapes, the first position–*farmer chords*–he remembers his father scoffing after the Peace Country cousins left, reviewing the hazel-eyed cousin's playing–C, F, G; G, D, C; D, G, A; A, D, E.

A minor. E minor. He moves between these two, begins humming under the sound, opens his mouth to sing, and can't stop the sob that breaks out.

He stops, puts the guitar down, gently, and bows his head to cry, softly, quietly. Not to disturb anyone.

Then he closes the guitar back in its case, pockets the dead battery, scrubs his face at the kitchen sink, dries it on a tea towel and heads out.

HAZEL: DREAMSCAPES

I'm standing at the farm gate, looking out across the snowy fields, waiting for my mother to come home. From the place where white field meets white sky, a snowy owl comes soaring, skimming over the snow. In the dream, it locks eyes with me, then turns aside and glides on. A stag snorts a cloud of breath that hides the scene.

I wake up, get up, go to the kitchen. Make coffee. Shanaya's still in bed, up in the Green Room. It used to be my kids' room. Missy chose the green paint. Frankie chose the linens. Green walls, blue and mauve bedclothes. Jim just moved in and used it like it was. And now Shanaya, staying with me while Édith uses her suite as a hiding place. Diya texts us daily updates on her progress.

Shanaya and I lie low, work from home, catching up on things, trying to work ahead.

That first night we returned from Banff, I made herbal tea for us and sat her down.

'You still think this is what we should do?'

'I do.'

'I mean,' I try, 'those kids might be anywhere by now, right? How do we know we'll find them? How does it make sense for the three of us to go hunting for them?'

She just shakes her head, her eyes aglow.

'It doesn't.' She drinks some tea, sighs long and deep. 'But with every fibre of my being, I *know* this is something that I need to do, that I was born to do.'

I just stare at her.

'It's a tiger thing,' says Shanaya, playing her trump.

***

I've always liked getting up early, before everyone else. I like to sit on my step and have a smoke, greet the day my way. In ugly weather, I sit at my kitchen window. This morning it's bits of gusty wind spitting cutting rain, and so I sit inside with my smoke and my first cup, and just wonder.

What is the world, even? It is more glorious and alive than we know. And we cannot live like parasites, we should engage with the holiness of it all. That's what my mother's voice had said in the dream, and I'm not at all sure I trust that it was just a dream.

Grieving again?

Standing around at the gate? Straining your eyes for a sight of a snowy owl in the winter fields because you think, if you see it flying, it will be a sign that your prayer has been answered and the one you lost will be returned to you. You will get home from school, and she will be there.

***

So much of life just goes by and we don't know it's going 'til it's gone and then we look back and see we didn't do anything remarkable, not really anything at all. To get any sort of endeavour off the ground is a long work of love and devotion and at the very same time, it's not so much at all. I am middle-aged, university educated, working between the pink-collar ghetto and my ad hoc occasional investigations. My kids are grown. My last investigation? It was pretty damn weird, if I'm being honest. I helped–*abetted* might be more apt–a shape shifter hunt down his missing daughter, when I thought I was looking into the murder of his daughter's mother, his lost true love. I shake my head. What a muddle.

Close my eyes, and I see the owl swoop past again, hear my mother's voice echoing *engage with the holiness of it all*. God, but my mom sounds like Sandra sometimes. Or vice versa, I guess. Huh.

A wasp buzzes against a window screen, seeking the way in. Why would it want to come in, when it has the whole world out there, and in here there are only people who don't want it near?

In here, I'm ready to smack it down before it knows what hit it.

Why do we move through the world as we do?

DEVIN: CALLOUSING

Devin waits three days before he picks up the guitar again. He loads the new battery in the tuner and switches it on. Then he plucks each string, watching the tiny light waver into green. Every string is in tune, on pitch. He checks again.

Then he turns the tuner off, starts playing chords. C, F, G; G, D, C... he's crying already, and he doesn't even try to sing, just runs through the majors, adding E, A, B; returns to the A minor E minor oscillation, then moves from each to its major.

It's another week before he lets himself try to sing again. No good. But he sticks with the daily chording, feeling the callous beginning on his fingertips, the pain ebbing.

Some nights, he comes home from work and plays, keeping the windows closed, playing soft.

Missy takes to dropping over.

'Do you mind?' she asks.

He shakes his head, clears his throat.

'I like it,' he adds.

Sometimes, Maengan comes with her, but mostly she turns up alone. She brings food sometimes, in case he isn't eating. One day, he surprises her by serving a casserole.

'What is it?' Missy asks.

'Vegan lasagna,' says Devin.

'I didn't know you could cook.'

He nods, his face owlish again.

'Auntie taught me a few things.'

Missy digs in.

'Hey, pretty good,' she says, hoisting her second forkful.

'I wanted to say thanks,' says Devin.

'For what?'

'For this,' he says, waving his fork at the space around them.

Missy shakes her head. 'You really are doing Frankie a favour here. I don't know what she'd do if she lost this place. It's… her…'

'It's a sanctuary,' says Devin, and they lapse into silence, eating.

After dinner, she notices the guitar out, the case lying in front of the bookcase.

'You playing now?'

Devin scowls, shrugs, doesn't reply.

She tries again.

'That was your dad's guitar, eh?'

Devin nods, looking away. She frowns a moment, and lets it be. Sometimes being good family means knowing when to let it ride.

HAZEL: FOR FOX CREEK!

Why am I going to go with my crazy friend, on the word of a woman that I only really know as The Embryo Who Broke up My Marriage?

Shut my eyes. *White wings. Unclear snatches of song. Something like a message and a feeling in the pit of my chest that the dreamworld hangs over me. Stag's breath in frosty air.*

Open my eyes, and Shanaya is descending, her magnificent hair more like a lion's mane than a tiger's, barefoot and glorying in the coolness of my floors. Guess this wild swimming thing toughens you up.

Will it help when we're out there, wherever the hell we're going?

'Fox Creek,' says Shanaya, gliding into a chair at the table, a glass of cold water in hand.

'Same to you,' I quip.

'That's where Édith says they will be.'

'Excuse me?'

Shanaya pulls her phone from her robe pocket.

'She's been…figuring out some things…she says that's where they'll be taken, to an old work camp outside Fox Creek. They should be there next week, maybe the week after.'

'Well,' I say, shaking my head, 'for Fox Creek!'

She looks at me quizzically.

'My brother used to use it as a swear word. We thought it was funny. *Fox Creek!* We'd run around yelling it, and Mom couldn't say anything. We used to think she didn't know what we were doing, but I guess it must have been pretty obvious.'

I look over into the empty living room.

'He taught it to my girls, too. I still remember Missy banging her toe when she came downstairs one morning and yelling out, *For Fox Creek!*

We both laugh. She drinks her water. I pour her some coffee.

Fox Creek. It doesn't feel so funny now.

DEVIN: BIRD WATCHING

After work, Devin sits out on the balcony. Up this high, he can almost see into the bird nests in the boulevard elms. He also notices there's a sparrow nest under the eaves of the house next to this apartment building. Sparrows shoot past him at a ridiculous velocity, ignoring him with great ease.

Missy calls.

'How are you settling in at work?'

'Okay.'

'Where are you? I hear birds.'

'On the balcony. It's a bunch of sparrows.'

'Frankie has sparrows?'

'They're nesting next door.'

'Noisy neighbours.'

Devin stretches past his shyness.

'Do you know that sparrows have lived with humans for about eleven thousand years?'

'Really?' Says Missy encouragingly. 'Cool. Are they from here?'

'The Middle East,' he replies. She hears him moving indoors, and opens her laptop.

'Hey,' she continues, 'It says here that sparrows can digest potatoes, wheat, all kinds of starchy foods. They came out of ancient Persia or something, and colonized the world. Little fuckers.'

Devin laughs at her easy profanity.

'I wonder if they built churches as they went,' he says.

'Apparently, they came to America in 1852,' she reads. 'Pretty specific about that year. Wonder if someone brought them deliberately?'

'They sure live like they own the place,' says Devin, watching two of them perch on the balcony rail, looking in at him beadily as if to ask what took him so long to get off their balcony.

Missy and Devin laugh together.

***

When Sandra calls to check up on him, Devin pushes his awkward bewildering anger aside and talks to her about sparrows.

'There's a whole bunch of them here. Apparently, they symbolize safety and industry and social harmony. And did you know they can fly up to forty kilometres per hour? And they have two or three hatches per year, and their young take about six weeks to leave the nest.'

He pauses.

Sandra wants to keep him talking.

'I recall,' she says, 'that they say if a sparrow nests in your home, that's good luck.'

'Well, they're next door.'

'Still,' she says, 'good neighbours to have. A little messy though.'

'Yeah,' he says. A silence falls between them.

'Well, gotta go, eh,' he says.

'Okay then, my boy,' she says, and he disconnects before she can add that she loves him.

HAZEL: DICK FRANCIS HERO

We go to Canadian Tire for supplies.

'I don't like that you're paying for things, Shan,' I say.

'Yes, but please remember, I am a Brahmin heiress with scads of money,' she replies, lifting her nose high and winking at me. 'Besides, I am living like a squatter with you, free room and board and all.' She laughs. 'Give it up, Hazel. Imagine what you'd say if it were the other way around.'

She's got me there.

I was raised to share, damn it, though I'm not a sucker–anymore–but with friends and family, you never go wrong sharing when you can.

We take both our vehicles in for a tune up. Hers is done first. Mine needs a little extra work, we leave it overnight with my garage pals.

'This car of yours, though,' I say, 'it's not built for the bush.'

She pats its gleaming hood, elegantly opens the door, elegantly starts the car purring.

'Patsy is sturdy as well as beautiful, you know. And she has the advantage of being unknown.'

She's got me there. George might recognize my Jeep, might have people watching for it.

'They don't know we're coming, though,' I say.

'Right,' says Shanaya, 'so why advertise?'

A sleek sedan in Fox Creek, though? That's going to draw

attention. Shanaya strokes her car a bit more, considering.

'I wonder if we might be wise to rent a car?' She says.

'What if something happens to it?'

'Insurance,' she says, brushing that away. I shake my head. I have never been able to be so free.

'You're the heiress, I guess,' I say, uncomfortably. I shake my head, and snort.

'What's funny, Hazel?' she asks.

'My brother,' I say, shaking my head. 'Did you ever read Dick Francis? He wrote mysteries set in the world of English horse racing. We read them all when we were young.'

'I think my mother has some in our library,' she says.

'Well anyhow, one day when we were at university, Frank comes over. And we're just visiting, and he sees a Dick Francis book on the shelf, and he grabs it and thumps it down in front of me and Sandra.

Do you realize, he says, *that these books are a neo-colonial fantasy? A lie!?* Sandra and me, we laugh out loud. *No no*, he says, *I hate these books now.* He's laughing, but he's got a head of steam. *I mean look at them*, he says, poking the book. *They are not written for us. We don't exist in their world. But Dick Francis heroes always have one thing in common!*

Shanaya nods. 'They are all basically him, thinly disguised as various jockeys, trainers, spies, what have you.' I shoot her a glance. 'So my mother says.'

'Exactly what we tell him. They're horse racing's answer to the James Bond fantasy. But he says, *No no, the thing that really pisses me off is, they never have to worry about having enough money to carry out whatever bold and clever plan will unmask the bad guys and save the day!*'

Shanaya laughs.

'Dick Francis, Ian Fleming, and all their sons as played by Arnold, Bruce, Jason, etc–'

'Me, I ran out of gas, Shanaya, chasing the bad guys this spring! Remember? And we had to walk.'

'Yes, I remember,' purrs Shanaya.

'Dick Francis Heroes don't run out of gas!' I shout.

'But we are Decolonial, Hazel, and so we have rights!' She is mocking me, her voice faux-anguished. 'Women of the Post-colonial era, finally achieving our rights! You have as your True Heart Friend, as my mother would call me, an heiress of the British Raj, and for this caper, there shall be no money worries! We shall go forth as Dick Francis would have.'

'You laugh, Shan,' I say, 'but I'm serious…it's…uncomfortable.'

She regards me soberly for a few long moments.

'Hazel,' she says, 'it's not Dick Francis's fault. He wrote the world he moved in. This is our world. And guess what? I want to spend my money on this.'

'But you see? There it is. You've got the money. You call the shots. You're the Dick Francis Hero.'

'Heroine, thank you,' she purrs.

'What am I then? The sidekick. The humble Indian Guide?!'

She looks a me wryly.

'No, my friend. Never that.'

And she drums her nails on the steering wheel, makes a little growling sound. I'm beginning to fume, actually.

'Hazel,' she says, 'I respect that you are a self-made person. I'm not trying to lord it over you. Why can't you see this? You have a house, you share it. You have knowledge, and skills and courage and honesty and you share these things freely. I have money, and why can't I share that?'

She's getting a bit hot under the collar too, her golden eyes snapping. She's driving a little more emphatically than usual.

'You cannot let your baggage about not being a no-good Indian bum get in the way here.'

I'm stunned. I've never said that to her, but she's got one of my biggest fears pegged, the thing I am always working not to be.

'This is not about you, can't you see? It's about a bunch of kids who need us. Not the system, with its protocols and paperwork, or they wouldn't be in this predicament. The system has failed them. We have a chance not to.'

'So, '*there's no justice, just us*' like they said in that stupid cartoon or rap song or whatever it was?'

'It was good enough for you and Jim. Why not for you and me?'

She's got me there. I sigh.

Silence falls. I figure I should say I'm sorry or something, but I'm kind of shook. *Why not? Because Jim died.* I say nothing.

As we pull up at the house, I manage a small smile.

'Well,' I drawl, 'I guess I'm okay with you bankrolling this expedition. After all, you have bummed about six figures worth of smokes.'

'Speaking of which–' she quips back, standing in the street, extending her hand over the roof of her car. I toss her the pack and it gleams almost heroically in the street lamp glow.

DEVIN: SOUNDING

One day, he is playing through the minors and he remembers D minor, his fingers finding it as if by birthright, and he feels something rising from his belly. He thrums with it, begins to hum. His fingers move to F, to C, to E, A, D. Back to A, to D minor, and he is playing memory now, eyes tightly closed, sound reverberating through him.

He remembers the third of the Peace Country visitors, only an 'honorary cousin' his father had explained later, dismissively. But that cousin, his hair Cree black, his eyes bright German blue, had not simply played, he'd flowed along the guitar neck, and song had been a river through him.

D minor, E minor, A minor, G, F, E. Devin remembers the cadence, the blues. Third time through, he hits the E and the sound bawls out of him, a great baritone wail. Wordlessly, he roars on, howling through the changes, riding his pain and entering it, melody coming over him without words. For a spell, he is found, and everything falls away except the glory of sound, voice and strings all painting great swathes of blue.

In the silence after, he whispers, 'Fuck you. I'm not stupid.'

Quietly, not to disturb anyone.

HAZEL: HOUSE SITTER

'I have to think about it, okay?'

'Well,' says Shanaya, 'it's either her or Miranda.'

It shouldn't be so hard, I know. I will just ask one of them, either my sister who lives up the street or my daughter who lives fifteen minutes away, to keep an eye on the place while I'm gone. I don't have to tell them where I'm going. I don't have to tell them I'm undertaking a ridiculously dangerous attempt to rescue a bunch of human trafficking victims, armed only with my ex-husband's second ex, recently beaten nearly to death and probably crazy–why go back again?–and my lawyer friend Shanaya, who knows we're skating pretty close to some legal edges doing this caper, and who is also probably crazy. Only in her case, I suppose she has some right to be, since she is not just a lawyer but also a part time tiger. Oh, and it turns out–how unrealistic and convenient–she's a freaking upper-caste Indian heiress who can afford to kit us out for this adventure with any sort of gear we might desire.

I don't know how to desire gear. I do want to take my midsized frying pan, my knife and a good pair of sturdy shoes. Probably a couple pairs. We're going up into the muskeg country, that land eats footwear.

But I digress. Shanaya is staring at me, waiting for my answer. *Who am I going to ask to keep an eye on my house?* Which of these two am I more okay with asking to mind my house, knowing that there is an outside chance, however small, that trouble will come looking for me there?

'Why would I expose either of them to danger?' I ask Shanaya, rhetorically. 'Who do I like less?'

As if in answer to my question, Maengan Nolan comes biking round the corner, all sleek braid and squared up shoulders.

He agrees a little too easily, and I go over it twice to be sure. Funnily enough, it's him who says, 'That's fine, umm–' he calls me 'umm' when he's nervous because he's never quite been sure how to address me. He's tried out Mrs. LeSage, and Auntie, but you can't really call your girlfriend's mother Auntie when you've gone and moved in with that girlfriend against her mother's best instincts. And there's no way he can call me Hazel. His own upbringing and mine, too, put that right out of reach. Unless of course I instruct him to call me Hazel, or anything else in particular. But I don't.

We've been through hell together, Maengan and I, and he's living with my daughter, and I still can't bring myself to let him off the hook. Yes, I'm an asshole.

But I'm a lucky asshole.

To my surprise, Maengan's the one who asks if it's okay if it's just him who comes and checks up on the place.

'Miranda's got a lot on her plate right now, ummm—' he trails off.

I pretend to have to think about it.

'Yeah. No. That's fine, just fine. And Roy will stay with Sandra, so shouldn't be much to check here. Thanks for doing this for me.' I hand him a key. 'We leave on Saturday, should be gone a day or two; no more than a week.'

He looks a question at Shanaya, who's stood by the whole time without a peep, just watching us. I am going to get a growling when he's gone.

'We're going on a driving tour,' she says jauntily to him. 'I've realized that I don't really know the countryside, and your–Hazel has graciously offered to be my Indian Guide.'

She smiles and winks at him, all jolly pals. He smiles in relief.

'Sounds like a lot of fun, Ms Bhattacharya,' he says.

'I've told you, Maengan, none of that,' she scolds playfully. 'We are strictly on a first-name basis, you and I. What?' A hint of Diya's phoney accent slips into her tone for just a moment, then she gives him a genuine beaming smile full of kindness. 'After all, we shape-shifters have to stick together in this world, don't we?'

And he smiles back and nods and rides away.

***

'There,' I say, 'are you satisfied?'

'Hazel,' she says, beginning to growl. No, I can't justify my attitude.

I can find a plausible retreat.

'Listen, Shan, I'd love to try to sort this out with you, but I feel like I really should call my sister. Check in and see how Devin is doing since he moved to Frankie's place.'

And I'm not just avoiding a growling. I really do want to know how Devin is, how Sandra is. Nothing like facing a potentially dangerous secret mission to make you realize, while there's breath in you, you should make sure to reach out to the people you love and show them you care.

Or whatever.

Yeah, I do. But I don't need Shanaya watching me do it.

'Actually,' I say, 'I think I'll walk over and see if she's home, organize about Roy. See you in a while, eh?'

And I walk off, listening for the door as she prowls into the house. I can practically feel her tail lashing.

DEVIN: ROSIN

The next time Devin opens the guitar case, he closes his eyes, caught up in the fragrance that wafts out every time he opens the case. He lifts the guitar out, brings it up close to his face, searching for the fragrance. He catches old tobacco, and remembers his father, smoking, drinking whiskey from a tumbler. He remembers his father's laughter.

He sets the guitar aside. The smell comes from the case itself.

He opens the small compartment at the top of the neck of the case. Inside, there are a pack of strings, and a small red box. Astonished, Devin lifts out the box and opens it. Inside lies something wrapped in a tidy soft cloth secured by a buttoned elastic strap. He fumbles it open and there in his palm sits a chunk of amber. Rosin. The fragrance seems to swirl around him, and he sits still, wrapped in its embrace.

Devin remembers Big Frank and his Mother singing, his father on the guitar, his mother playing fiddle. Their voices and the smell of rosin and the music made him feel that he was home. A child doesn't judge, they haven't the capacity to discern nuance–they judge simply, by gut, and rosin is the smell of home, of his mother.

And when she died, everyone told him how much she was loved, how beautiful she and his father were together. Children have their gut, but are too easily taught to discount that, or at least to dissemble as if they are putting aside their true feelings to mirror what others say, what others profess to know.

His beautiful mother, how much their father loved her, how proud he was of her talent. His mother, her voice, her fiddle. But he remembers them shouting, too. Remembers his father jeering, his mother crying. Remembers his father throwing the rosin, throwing everything in her face, nights when too many people, especially other men, cheered for her leads, her solos.

Music brought them together. He remembers so many people saying that. And in public, it was harmony, rhythm, old songs made new. Backstage, at home, the arguments about genre and authenticity, the flaring anger from them both. Frank and Evelyn had vowed never to be without music, but soon enough the songs were eclipsed by thunder. The broken fiddle his father burned.

Devin wraps the rosin, puts it back, entombs the guitar in its shroud without playing it, and goes for a long walk. He's got to work tomorrow. When he gets back, he puts the guitar back in the closet, back into the dark. He checks the fridge.

'Should've bought eggs,' he mutters to himself, and goes to bed. Sleep comes and goes, and he dreams wild strains of melody, wakes with them just beyond recall.

HAZEL: ONIONS

Sandra is in the garden, of course. But she's not alone. She's crouched among the beans chatting with a man. They stand up when they hear the gate, and it's Father Efren Mannfredsson, his lanky ponytail and sun bronzed face looking much younger in this context than I've ever seen them.

He wipes his hands on his jeans as I approach, reaches out.

'Ms. LeSage,' he says.

'Father Mannfredsson', I reply, shaking his hand.

I turn to Sandra, catch the wary, guarded look on her face. My own hackles start rising, but I force myself to remember *I thought you were judging me because I'm not a real mother*. I make myself smile, give her a half-hug.

'Hey, Sam,' I say. I haven't called her that in eons.

She looks startled. But then she smiles back.

'Garden's looking good,' I say, as if I'd know the difference.

'You too,' she says offhandedly, and I wonder for a second, *good like a cornstalk? A pumpkin? A bean?* I hear my father's old joke, the first ribald one I can remember him reciting in front of his children. I can't help myself, I blurt it out:

Mary Mary quite contrary
How does your garden grow?
With blue bells and cockle shells…
And one great big fucking onion!

There's a beat of silence, and I wonder why I had to go there.

Then both of them laugh.

'Sorry, Ef,' says Sandra, 'that was our father's garden joke.' She shakes her head, still chuckling, tips her head at me and grins. *Well, there you go... but 'Ef'?!*

'How are the onions?' I say, looking around for them as if they matter to me deeply.

'Boisterous,' replies the priest, waving his hand at the bed of green stalks. Several of them bear small clusters of bulbs up high, not in the ground. My puzzlement must show.

'They're called Egyptian Walking Onions,' Sandra explains. 'They perpetuate themselves by growing bulbs up high, tipping over, and rooting down again.'

'Walking' I say. 'Huh. Well, speaking of travel, just wanted to let you know I'm going on a little road trip for about a few days, maybe a week or so, just taking a friend to see some rural sights.'

Several expressions fleet across Sandra's face.

'And, uh, Maengan happened by, so I've asked him to look in on my place while I'm gone. So you'll probably see him in and out.'

She nods, still looking a bit inscrutable.

Efren reads the room, or the bean patch or whatever.

'Okay if I go in and set on some tea?' He asks Sandra.

'You know where things are. That would be nice, thanks.' And he makes long strides for the back door, leaving us alone.

'So–' I stop myself. I can feel her bristling. Not my place to ask he if she's dating a priest. I'm out of my head curious, but it's not my place.

'Speaking of house-sitters, I was also wondering, how's Devin doing? He liking the job? Enjoying Southside life?' I keep my tone light.

She doesn't answer me, just looks away.

Oh God, what have I said now?

Then she sighs, rumples her hand through her hair.

'I don't know. He says he's okay. Never wants to talk. But he says he's fine.'

I pick at a random leaf of some kind. This really is a thriving jungle of a garden back here.

'Mint,' says Sandra, and I nod 'mmm' as if I knew that, and crush it between thumb and finger, and bring it to my nose.

'Sounds like he's enjoying stretching his wings.'

She still looks gloomy.

'I know, he's been through a lot, but hey–he's working, right? And he says he's okay.'

'I feel like I need to go see him, but I don't want to crowd him either, you know?'

'I tell you what,' I say, 'why don't you ask Missy to stop by sometime? Not to spy on him, just so someone's there. It would probably do her good, too. She probably misses Frankie.'

Sandra nods, thoughtful.

Father Efren comes out with a tray of tea things. Now I'm stuck.

'I tell you what else,' I say,' I have to go over that part of town tomorrow, take care of a couple things before we leave. I could maybe pop in on him on my way by, how about that?'

'Thanks,' she says.

'Well, look, guys, I'm sorry, ' I say, looking at my phone, 'I have to go. I'll have to take a rain check on that tea, Father. Sometime when I get back.' I hate the forced jolliness in my tone. Sandra for sure can tell how hard I'm faking a mood here. But I suddenly find I cannot stay and make small talk with them.

Never mind my ambivalence about that priest's long friendship with Devin, seeing him in the garden with my sister, fawning over her? It's just too weird.

But she's willing to keep Roy at her house, so that's to the good. Walking back, I imagine Shan asking why I don't just have Sandra watch the house, since she'll have the dog? I hope she doesn't. It's not a thing I can explain. Sandra lives just down the street. But she's not set foot in my house since our brother died. That's a whole other story. Not for the first time, I kick a bit of dust in disgust as I walk. *Is every family like this? Full of secret traumas and fights and stupid accommodations we just silently agree to never talk about, not ever again.*

DEVIN: HORIZONS

'We've been through this before,' says Maengan, ruffling his hand through his hair.

'It wasn't me saying it,' says Missy, chewing.

He quirks an eyebrow at her. She bobs her head.

'This time,' she amends. She swallows, thinks for a moment or two.

Missy and Maengan sit opposite each other at Frankie's table, Devin between them with his back to the window. He keeps his feet tucked back, having accidentally bumped against their intertwined feet stretched beneath the table.

The little formica table holds the litter of their meal, compostable boxes with the dregs of sushi.

'So why–?'

Devin speaks slowly, and Missy smiles to herself. It's his natural way, not like Maengan. When she winds up into a rant, he gets his patient voice on, the one that she's come to realize is him making the effort not to be needled by her provocations.

'The thing is, Devin,' she says, 'It kind of pissed me off. '

'Oh?'

'Yeah. The way they put together two things that don't necessarily belong together. They said this kid they knew liked manga and anime.'

'Cool.'

'But they said they figured it was because that kid didn't like being Anishinaabe.'

Devin says nothing. She's winding up. Maengan holds his tongue.

'But those two things don't necessarily correlate,' says Devin. 'Why would they? Why would being Anishinaabe mean you can't be a Japanophile?'

'Exactly,' says Missy, thumping the table, 'I mean, what the fuck would they say if that kid liked…hamburgers? Mainstream TV? American pop? Would they say that's because she doesn't like her own self, or would they just accept that everyone likes that stuff because it's the water we swim in.'

Devin nods.

'For fuck's sake, people around the world are xenophiles without it meaning they hate themselves. Why can't an Ojibway just be curious and open-minded and interested in things that resonate with our own world view?'

'Why does anyone still assume that Ojibway equals no horizon? That to be Authentically Ojibway–sorry, Anishinaabe–means you don't try new things, you don't want more than the shit hole you might be stuck in. Especially,' she cries, waving her spoon now, 'if you are stuck in a shit hole, in one of those places that still–*Still!*–don't have clean water or decent infrastructure. You can love being Anishinaabe and hate the poverty, hate the crime, hate the fucking denial of horizon! Look at…what's his name? That sumo wrestler that Hakuho recruited from Moose Factory…what's his name? Winter something…'

'Fuyunokaze,' says Devin, and she nods.

'Yes, The Winter's Wind–what a great name!–you can't say he isn't proud of being Anishinaabe, just like Hakuho was proud to be Mongolian, but not making the mistake of thinking that Mongolians needed to stay home and be poor when there's a whole world in which to prosper.'

'Well,' hazards Maengan, now that her rant has morphed to discussion of one of his great loves, sumo and its greatest champion. 'Hakuho wasn't from a poor family. Most of the guys who went and took over sumo weren't.'

'True, true,' says Missy, 'but I gotta say I'm so glad you introduced me to that sport and that world and particularly Hakuho. Look at everything he did! He transformed sumo, and opened doors and–'

'And he took a few beatings doing it. The guy was the greatest champion to ever step onto the dohyo, but all the records he set didn't mean he could escape racism, fear of change, suspicion that he would ruin the more subtle aspects of the sport. I mean,' says Maengan, 'sumo is a religious ceremony, not just a wrestling match. So the old guard who opposed Hakuho at every turn, they weren't entirely wrong. The deeper things are worth protecting.'

'But Maengan!' cries Missy, re-inflamed, 'there is nothing deep or worthy about forcing people to live in poverty like Mongolian nomads. Nothing noble about maintaining disparity, about writing off people and places as sacrifice zones–like the Reserves basically were seen as, places without resources, without access, no freedom of movement, languages and religions outlawed–even when people got off the Reserves?'

Maengan says nothing. His jaw tightens and he looks away.

'They still,' says Devin, '*We* still carry the wounds with us.'

'I remember when I went to Korea,' Missy continues,' how shocking it was, that double edged thing. People there, if they knew anything at all about so called 'Indian' people, knew only themes, ridiculous broad stereotypes–good and bad!'

She's waving the spoon again.

'But they wondered why I was there, more so than any of the other foreigners. And those guys, my fellow ex-pats, felt entitled to question my pedigree, too.'

Maengan shakes his head, catches Devin's eye and winks, his smile waxing a little wolfish.

'I pity the fools who'd get you riled,' he says proudly.

'But, Love,' she says, 'that's the shocking thing. I wasn't immediately riled. I caught myself answering to them, at first. I hadn't realized how much I'd internalized that sick thing that assumes that being 'Indian' means your own validity, your own authentic real human self itself, is something that everyone and anyone else has the right to question you on.'

Her face is red now, angry, but she needs to draw breath, so Maengan speaks up.

'I know,' he says. 'I mean, yeah, I grew up on the Rez, partly. I look the part, so to speak; but there's more to it, right? Even with all the doctors we have out there, so many people still don't expect an Indian to be a hospital worker and still be an Indian. I mean, every kind of people get picked on for something. But who asks a Chinese person, can you work here and still be Chinese?'

'That's the thing,' declares Missy, 'We still have to beat that, Maengan. We still have to beat that idea that Authentic Indians can't take part in the larger world.' She bangs the spoon rhythmically on the table as she rants. 'And beat the idea that me saying that just proves I'm not Authentic, that must be my White side talking. God, when do we get past these boneheaded ideas?'

'Well, don't get too riled. I'm with you beating ideas. But just, you know, not me.'

She stops, puts down her spoon, and just looks at him a while. She hasn't the words to talk about the elusive truth that he embodies ways and means, traditions of connecting to the earth and all of life, that are profoundly different than her own. And that she feels bereft of all that, that she fears that sometime, somewhere down the road, it will matter too much, and he'll turn away from her, for the sake of something she can never quite comprehend.

Maengan smiles and says nothing.

Devin pushes his chair back, stands up.

'Dessert?' Is all he says.

HAZEL: PRE-DEPARTURE

Diya phones me. She wants us both to join her and Édith for dinner. Shan looks a bit weirded out to be invited to come as a guest to her own home. And I am a bit weirded out, if I stop to think of it, by how natural it feels to obey Diya, to fall in line with her plans.

Shanaya shakes her head at me.

'What happened to our Girls Night In with a movie?'

Driving down to Mill Woods, I consider that. Diya phoned me, because maybe Shanaya would have declined. Guess Shan had to push back against Diya's strength, to establish her own sense of who she is in the world. And to feel like an adult while living in her mother's house.

Not that that's so strange. We got past the twentieth century's nuclear family isolationism, thanks be, and spiralled onward into something more realistic. Intergenerational homes are more normal than not around here again. I think about my girls. They couldn't get away from me fast enough, and I am glad of it. They're fiercely independent and have managed on their own for years. I wouldn't want them to come back to me. Sure there's something powerfully appealing, just for a moment, in the notion. But we take up a lot of space, each of us, in our own ways.

'And you're thinking...?' says Shanaya as we drive.

'About intergenerational housing.'

'It's not so bad. You thinking of trying it?'

'Not even a little bit.'

'You're thinking that you could bring Missy home–and her wolf-boy with her–if they decide to have a family, so you could be granny on the spot.'

'Doesn't sound like me at all, granny on the spot.'

Shanaya laughs out loud.

'Famous last words.'

'Fuck. I am not cut out for grandmothering, Shan.'

She keeps right on laughing.

'I can see it though,' she purrs. 'You'll be that rogue granny. The same sort as Diya would be. If I had ever married.' She pauses, then goes on, 'If I weren't terrified of being a mother because I might birth a tiger, or worse of course, turn into a tiger and eat my own child.'

She says it quick and light, but it's not light. She has come eerily close to my fears for Missy.

Except Missy's not the one who's a werewolf. That's the potential father of her children. And I can't bring that up. It's way too early for me to have any sort of opinion about the shape of any family they might decide to make. My place in it is the least of my worries, though.

We arrive in Mill Woods, park inside the attached garage, and go in to find Diya and Édith have prepared something of a feast.

'This girl,' declares Diya, 'is a natural-born chef. Look at what she has made.'

'What *we've* made,' says Édith, and she must be recovering, because that little burble of smugness is back in her voice. She looks fabulous, her hair sleek and well-combed, dressed in an Indian style tunic and harem pants (as we called them in the ignorant 1980s) in an unfairly becoming shade of rose. I find myself ready to recommence hating her.

But we make it through dinner, and then Diya springs another surprise on us.

'Your car is all packed, yes, Beti?'

'Yes, Mom. Except for Édith's bag. We left room.'

'I hope you have brought your dry robes?'

'We have,' I reply, uneasily wondering if she's going to take us through our packing list. I wouldn't put it past her. I think of Shanaya's story of how she met her husband on a trek in Nepal, back when most women didn't trek.

But Diya has just handed Shanaya a bundle I recognize, her own dry robe, rolled and tied with webbing straps.

'Beti, stow this one for Aditi, along with her bag. Aditi, give your bag to Shanaya.'

Aditi, she calls Édith. How much longer have I known Diya, and I don't have a nickname? Huh. I must govern myself, remember our mission. In my mind's eye, I see her again, wet, haggard, bruised and afraid, stumbling in out of the storm. I blow out a breath. Diya quirks an eyebrow at me. I feel my cheeks growing hot. I am too old to blush, aren't I?

'So,' I say, 'do you know where we're going?'

'Fox Creek,' Diya replies. 'Oh yes. Aditi told me. I've been helping her study maps of the area.'

Of course she has. The others are back, hovering. Diya springs her trap.

'Now,' she says, 'it will be best if you all stay here tonight.'

Shanaya and Édith just nod, and I realize I'm the only one for whom this is news. Why didn't they tell me? I'm beginning to steam. They appear not to notice. I need a smoke.

'Now,' says Diya as if on cue, 'we can't have the neighbours noticing you, Hazel. So, you are going to have to smoke in the garage. Please be very careful not to burn anything down.'

'Mother,' Shanaya chides.

'You will find my daughter's secret ashtray on the shelf next to the potting soil.'

'Mother!'

Diya just laughs, and shoos both of us toward the garage.

'Aditi and I have prepared the maps you'll need. Come and find us in my office when you are done with your filthy habit,' she says, cheerfully imperious.

We spend a solid hour going over onscreen and printed materials.

'Where'd you get all this?' I ask, looking at what appear to be proprietary maps of well sites and work camps, 'aren't these confidential or something? Don't the companies guard them with their lives?'

Diya twinkles.

'I cannot disclose my sources, Hazel,' she says, then bends her head back to the task of plotting each one onto a folding road map.

Shanaya catches my eye above Diya's head, flashes me a warning. *Okay*, I think, glaring back at her, *I don't want to know anyway. Just our lives might depend on the reliability of these maps.* Then I watch Diya directing Édith, correcting her notation, and realize I've got nothing to fear on that score. Whatever her source, no map of Diya's would dare to be inaccurate.

Diya turns out to have a laminator in her office. I don't know why. I decide it doesn't matter.

Once the mapping is done, the results plasticized against inclement weather and muskeg, Diya claps her hands.

'Now,' she says, 'let's all have a proper night cap, and then a good night's sleep.'

She hustles us into the kitchen where we perch like a line of birds on the stools at the granite-topped island (of course Diya has a kitchen with a granite-topped island) while Diya whisks around preparing some concoction that smells great.

'It's Ayurvedic,' she says as she hands us each a mug, 'specially formulated to enhance your sleep, so that you can be fresh and ready for your mission in the morning.'

I have no idea what all is in it, but I drink it down, we all do, obedient line of birds. She drinks hers sitting in the little breakfast table in the window, all the blinds drawn snug. (Of course Diya has a breakfast nook).

'All done?' She chirps. 'Beti, put the mugs in the dishwasher. Then off to bed we go. Shanaya, you will share with Hazel. Aditi will sleep in my room.'

And she bustles out, Édith following as if on a leash.

The Embryo turns in the doorway of the kitchen, looks at us both and takes a deep breath.

'Thanks,' is all she says, but there's a world of subtext in that word.

Shan and I get our overnight kits from the car, resist the urge for one more smoke, and I follow her up the stairs to her suite of rooms.

'A sleepover, at my age,' I mutter goofily, and she grins.

'Don't worry,' she says, 'I don't bite.'

'I might,' I grumble, 'if you snore.'

I wouldn't know if she did. Whatever was in that Ayurvedic potion, my head hits the pillow and I'm fast asleep.

SHANAYA: HABITAT

Shanaya looks around her study, sees it a different way. The books align like light-striped forest, law and philosophy and Rabindranath Tagore. The plants her mother insisted on look a little dusty, as if waiting for a breeze. Here is her habitat.

Shanaya frowns, remembers a voice whispering to her that *it will be alright, even here. Life is life anywhere, beloved. We can make this work.*

She remembers a dream where a woman strokes a tiger's head and sings to the beast tales of Durga the all-protector.

She curls into her wingback armchair, pulls an orangish plaid throw over herself.

DEVIN: BLIND

Shall the blind lead the blind then? A voice echoes in the dark.

Devin wakes up from another bad dream, his head full of angry thoughts.

We can't follow the Christian Churches anymore, because they have too long a history of cheating and beating and defeating our people.

Shall I be a destroying force?

Shall I be Genghis Khan, the wrath of God visited upon the cities for their sins?

He shambles out to the living room, turns on a lamp and stands gazing at Frankie's bookshelves, all the pre-Columbian evidence for urbanity among the Indigenous people here in Turtle Island the same as anywhere in the world, societies rising and falling, empires and dust in epochal seasons. He hears the strange voice from the dream.

What does it mean to live at this point in the turning of cultural epochs? Are you here to be the Destroyer? What is the Indigenous God who does this work? What is the name? How can you call on a Name that you do not know? Who will replace the Church when it is broken?

He sees the dawn is lightening the East, so he pulls on his hoodie and shoes. His large form shrouded in a hoodie and grey trousers, his big feet quiet in slip-on sneakers, Devin sets out to the East, walking down the elm-lined street, just breathing, and observing his mind as it latches onto things along the way–the new bike route, the evidence of guerrilla gardeners expanding their war against grey and monocultural city depths.

He thinks about the conversation with Missy and Maengan, considers the young man pulled out of northern Ontario, Hakuho Sho's recruit, the first Indigenous sumo wrestler, rising through the ranks to become a salaried wrestler–*a sekitori*–and now gaining fame under the name *Fuyunokaze*, Winter Wind. He wonders what might have happened if there had been less policing, more scouting. How many other big boys might have had a future in sport, in football, in basketball, in baseball... He remembers his father showing video of a superstar of bygone days, the Mexican Fernando Valenzuela.

Valenzuela breathes through his eyes, said Big Frankie to someone else in the room, not his chubby son perched quietly nearby. The thrown ball lances through history.

Devin breathes through his eyes as he crosses the arterial at 99th and turns North, zigzagging to the edge where he can descend into Mill Creek Ravine.

The ravine is rife with sound, birds, squirrels, gentle rustling in the middle distance and something like a bell he can hear. He lifts his head a little higher, scents the wind and catches wood smoke. Someone has a fire going somewhere in this little alternate universe that is Mill Creek before dawn.

Devin crosses the creek and turns South along the off-leash dog path, following it up through the spruce, traveling by feel and by smell and listening to the water. His heart beats strongly and his neck tingles with the sensation of lives around him, hidden eyes watching his passage. For a moment, he feels the unease that rides with him always among groups of humans, but then he catches his breath, focuses and chants in his mind: *Mitayuke Oyasin, all my relations*–a phrase his father would say–and calm rises up in him again through the soles of his feet, calm descends from the branches and the gloaming sky beyond, calm sings in water over stones.

That morning, he feels his way down toward the water, stands there a long time before he decides to take his shoes off, push his pant legs up, and step cautiously into the half-seen water.

He hears his mother's fear in his mind, and stills that. *No, I won't fall. The water is not deep. There is no broken glass down there, no rusty metal. I feel the earth under me. I feel the stones, the sand, the mud.* He manages to stand for several minutes, listening, breathing, proving to himself that he is safe. Then he cautiously steps back out of the water, dries his feet on his pants legs, puts his shoes back on and walks home.

The sun has found the western edge of the ravine, and he lets himself become aware of the city waking up, up there and all around him, forest sounds and human sounds, wood smoke and diesel.

HAZEL: CLEAR BLUE

Saturday dawns clear, a little windy, that kind of wind that lights up the grain fields out in the country. Here in Mill Woods, it blows a pine cone down and bounces it off the garage window. At least I think it's just the wind. Could be a resident squirrel. Could be worse. I finish my smoke and go back inside.

Diya is a sergeant-major, rallying us.

We've agreed on code phrases to text back to her if we are in trouble we can't handle; and if we are in range of a cell tower. I don't mention the fact that Fox Creek, despite all our technology, lies in a zone where radio and cell reception is bad to non-existent. I'm not being kind. I'm just sure we all know that already.

Diya hugs us each, and we load into the car, Édith again under wraps in the back seat, just in case. Then Diya surprises me again.

She reaches in through the open window and hands me something, a small rectangle wrapped in cloth. Then she passes something smaller to her daughter.

'Hang this on the rearview,' she says. She holds up her hand before Shanaya can speak.

'No, Beti,' she says, and her voice is suddenly shaky, 'don't argue. Maybe it's just superstition, but think of it as me, going with you.'

Shanaya hangs it on the rearview, and I peer at the little icon spinning on its ribbon.

'Durga and her Tiger,' says Diya, her voice again firm.

Diya put me in a mood, and as we roll around the Henday ring road and take the Yellowhead westbound, I scan the roadside for sage. Not that I'd make us stop to pick some, to make sure this journey is also blessed in an Indigenous way. That sort of thing is just superstition, the kind of hokum that gets people killed as often as it saves them.

On the other hand, when I unwrap what Diya gave me, I find it is a pack of Mohawk Ceremonials, the organic blend cigarettes that all the upper-class Indigenous Traditionalists smoke. I can't afford them. But I crack the pack with alacrity now, unroll my window, and light up a traveling prayer, the cool blue smoke flaring out behind us, up into the clear day.

DEVIN: MORNING SINGING

The summer simmers down into autumn. Devin is settled in his work, in his home, in his morning ritual. He has quelled his mother's fear when it told him *You should tell someone where you're going*. Her voice in his mind blends into Sandra's voice.

You should leave a note or a text. What if something happens to you?

Something is happening to him. And he keeps right on going out to meet it.

Soon enough, he reaches a spot he knows well and then he turns aside from the path, pads down and across the small silty beach and at the edge, removes his pants and hoodie, moccasins and warm socks. Clad only in briefs, he steps into the cold frothing water, walks out to the middle where there is enough depth, and sits down.

Mill Creek's tea-dark water washes him. This is an urban stream, much deepened and improved by constant conservational care if still not strictly potable; but ducks swim here, and dogs splash, and there are minnows and other little aquatic denizens, and so he murmurs 'good morning' and considers himself taking part in their world, in their ritual lives, in their day to day.

Devin stretches his legs, lowers himself further, resting his back against a broad sandstone boulder he spotted underwater when he first found this spot. He sinks until he can tip his head back and feel the water wash the back of his skull, lap at the edges of his ears. Overhead, the very last of the stars are still visible, but losing ground against the oncoming dawn.

The cold bites, awakens, welcomes him.

Devin sings softly then. He sings the Water Song of the Ojibwe grandmothers, *Nibi, Gi Zha Ge go softly*, crooning to the water and her creatures, affirming to them that he loves them and their lives. He smiles in the dark, considering the story his auntie showed him online, about how an Ojibwe grandmother and her grandson wrote the song after hearing of the Water Walkers, about how the grand-mother's daughter, the boy's mother, having learned anew Anishi-naabemowin lost to the grandmother in the schools, translated their simple song–*Water, I respect you, water I thank you, water I love you.'*

This morning, as so many others, Devin cries a little as he sings. Tears keep flowing as he sings George Paul's Mi'gmaq Honour Song, *Kep n mite'tuh muh nej da'n deli ull- nuwulteekw*…calling softly his commitment to honour all of life, to live as Creator meant for him to live…however that proves to be.

And then he sings a Gathering Song–*Wejkwita'jik nkikma'q wula tet nike' a*–marvelling at the meanings in *Mawi'omi*, how his Auntie Sandra explained it to him, verb and noun and cloak of belonging, a word of administrative practicality and of spiritual connection.

And then he sings a song of his own devising, a wordless med-itation on water, bears, manatees, generations, loss and renewal, loneliness and belonging.

He sings softly on until the last of the stars bow out, and then he rises and stands for a moment shivering in cold dawn air, shakes himself off and uses his hands to scoop most of the water down from his skin.

He dresses without drying further: first the long sleeved t-shirt, drops wet trunks, pull on fleece-lined track pants, wring trunks and wrap in plastic bread bag from hoodie pocket. By the trail side, he rubs his feet on the grass, and on the legs of his sweatpants, and leans against a tree as he slips back into his shoes.

They are a little snug still, but this constant ceremony is stretch-ing them to accommodate his big feet. He pulls a fleece toque down over his head, the hoodie up to protect his cold neck.

By the time Devin returns to Little Frankie's apartment, the sun is streaming down the street at his back and Whyte Avenue has begun to thrum with daytime traffic. Devin walks quietly, shivering slightly but wholly alive, absorbed in the world orchestral.

HAZEL: FOX CREEK ACTUALLY

So we go to Fox Creek, and there's nobody there.

I mean, the town is there. And in fact, I am bemused to consider that this is the first time I've ever seen the town. I've spent most of my life, child and woman, passing intermittently through Fox Creek, gassing up and buying snacks, and never ever thinking about where the houses are. Fox Creek? That's an airstrip, a couple of blocky hotels, an A&W for burgers, lately a Freson's which is awesome, and a couple of choices for fuel/conveniences.

There are always a few big rigs parked along the service road, and though some of the names on the doors have changed as South Asian immigrants made inroads into the trucking industry, those rigs have been there as long as I remember.

Fox Creek.

It's where the weather changes. Where the edges of two systems knit up. Something to do with the geography, the way the hills channel the clouds, stop the weather that comes over at Jasper from going north, so they drop their rain there.

If there is rain, it falls in Fox Creek. It's the weather changer.

Everyone who knows the province knows about Fox Creek. But they didn't expect it to be the place where everything changed. When the fracking began to happen, nobody expect the first earthquakes. At Fox Creek.

But they should have, because the way the hills fill in there, that just tells you that there's a crack down there somewhere. And then the first earthquakes happened, and the frackers said it was just normal, just the expected result. Nothing too big.

But then they kept building, 4 on the Richter. Then 5. Still nobody realized this was not settling down. When the big one happened... well, Amiskwaciy changed a lot in response. We built UpTop geothermal power plant, for one thing. Shrunk the city's footprint. So many changes started with the ground shaking in Fox Creek.

Fox Creek is a lot of nothing, for all that happened there.

I simply never thought of it as a real town, where real people live, with schools and a rec centre and a tiny hospital and all. Probably a dentist. Maybe even a law office, I muse, glancing at Shanaya. She doesn't look as astonished as I feel. I guess if you've just never been somewhere it is not nearly as surprising to discover it as if you've threaded the edge of it all your life without realizing how much more there was to it.

Not that it's huge. It's just a typical Alberta town, somewhere between 1-5000 people, mostly modest homes, lots of nice vehicles, its fair share of gangling teenagers at various hangouts, looking like they cannot wait to get out of this dead end town. Is that me in their eyes?

We don't make a big show of driving around, you never know who's watching for strangers. After we've made a circuit, I get Shan to pull up in shouting distance of a scruff of teenagers kicking something.

'Hey,' I holler, 'where's the road to Iosegun Lake?'

They point and I holler thanks, close my window and we head in the general direction indicated.

Now, if anyone was tracking us, they'll hopefully just write us off as a car of day-trippers looking for the picnic grounds. Not their problem. Not anyone's problem.

Once we're on the lake road, it's an easy matter to take another random-seeming turn and find ourselves on a gravel road leading off through the dense bush.

The first camp is so close to town you might feel you could chuck a rock and hit the townies. We slow down and Édith whips out her binoculars and scouts from the back seat. It's empty. We turn in, drive up close and park. No tire tracks in the dirt. The trailers are locked, their eyes blank and empty. We carry on, checking a few more sites, ready to do what I don't know. I've got sunglasses and a ball cap on, in case we see George. He may not recognize me if I let Shan do the talking. God, we did not think through how to answer questions.

It doesn't matter, in the event.

Nobody questions us.

We find a few camps with people in them, stop at the Security shack they all have up front, and Shan's cheery tourist-waving-the-map thing convinces them that they are not interested in us.

I start to worry as the day draws on toward evening.

'What if they think we're here to entertain workers?' I say.

'Ew,' says Édith in a perfect teenage voice.

Shanaya laughs. 'Then I guess we are a lesbian couple lost, and we ask the way back to town and we get the hell out of there before they can insist, thankful for Patsy's powerful engine…if it comes to that. But it won't. People aren't that stereotypically evil,' says Shanaya the barrister, entirely too breezily considering we are on the hunt for a human trafficking ring that beat one of us nearly to a pulp.

This *I'm a tiger I will destroy you* business may be going to her head. I figure people are evil enough for most anything.

'You sure you don't remember exactly which camp?' I say, staring at the wall of autumnal muskeg out the window.

Édith shakes her head ruefully.

'Well, at least we won't get lost,' I mutter, tapping the plasticized maps with their military-precision indications. And we drive for hours, and Patsy gets dirty, and we don't get lost.

But in the end, we find exactly nothing. And we decide not to stop in one of the blocky hotels, and we sure aren't going to sleep on the side of the service road with the semis.

So we buy a bunch of mediocre coffee for the three hour haul back to Amiskwaciy, to my house, not Diya's. We get home late, and I let them each have a bed and I claim the sofa and they go right to sleep. Me, I sit up almost longing for the nights I wasted on the internet, worrying about the trouble my daughters might be in.

When I'm sure The Tiger and The Embryo are firmly asleep, I go online, and simply type in *The Harvestmen.*

The arachnid (not precisely a spider) colloquially called *harvestman* or *daddy longlegs* is of course first. I learn that their scientific name, formerly *phalangida*, is now *opilliones.*

Next…Aha! A wiki about The Harvestmen as a conservative, militant religious cult?! Nope, it's a fantasy role playing thing, can't make heads or tails of it. But it's not what we're after. Back to the search page.

We're back to the not-a-spider, which turns out to be utterly fascinating to a long list of content creators. There are daddy longlegs from Minsk to the tropics , and they're as old as dinosaurs or something, fossils in France… I fall asleep in my chair sometime before dawn, but I'm still the first up, so I slip out the door and up the street to Sandra's. She'll be awake, either in the garden or playing with Roy.

She meets me at the door, Roy at her heels burbling and bouncing to get at me.

Sandra's glare could make a spider's blood run cold.

'Your dog has destroyed my garden,' she says bluntly.

Roy, sensing she's talking about him, bounces back and laughs up at her as if he has no idea why she's mad.

'You!' She growls. Then she gives in and scratches his ears. 'Dogs will be dogs, eh, Roy?'

He responds to her sorrowful chagrin like he responds to most things. He just licks her hand and grins, wagging a little.

'How bad is it?' I chance.

'Come see for yourself.'

And we step around and go in through the gate, but Roy squeezes past and galumphs through the paths, his ears flopping, then leaps into a bomb-struck garden bed and starts right in digging.

'Roy! NO!!' I roar.

Sandra's face is in her hands.

'Just take him and go,' says a muffled slightly shaky voice.

I grab Roy, lift him physically out of the hole he's gotten so invested in, and pick up the leash Sandra has dropped on the path. Roy makes one last lunge toward another of his artistic endeavours, but a snap of the leash transforms him into the meek and obedient charmer I've never suspected he was not, until now.

'I–'

'Go,' says Sandra. 'We can talk later.'

Oh boy, Roy. I shake my head most of the way home. But you know, when your former canine companion is a vengeance-obsessed shape shifter, most sins of the ordinary canine sort take on a different hue. Still, Sandra and I were just starting to get along. *Dogs.*

Roy is just happy to see me, happy to saunter into the still-sleeping household and curl into his dog bed and lie there grinning while I make coffee.

The smell wakes them, that or Roy's offhanded bark when he discovers their shoes. So they descend, we sit down to coffee, and now we have to figure out what to do next.

DEVIN: THE MAN IN THE FOREST

Devin has been aware for some days now that somebody has noticed him; it's more specific than the general wakefulness of the predawn ravine. He smells the woodsmoke every time he goes now, and wonders where the fire is.

One morning, he rounds a corner in the trail and sees a man leaning against a tree. His hackles go up, but then the man speaks:

"Hi."

The man lifts a hand in acknowledgement, but stays leaned, at ease. Devin stands for a few breaths, considering.

'Hi,' he replies, nodding. 'You build the fire.'

'You sing in the water.'

They look at each other.

'I figured,' said the fire builder, 'that it was about time to meet, rather than tiptoeing around each other out here. I'm Kjell.'

'Shell?' Devin repeats.

'K-j-e-l-l, but pronounced 'shell' as in 'seashell,' the big man says, 'Kjell Kristiansen.'

'Devin Buck.'

Kjell nods.

'I heard you singing, figured you were Native.'

Devin nods.

'I wondered if you were, too, making a fire out here every day.'

Kjell smiles, a slight glint in the shadow of the spruce.

'Well, not every day. Me, I'm Norwegian a little ways back. So, from a long line of forest folk too. Shall we walk?'

They set off side by side, down the ravine in the growing morning.

'In the long ago, *Kristiansen* would have told you that my father's name was Kristian.'

'Buck's is my mom's family name. My folks were married Traditional style; she kept her name, Buck. But that's not her Traditional name.'

It's easy to talk to this stranger, until he asks,

'Your mom teach you to sing?'

Devin looks away, embarrassed.

'You're good, you know,' says Kjell. 'I mean, at least to a Norwegian Forest Cat like me, you sound good.'

The boy is still looking down.

'Did you know they have those in Norway? A separate kind of cat, the Norwegian Forest Cat.'

'What are they like?' Devin welcomes the subject change. 'Big cats? Or house cat size?'

'I've never seen one, myself, but they are cat sized. A little large.'

'Like a Maine Coon,' says Devin.

'Yes, like that,' says Kjell. They run out of chat and walk in silence, listening to the ravine sounds. Devin hears his mother fear voice warning him *why is this man interested in you? A strange man in a forest. What does he want from you?*

Devin feels his shoulders coming up, begins thinking about what he might do to protect himself, if this turns out to be a stupid idea, to talk to a strange man alone in the forest. A big man, who moves like he is fit and strong.

Kjell stops at a fork in the path.

'This is my turn,' he says, nodding at the trail leading Eastward up the bank. 'See you.'

Devin nods.

Kjell takes a few steps, turns back.

'Hey. Listen… I come here for time alone. Obviously you do, too. I will stay out of your way. I'm not…looking for boys in the woods, okay? I just thought you must know I am out here, and it seemed creepier not to meet.'

Devin's shoulders drop a bit.

'Also, I wanted to know you won't come looking for my fire.'

In the growing light, Devin can see truth and darkness in Kjell's stern gaze.

'I won't bother you,' says Kjell, 'You don't bother me. That's all.'

He turns and strides up the path.

HAZEL: ACCOMMODATIONS

'*Now* will you two listen to me and go to the police?'

'No,' says Shanaya. 'We've got nothing to tell them.'

'We've got pictures of her,' I say, nodding at Édith. They blink.

'Yes, I took pictures and no, I didn't ask permission. When you don't know why a woman is covered with bruises, you document it, then you tell her. Okay, maybe I should've asked her first.'

Their stony silence stretches until Roy looks up and gives a little anxious whine, cocks his head at me. He doesn't telepath at me, but it's clear he's telling me to fix this.

'Sorry, eh?'

Édith is focused a long way away.

Shanaya is gearing up to growl at me good, but then the little woman speaks.

'No. It's okay. You did the right thing.'

She drinks some coffee and gives me a wan smile.

'Thanks.' She actually winks. 'Especially considering I thought you were going to deck me when you opened the door.'

She sighs, and there's a lot in it, rubs her skinny arms.

'Now what can we do with evidence like that?' She muses.

Shan's staring and I know I am, too. Édith's talking about herself and her injuries as if they are just a tool, just information outside of her. I blink. I've been there. You put it outside yourself and that is how you survive. It's a thing that happened, it's done. You go on.

'I mean, we could get them looking for George, but that might put those kids in worse jeopardy.'

She pauses, looks around at us seriously.

'Or the next batch.'

'Oh?' Shanaya breathes.

Édith's voice goes hoarse.

'This isn't the first time.'

And now she's struggling a bit to keep her head. My eyes sting and I push back from the table, open the window, light a smoke. I don't look at her. My tears of sympathetic horror she does not need. I glance at Shanaya. Her hands are laid flat on the table. No, her hands are forced down flat to keep them from drumming, keep her grip against claws and brindled fury. She makes a small noise in her throat and Roy springs from his bed to my side in a flash, presses against my legs. He's shaking. I take a drag, blow smoke into the room, force my voice calm and neutral.

'Of course. We have to face the possibility that they've shipped that bunch of them away. So, where do they send them?'

The morning tilts. Édith drinks her coffee, draws breath.

'That's the thing,' she says, 'I have no idea. Could be anywhere. Anywhere.'

Roy trembles against my leg.

'Hey boy,' I say. 'You need to go outside?'

'I'll take him,' blurts Shanaya, but when she pushes back her chair he just shoots past us to the door as if the devil is on his tail. He ricochets off the back door and Shanaya blandly ignores his terror but I can see her taming herself as she stalks through the house, and her voice is her own as she opens the door.

'There you go, Roy,' she says gently. I pour us more coffee. She comes back to the table. The morning rebalances.

***

'How about we just think about it a bit then,' says Shanaya. She runs a hand through her mane. 'I know some people who work in Immigration law, and who are probably more up than I am on agricultural workers in particular.'

Now she's talking sense. I've opened my laptop and we're browsing together through government sites. So much has changed in the world, but bureaucratic language is tougher than cockroaches. No matter who's in charge, the jargon inserts itself and overruns things. I'm used to reading through it, used to legalese, but the clauses available to the public are at once dense as a thicket and frustratingly vague.

Roy comes back in, pads around the table counting us with his nose, and you'd never know he'd ever had a problem with Shanaya. Édith, he nudges and licks, his soft brown eyes worshipful. Great. He trails after her when she excuses herself, parks in front of the bathroom door. Just great.

'This could take awhile. So what about Édith? Where is she going to stay?' Shanaya asks as soon as she's gone.

'You content to let her go on worming her way into Diya's affections?'

Shan shakes her head reflexively, then sighs.

'Well, I mean, we could make an arrangement. It has worked out so far.'

'Uh uh. That just means your mother gets deeper into this than she already went, and do you want that?' *Not to mention being pushed out of your own bed.*

'No.'

'Okay, so let's think,' I know I am grasping at straws. Shanaya tries to help.

'Sandra's got space now that young Devin is subletting your daughter's place, yes?'

'No. She's as bad a Diya for nosiness…and she hasn't had the benefit of really getting to know Édith like we have. She still thinks of her as The Embryo that broke up my marriage and took our farm. So no. Even if I hadn't unleashed pure destruction on her in the shape of Roy.'

At the sound of his name, Roy perks right up, uncurls and bounces over for some love.

Shanaya looks questioningly at me.

'He dug up her best squash. It was a massacre.'

Roy grins as if I'm describing his win at the local dog show. What a guy.

I bury my face in his furry neck for a moment. There really isn't any way out of this.

'She can stay here.'

'She can find her own place, thank you,' says Édith, entering the room with deadly timing.

'No,' I say, holding onto Roy's collar so he doesn't bounce over and knock her down and dissolve her in drool or something. Unbelievable. As is the prospect of me, trying to convince The Embryo to be my guest. But I do.

'Think about it. Nobody knows where you are, and that's a good way to keep things.'

'Hazel's right,' says Shanaya soothingly, 'we must consider you still in danger.'

Roy breaks free and goes to Édith to lay his big head upon her knee.

She pets him and he looks up at her adoringly. *Gaah*. Then he peers at her more closely, and slinks back over to sit on my feet. (Not at my feet, Roy is an on-the-toes sort of fellow).

He makes a tiny noise that I choose to interpret as a *sotto voce* growl. *Huh*. And yes, I confess it warms my suspicious little heart just a bit that he is so obviously making a point about whose dog he is; but he's still grinning at her, like a living welcome mat.

'And the second you go around looking for a place you expose yourself to the possibility that George can track you,' says Shanaya.

'But I can't impose on you any more than I already have. Mama Diya wouldn't let me contribute at all while I stayed with her. I can't–I won't–take that from you.'

Mama Diya!? I see Shanaya flex her fingers at that one.

'You don't have much choice, chicken,' I say. No, I'm not in the habit of calling people 'chicken' but Édith just looks like a comical little hen puffing herself up like that. Or a sparrow. *Le Piaf*. I shake my head. No way I can't handle her, Roy or no Roy.

'Besides, Dick Francis can pay for you.'

Shanaya laughs, and I start laughing too, and Édith frowns from one to the other of us.

'I'm rich,' says Shanaya.

I wish she hadn't said that, so free and breezy. This is still the woman who stole my husband, I am not at all sure she's a safe person to be telling that you have oodles of money.

Shanaya catches my frown and just winks. I sigh and play our ace.

'He'll never look for you here.'

***

And so it's settled. Until we sort out what we can best do about all this, I have a house guest, whom I do not quite trust. And to help me protect her I have the dubious might of Roy, who has commenced carrying his bowl around the room and dropping it pointedly beside each of us in turn.

'Aw, how cute!' says Édith. 'Can I feed him?'

'Be my guest,' I say, nodding at the open pantry where some cans of dog food lurk.

'How about us?' Shanaya says. 'What if I whip us up some eggs?'

'If it's in the fridge, fill your boots,' I say.

She starts rummaging in the fridge and before long she and Édith are bustling and chopping and whisking, building breakfast. I pour myself another coffee and get out of their way. Back to the computer.

'You want me to read you the latest on the *leiobunum rotundum?*'

'The what?' Shanaya asks.

'The most recently discovered species of *Opiliones*, commonly known as Daddy Longlegs or Harvestman.'

'Oh.'

'I felt like browsing before bed last night, thought there was a million-to-one shot our group of bad guys might have a Facebook page–'

'Or a web site?' quips Édith.

'The harvestman is not a spider,' I reply loftily, 'more spider-adjacent, if you will.'

'And?' Shanaya asks.

'And nothing. A lot about the not-a-spider and its worldwide varieties; nothing about our shadowy gang.' I'm typing and scrolling while we talk.

'Also nothing, you'll both be interested to hear, about a missing woman named Edith Jones, or Édith Pomeroy, or anything like that. And no reports of missing agricultural workers either, come to that.'

As they serve up the breakfast I consider that: temporary farm workers are a category of people that, if you think about it, would be easy to traffic, hard to keep track of. Anyone itinerant in this world, despite all the digital surveillance we all bemoan, anyone itinerant could fairly easily disappear.

And if they don't have family to look for them, maybe they never get found.

I grab a piece of toast.

'Édith, by any chance, do you have a list of names? What if we start by trying to find their families? Someone has got to be wondering where they are.'

DEVIN: UNDER

Devin walks on, unnerved and unsure what to make of the encounter. He's known for some time that there is someone else using the ravine some mornings. He's been so careful to sing quietly.

He walks home slowly, his big feet clumsy and his spine uneasy.

The next day, and the next, he avoids the ravine.

By the third day, he is angry enough to return, but he finds he cannot follow the path. There is no smell of smoke in the air but now he knows there is another man in this forest. A man who says he means no harm, but Devin doesn't know him. And Devin's not LeWayne, charging into the dark alone. He's big but so is that man Kjell, and Devin never learned to fight.

Until now, being big has meant that other men assume he is dangerous, and don't challenge him. And he has kept himself out of situations where they'd see him as a challenge against which to prove themselves.

When LeWayne and Cody and Tomlin started running rough, Devin went to his aunt's garden, to the library, to Father Efren's residence. He studied on things, set his mind to complexities, read history, read lore, listened hard. It's never appealed to him to do the obvious and hit something. Until now.

Now he stops, under the bridge where Whyte Avenue crosses the ravine. There are probably people camping under here. He's never seen them, but they're probably there. Probably been listening to him. Probably haven't bothered him because they've been afraid.

But one day they will. They will come out of the darkness like his father's pointless anger.

They are what his father ranted about:

I'm so sick of it. All the people fucked over and fucked up by the Church, by the government, by the broken treaties and the Residential Schools, and so accepting of it, wallowing in their fucking brokenness! And hanging on me. And no matter how hard I work they want more from me! And everyone who knows I'm Indigenous thinks I'm them. No matter what I do they want me down!

His mother trying to comfort and cajole. His father turning on her. Stop making excuses. *Stop trying to make this small! You don't know how it feels, you don't know how it is for a man!*

His father banging the table, getting louder. His mother trying to break through. Then her own anger rising in response. *However hard you think you have it, Frank, women have it worse!*

And she would get all feisty and up in his face and then they would either start throwing things, or she'd break through his rage and he'd laugh and sweep her up in a rough embrace and either way, Devin would be left out of the whirlwind of their passion.

Devin stands alone under the bridge, staring at the darkness.

From the darkness, a creature springs, snarling and whirling and speaking in a terrible flat condemning voice.

'*Fuck you all. You world-destroying cunts of evil. Fuck you all in every detail. You have no love for anything sacred. Fuck you entirely from stem to gudgeon. And the dogs of your mind, which are nowhere near as dignified as real dogs, but cringe and bite along the lines of your poisoned thought. Fuck you.*'

So says the angry creature under the bridge. The creature spins and snarls and curses clawing like a bear caught in a cloud of bees, clawing as the rage bites deeper. And that is not what Devin wants.

So he drops to the earth and lies panting in the dirt a moment. Then he sits up, back against a bridge footing, and peers into the darkness until he can rise again, himself again in the growing morning, and he takes himself home to his sanctuary, lies down on Little Frankie's sofa and falls asleep, dirty and exhausted and for once dreamless.

HAZEL: ARMS

Okay, we only sort of have a plan. Really, a lot depends on things we don't know yet. Where are they? How many prisoners are there? What state will they be in when we find them?

How the hell do we get them out?

What do we do with them once we've gotten them out?

Diya has arranged for someone to receive the stolen ones in Amiskwaciy. She calls, of course, just after noon, and insists on an update. She expresses no great surprise that our first foray has been inconclusive. What's surprising is that she agrees that Édith is as safe with me as with her.

'Nobody would suspect to look for Aditi in your house. But my own daughter must come home,' she says. 'She must help me make some arrangements.'

I guess I'm not surprised that Shanaya goes straight home, leaving me hanging around the house with my husband's second ex-wife. I've come a long way in a short while, but realistically? I am not going to hang around with the woman my husband left me for.

'Make yourself at home,' I say to her, as she lounges on the sofa with Roy curled on her feet. 'I've got to go see my sister about some vegetables.' I shoot Roy a dark look and he just grins back.

'Wait,' says Édith, 'I-I don't want to drive you out of your own home.'

I can't see my own face but I must be a sight.

'Again?' She adds softly, with a pained little sideways grin.

It strikes me that I could choose to find that funny.

'Huh,' is all I have to say, but I do manage to raise what is either an answering sneer or the other half of a wry acknowledgement of our strange common ground. And I hightail it down to Sandra's, where there is plenty of dirt that needs shoving back into order.

'It has to be discreet,' Shanaya says. 'We don't know if they'll be willing, or able, to go to the authorities right away. We don't know their legal status.'

'La, la, Beti,' says Diya, 'just bring them where I told you, and they will be safe enough.'

***

I have smuggled The Embryo to Mill Woods in a hat and sunglasses, and we've had some excellent food and now we're down to business.

'Shouldn't we all know the address?' I ask, awkwardly aware of the thought behind that, *in case any of us don't make it back.* Diya gives me a shrewd glance, her eyes flaring just for a moment with what might be a mother's fear for her daughter. Then she shrugs.

'Of course, of course. Better yet, let's all go for a little drive and I will show you.'

'You sure about this?' I ask.

It doesn't look like a safe house. It's a daycare, garishly painted with a god or goddess featuring about twenty arms. *One for each kid*, I think, stifling an irreverent grin. Diya catches my eye, though, and I know she's heard my thought. She twinkles back at me.

'You see, Hazel,' she says, 'enough arms to hold all your little refugees.'

I almost ask more, but Shanaya shakes her head just slightly. I guess I do not need further details, really. This is not my part of this caper.

I'm the Native guide, for when we get out in the bush and the back country.

Mill Woods is not my territory.

'Shanaya's friend Ramesh will be ready to help with legalities,' says Diya archly, and Shanaya shakes her head.

'Mother, don't bother with saying *friend* like that. We're colleagues. That is all.'

'Then how can you trust him?' I can't help myself.

'Okay. We're friends. Long time friends.'

'*Family* friends,' twinkles Diya.

'Mother,' Shanaya chides, then shrugs. 'But yes, I've known Ramesh and his family forever, and I know he can be trusted in this matter.'

She's still a bit annoyed, and I can't blame her. It's a bit of a thing, after all, to be a shape shifter. You can't just go out with anyone. Not that I know from being one. But I lived with one. And sure, I thought about it. Fortunately, I met him as a dog and by the time I found out he was also a man, well, I'd gotten used to thinking of him as a dog. And I'm just not that broad-minded.

In Shanaya's case? God I don't know what I'd do. I shake my head. That thought leads nowhere good. I do not wish to think about the pitter patter of little paws.

Let's get back to the practical.

Hardly less scary. What if they are all as beaten up as Édith was when she arrived? Was she that utterly battered because they all were, or was it personal? Someone should ask her. I hope someone asks her. I suppose I'll fucking have to ask her.

DEVIN: PIECE OF WORK

Devin likes best to work in the back where it's quiet, with the shrubs and young trees. He also fears it some days. He can't help it, the drooping saplings make him choke up, and then he is thankful that at least he's on his own out there for the most part. But he also can't help feeling watched there, feeling like at any moment, someone either staff or public is going to spring out at him from a line of cherry saplings or something and shout because they've caught him out, the big weirdo crying over potted trees in autumn.

Whenever he has to clean up after a weekend, he sees what it is that bothers him: the trees, their roots shrouded and stunted, can't stand up for themselves, and are so easy to knock down and break or blight. The metaphor is obvious. That doesn't make it easier. He still sees LeWayne lying in the grass, Tomlin and Cody sobbing, one of them crying for his mother, Rabbit's eerie voice crying too, somewhere in the bloody stinking darkness.

Whenever it hits him, he tucks his head down and concentrates on lifting the broken tree, even if his hands shake. He goes down the rows, resetting the fallen until it's done. Some mornings, he doesn't hear his colleagues tell him it's time for a break. Soon enough, they learn not to bother him when he's straightening trees.

'He likes it. Let him alone,' explains the shift supervisor to Akasha, the new girl, when she makes to go and physically fetch him, and asks why nobody's brought him in for coffee. Akasha doesn't let it go at that. The next morning, she takes two coffees and goes out to him.

'Uh. Thanks,' he says, looking down, looking away, shuffling his big feet.

She smiles, reaches out a hand and pats his sleeve.

Startled, he looks up.

The smile slips a little, then ups wattage to a full beam.

'No problem,' she says, and walks away slow, as from a bear surprised at a berry bush.

'Sawitsky wants to see you.' It's Akasha again.

Devin puts aside the cedar he's been grooming and ambles up toward the shop. To his astonishment, he rounds the corner and sees Sawitsky seated at one of the frou-frou wrought aluminum cafe tables set out in the front now to welcome customers. On her rough pallet patio, she looks at home. On the little public chairs, she looks awkward as a circus bear on a bicycle. Across from her sits his Aunt Hazel.

Devin's spine runs with chills. This can't be anything good.

It's not that he doesn't like his Aunt Hazel. It's not exactly that he fears she does not like him. She's never said or done anything mean, but she's sharp-edged in general and being near her feels like…a metaphor fails him. She's uncomfortable.

And yet, when he discovered strange tally marks on a brick wall that coincided with the deaths of three men connected to their community, he knew to take the problem to Hazel. He knew that she would take him seriously. However off-hand and aloof she is to him, she has also always spoken to him as if he were a full person.

She doesn't condescend. Hazel is prickly and surly to everyone.

And she does not wheedle.

But as he draws near, his fear gives way to puzzlement as his Aunt smiles warmly at Reg Sawitsky, and speaks to the broad-beamed, matter-of-fact greenhouse manager with a tone that Devin would have to classify as wheedling.

It's hardly necessary, because Reg Sawitsky is only half paying attention to Hazel. She keeps dropping her gaze to where a big golden dog lies panting and grinning beside Hazel. Sawitsky's expressions mirror the dog's, her greying blonde hair flopping a little like ears as she tips her head in unconscious simpatico with the reddish blond dog.

Hazel looks up and nods at Devin.

She's smiling, which does nothing to allay his fear. *Who died?* He thinks breathlessly.

***

Later that night, as Roy curls up on the sofa grinning at him, Devin doesn't know what to feel. He's agreed to take care of Roy while Hazel goes on some unspecified trip. Something about that lack of details worries him. On the other hand, Roy is undeniable. And, after losing her bid to just adopt him herself, Sawitsky has eagerly agreed that Devin can bring the dog to work with him, so no need to worry he'll be lonely in the apartment.

'Not fair to do that to a dog,' Sawitsky had said gruffly.

'Why isn't–?'

'Your Aunt Sandra has a bunch of meetings about the next phase of this project,' says Hazel. 'And you know her. She's been worried about you.'

Devin blushes.

'So I suggested having Roy for company would do you good.'

She's got him there. He's been ducking Sandra's calls, aware that if not for his contact with Missy, his aunt would descend upon him in a panic.

'It'll stop her descending upon you,' says Hazel.

That's one thing about his Aunt Hazel, she understands the need for personal space. Devin smiles at the sudden realization, but hides the smile. It would be too weird, and she might start grinning back like Roy.

Hazel surprises Devin again by looking around the space and asking whether he might have a use for something else.

'It's in the jeep. Come help me carry it in. I brought you gloves too.'

And now, Roy sits grinning next to him, and in a corner of Frankie's bedroom stands a well-used heavy bag on a floor stand, hulking like a bear at a tea party. Like Devin himself in Frankie's blue and mauve she-cave.

He tries leaving the big dog at home when he slips out to walk the ravine, but Roy begins whining and hopping about, his tail thumping randomly against the walls, and Devin sighs, finds the leash and the dog bags.

'Come on, Roy,' he says and they head out together. To Devin's surprise, Roy sticks close to his side, the leash slack. In the dark, he moves like Devin's shadow, and when they see a cyclist approaching, Roy mutters a tiny growl under his breath.

'No,' Devin whispers. Roy mutters again. The cyclist rides past, ignoring them, and Roy gives one parting low grumble, but makes the rest of the trip to the ravine in silence.

Devin knows that most of his habitual walk passes through an off-leash park, but that first morning, he leaves the leash on, appraising Roy's attention. No way does he want to have to try catching the big pup if he should decide to light out for his former home. If he even knows which way to go, Devin thinks. Dogs, he knows, have a powerful instinct for home, but Roy? Where does he consider his home to be? Devin doesn't know.

He knows Frankie got the big-pawed pup from somewhere undisclosed, gave him to Hazel for reasons unclear, and Hazel left him just the once with Auntie Sandra. Devin chuckles in the dark and grins at Roy. 'You made a mess in Auntie's garden, boy. Better not do that at work.'

***

They circle back, eat breakfast and head out again.

'Ride my bike with you?' Devin asks Roy, a little rhetorically. 'Nope. At least, not 'til we're a little better acquainted.'

So they walk, as fast as Devin can stride, and arrive at work a few minutes late. Sawitsky is all smiles though, and falls upon Roy with caresses, treats, and a ridiculous rubber chicken squeaky toy.

Sawitsky unclips Roy's leash without asking and sweeps her arm wide, toward the encompassing limits of the fence around the Civic Gardens Greenhouse grounds.

'All this is yours to guard, good sir,' she says to Roy grandly. 'Now, come along and let me show you.' And the big dog trots off with her, content to nose politely here and there as they go. Devin stands with the leash hanging from his hand, unsure what to do. Then Roy barks.

'Well, come along, Devin Buck,' calls Sawitsky, 'help me show your dog his worksite.'

They make an hour of the trip, and customers roam the aisles of the front shed.

'Of course,' says Sawitsky, for once looking at Devin rather than the dog, 'we will wait to see how he handles the busyness of the working day, before we let him have full run of the place.'

Roy shows zero evidence of inclination to attack the strangers pottering among the greenery. He just sits and grins contentedly.

'Now, sir,' she says, addressing the dog rather than Devin, 'you will come with me.' And Roy trots meekly after her, Devin trailing. Sawitsky has set up a place for Roy on the pallet patio–a big outdoor rug, a water dish and food bowl–and fashioned a gate from a chunk of another pallet. She leads him into his playpen, tosses the chicken to him, and ties the gate, all the while crooning to Roy about how much he will love his new job, watching over everything.

'Such a good dog you are!'

Sawitsky straightens up and turns to Devin.

'Now,' she addresses him, 'help me bring this for him,' and she points at a big ugly plastic igloo squatting in the back of her pickup. 'Every dog needs a den.'

HAZEL: CUBITS

We are driving through the breadbasket. Fields full of ripe wheat, barley, oats. Lentils. Fucking soy. What's wrong with us as humans? Why can't we recognize a good thing? Got to keep tinkering, us.

We went from lives in contact with the land to living in cities and abandoning the fields and then wondering why our food supply was so messed up. Mad Cow at the turn of the century. Automation. Caribbean apple pickers penned like slaves during the pandemic. Freight trains full of oil tanks driving up freight prices for grain, because we hated pipelines.

Even after that deadly train collision and fire at Lac Megantic, we couldn't muster the political consensus to build proper pipelines and use drone technology to maintain them, rather than shoving them haphazardly through 'empty' land where nobody but wildlife and Indigenous people lived, so it wouldn't matter if they leaked. Even though every single city in our land was fuelled by pipelines running under and into our hospitals, offices and homes and we manage that without leaks, it took us far too long to commit to using the best of our ingenuity to use fossil fuels cleanly, along with other sources, rather than in an endless strident debate about the better way to exploit the world for our own luxury.

I'd like to say we got it all fixed, when the earth woke up at Fox Creek and fires ravaged the Gnarly Hills and people nearly starved here that one dark winter, before we pulled our heads out of our asses, took a deep collective breath and got on with being a responsible keystone species rather than a spoiled jumped-up disaster train of narcissistic naked apes killing the world and arguing about who among us was going to wear the blame.

I'd like to say we woke up and got on with doing our best.

I've said that, but the fact is, that's not true.

We made a deal got more migrants coming, got more people to work in our fields. Yes, we revitalized some towns. Yes, we improved our train systems. But no, we haven't solved things yet, we're just working on it.

***

We turn north onto highway 43, rolling through the harvest lands and I gaze out on the grain and cattle and think about what was lost.

For society.

For me. Except I've never counted that cost, for me.

The thing is, agriculture is probably the biggest gamble we ever undertook, making deals with animals and plants to become in relationship to them. We tamed animals and bred them to be more amenable to us and our needs, we selectively bred the plants we like best. We worked toward symbiosis. I want to believe that is true.

'Hey Shan. In India, cows are sacred, right? And the people eat butter and cheese and milk, and the cows live free.'

'Mmmhmm.'

'Don't you ever think we'd be better here, too, if we treated cows as sacred, lived more slowly, sanctified our dal and ghee and greens?'

'That slow sanctity made them vulnerable to the British,' she replies firmly.

'Gandhi himself experimented with meat eating when he went to study in London as a youth.' I say.

I remember the weird old poem quoted in his biography then:

'Behold the mighty Englishman, he rules the Indian small
Because being a meat eater, he is two meters tall'

'5 cubits, actually,' pipes a voice from the back seat. Édith is awake. 'And Gandhi went back to strict vegetarianism. There's no one right answer.'

Whatever.

I turn back to the window, not sure what I want to say to them. I think about buffalo, about cattle, about Europe trying to re-wild, about Poland having its own wild bison. In the waving pale gold fields, I imagine horsemen riding. Imagine my grandmother stooping and tying straw into stooks. Imagine her grinding grain. Imagine whips and slaves and fire. Tanks and guns and reams of doctors doing talking head videos braying about optimal diets, without any real regard for life as a whole thing.

Who can hold all life in the balance in one mind?

I try to imagine one thing. *A bear. Picture a bear. What's more fundamentally real than a bear?*

Can't even hold that image in my mind.

I see Jim's human face dissolve into Spider's dog visage and that into a flare of fire in the night and then a girl takes the hand of a tall wild creature and they step through the sudden crack in the very air and walk away into nothing.

A bear. Picture a bear.

I see a tiger. A shivering woman bleeding and bruised. I see blood spray the air. I see flames. I see wild and tattered muskeg, and bodies lying in unnatural angles, discarded in the moss. Cold breath and everything dissolves.

I shake my head and look around. We're still just driving up Highway 43, all of us awake now.

Out the window, I glimpse something dark moving through the pale autumn fields, but I don't know what it is, so I don't call anyone's attention to it.

It turns out I'm not sure about anything. Least of all whether this is a fool's errand.

DEVIN: GETHSEMANE BREAKDOWN

He grabs the guitar by the throat and straps it on. He prowls the room, scowling and muttering. He starts a blues riff, chunky and thunderous. He thinks about the Pope's assertion that Reconciliation looks like Indigenous people deciding to consider all those kids killed in the Church Schools as a symbol of Christ Crucified. And he begins to sing, growling, prowling.

'Do you think you were the only one?
Crying in Gethsemane.
Take this cup away from me.
I wanted us to live.
Pontificate about us, we should thank you for the deaths
For all the tiny voices snuffed out in the dark.
But we lived! And while we lived
We were the heart
And it's still beating
No, you were not the only one
Crying in Gethsemane
Take this cup away from me.
I wanted us to live.
I wanted him to live.
How much love?
How much love?
How much love does it take to save one life?

How much stardust? How much will?
How much?! How much?! How! How? How?!'

He screams now, roaring, thrashing at the strings; he gnaws the air, and beats on the guitar, body blows that thud and grunt and stutter. His hand tight on the neck, he almost rips it off over his head, but the strap is caught under his elbow, and he is not a 1960s rockstar with guitars to spare. He doesn't reckon Robert Johnson or Robbie Robertson or Link Wray or the Vegas brothers ever wrecked their guitars.

This is his legacy and he pulls it hard against himself, wraps his arms around it as he sinks into the sofa, and he holds the unresisting body of song against his heart and cries, rocking himself through the grief and rage, head on the shoulder of the guitar.

He looks up in a while, wondering whether he should see his father's ghost standing before him, either to praise or to blame him. But the night is quiet, and it is his breathing that moves, his own heart beating.

'*Where are you?*' He whispers, crying again. '*Why did you leave? Wasn't I enough?*'

He cries on.

'*Why do I have to go on alone?*'

'*Mama. Mama Mama Mama,*' he sobs, the first and oldest refrain, the deepest love and the deepest loss.

And there in the dark he slowly becomes aware of a wordless feeling of love, a memory from before words, a voiceless voice speaking.

You are loved. You are born of love. You are here because you are love.

And he drums softly, so softly, and sings a phrase that tumbles from him

Aihai hai, mmhmm mmhmm hmm

Over and over he sings and hums the little thread of song, and finally gives voice to the sensation of arms around him, of an unbreakable truth

That you are loved

That you are absolutely, absolutely loved

That you are love...absolutely absolutely... He slowly subsides and falls asleep, but not before he eases his guitar down onto the rug, safely, reverently, with a poor boy's respect for his limited treasure.

And Roy, who has witnessed from under the kitchen table the whole time, comes softly stepping and nudges the guitar neck gently aside, makes room for himself to cuddle up next to the sofa, his big head pressed against the boy's trailing hand.

HAZEL: RADIO AND STATIC

'You know what I never realized 'til now? His name is George Jones. Like the country singer. God but I hate his music.'

We stare at Shanaya.

'How do you know George Jones' music?'

'Diya,' shrugs Shanaya, changing the station.

Nobody listens to the radio in cars anymore, do they? Most cars just have docks for your phone, wifi hotspots, whatever.

'Is Diya also why you have a radio in your car?'

'Mmhmm,' purrs Shanaya, who has found a classic pop station playing that old Hanson song. Édith joins in, shout-singing '*MMBop! bop bah doowop!... doobie da da doowah babadoooo!*' or something like.

I look out the window, eyes stinging a bit. Damn it. Think of Frank singing, Sandra and I trying to join in, him correcting, criticizing, huffing and making exasperated noises. At the time, it crushed any love of music right out of me. Took a long time to ask myself, how could he know any better? That's how our dad taught him, the old army way, never heard of positive reinforcement.

Not that Dad was mean either. He just learned how he'd been taught, by the Church school teachers who, let's face it, weren't in the job of teaching little Indians because they loved kids. Mostly, they were there because nobody else wanted the job, and they couldn't get the jobs they really wanted. So they took out their shame and inadequacy on these benighted heathen savages, who learned–those who survived at all–to teach the same way, by reflexive criticism and expressions of frustration over mistakes.

None of this *failure is wonderful, you need to make mistakes to learn* twaddle.

Get it right was the mantra, along with *What are you? Stupid?* And I'm not even saying I understand what those schools were, or how the poor bastards who ran them became so sick, or where the line of abuse began, or if you could solve it by unraveling that... and anyway, lots of people are just poor teachers for their siblings, anyway.

I loved Frank, but he acted like we were intruding on his private domain. He had the guitar. He was the oldest. He was the one chosen to sing. He had to share everything else with us. This, he wanted for his own.

I guess, if I were to look at that, I'd say it's kind of sad. More than kind of. It's tragic. He missed out, because he was so in need of something to define himself, some way to be better than the mongrel hillbilly mutts we were, that he curled around the beauty of singing and pushed us away. He'd never have articulated it that way.

To his dying day, he couldn't resist pointing out that we just weren't good at it, not like him.

I remember him laughing at George, too, shaking his head at George's skinny voice trying to sing. He was right, George sang like a goat, but he didn't find cause to sing except to try to impress Frank. Frank didn't know how much I paid for that scorn, after he'd left.

It's so complicated.

Music shouldn't be complicated.

Shouldn't make you angry and scared and scornful and elitist.

So I don't sing.

But I'm also damn sure I'll never criticize anyone, however ridiculous their harmonies. I smile now, thinking of my little girls singing along to Alanis Morissette. Singing U2 songs. Barging around the house playing air guitar to Murray Porter, shouting '*1492, Who Found Who?!*'

I don't sing, but I'll never stop anyone else from it.

Shanaya and Édith sing all the way to Fox Creek, even as the radio reception goes crackly–satellites and cellphones, all the tech you want, the hills in that country just block the signal, force you to notice you've left the tame agricultural lands behind, you're in primary resource country now.

I wonder what those kids we're hoping to rescue can hear, wherever they are out here. Do they have radio or just the noise of the living bush? And does it comfort them or add another layer to their terror and sense of helplessness. I wonder what I was thinking, letting Frankie go off alone, when things happen to young people, especially young women. I measure myself, my trust in the world, in God I suppose. My girls are grown women. I can do nothing more for them now but stand aside and trust, however hard it feels.

But these kids? I don't know who they are, where they're from exactly, how they are vulnerable.

Édith is humming now, that stupid tune she likes, the French one I can't quite identify. Ridiculous. I can't stand it, and as much to stop her humming before Shanaya joins in, I speak.

'Édith,' I ask, 'how does it work? How do they catch these kids they traffic?'

'I don't know,' says Édith, not for the first time. 'Some of them come from families of labourers sent here to pick crops. Some of them...'

I look back. She scrubs a hand through her spiky hair.

'There was this one boy,' she said, 'who told me he came out here by himself, looking for his sister.'

My blood runs cold. Seriously, I have no knowledge of how it all works. I'm in over my head. We all are. But I look from Édith to Shanaya and back again and they have the same grim, closed look on their faces. They do not care that they don't understand how it all works. They are not out to dismantle the system...

'Hazel,' says Shanaya, as if reading my mind, 'stop brooding on the context. Don't you get it? Those kids matter. *Those specific kids.*'

'Yes,' I counter, 'but it's been weeks. Those specific kids could be anywhere. Logically, they are not together. Logically, this will be another set of kids.'

'Does that make them any less worth saving?!' Édith's voice cuts like feedback through static.

She starts humming again. I turn on the radio, hunting for a clear voice in the wilderness.

DEVIN: FIRE

Devin is in the yard moving some saplings into a different arrangement, filling in for the holes caused by people buying one or two of this or that type of tree or shrub.

He finds it relaxing despite how it's a bit sad, as if the saplings are puppies in the window, wondering if someone will come take them home, or whether they'll be vestigial plantings, weeded out by attrition at the impending close of the season, finally too big for their containers but with no new home in view.

He is lost in his thoughts when he hears Roy bark. And then he smells smoke. His thoughts turn to the man in the forest, with his unusual name, Kjell Kristiansen. And then he hears the alarm.

He shakes himself, turns and walks out toward the barking. The Muster Point, he remembers, is just past Sawitsky's office trailer.

He strides long-legged through the gardens. Some of the staff are running.

He hears Sawitsky bawl, 'Muster!' And Roy barks for emphasis.

Devin sees a little knot of people and walks past them, nodding to Sawitsky. She's got Roy out of his pen, and the big pup is standing tight against her leg, uttering occasional barks and waving his plumed tail uncertainly. Sawitsky passes the leash to Devin, pats Roy on the head and begins calling the roll. He answers in his turn, as do they all but two.

'Where are Akasha and Leandro?'

And then sudden explosions rock the scene. The staff spin as one organism.

'Fertilizer,' breathes Sawitsky, mouth agape. Flame blooms up-ward, sound follows.

Devin feels it again, the sense of time slowing down like in the park in the dark as LeWayne drew his knife and ran headlong into the night, too fast and unstoppable. Devin presses Roy's leash back into Sawitsky's unresisting hand.

'Stay, Roy,' he says.

Then he drops his shoulders and runs toward the balls of flame roiling up into the sky.

Devin is dimly aware of shouts, of figures moving rapidly to-ward the burning building, but his mind is laser-focused. *Akasha and Leandro*. Where had he seen them last? He remembers Akasha bringing him coffee, telling him with a grin that Sawitsky wanted him the day Roy arrived.

He knows Leandro by his gentle laugh, the way he'd never crowd-ed Devin. How Leandro had taken Akasha under his wing. The way their smiles and strides matched. They always work together, for preference in the Tropical House.

They will be in the Tropical House now, surely. But they are not.

Devin runs on, toward the burning supply building.

Shouting follows him. He hauls open the door, charges into the dim, reverberating building.

The sprinkler system flares, and for a moment, Devin thinks it's going to be alright. But then the water fizzles, inexplicably. He stares. Then he thinks of the standpipe that morning and the forklift and the delivery man—just a boy, really—shouting and running, al-most comical, as water sprayed everywhere. But surely they'd gotten the system fixed since then?

Sirens announce the arrival of the fire department.

Devin staggers, stops.

Drop, says the voice in his mind.

He hits the ground and crawls forward, toward the figures lying there, just there, surely that is them lying among the shattered and scattered buckets, plants, wires and leaves and choking dust.

Surely they are alive, not too close to the blast. Surely they are alive.

'Akasha! Leandro!' He calls. A movement, a cough.

Devin rumbles through the mess, heaving aside detritus, growling and panting.

He blinks his eyes against the thickness in the air. There. One of the figures lifts a hand, moves their head.

'Leandro,' he barks. 'Can you move?'

Leandro looks up at him wildly, shakes his head.

But then he taps his ear and gasps raggedly, 'Can't hear you.'

Leandro pulls himself up to hands and knees.

'I'm okay,' he pants.

Devin knows Leandro can't hear, so he just reaches for Akasha, pushing aside the broken things that pin her to the ground. So many broken things. He cannot get her clear. His vision is burning.

'*Hey!!*'

He hears a roaring voice. Out of the roiling dark come the firemen, advancing in a rapid crouching run.

'Over here!' Devin bellows. 'One hurt! Help us!'

HAZEL: HUNT

I do my best hunting in supermarkets. I remember some wiseass friend of mine at university teasing me. Della was really something. Six feet tall, daughter of Korean immigrants, she was impossibly beautiful and always immaculately groomed. And yet somehow we became friends. Over footlong hotdogs and pitchers of cheap beer, we'd discuss the world. She called me Farm Girl, like it was a joke, a super-heroine who never was, Farm Girl with her tales of home-grown meat and wild game shot in season.

And now I'm here in the bush, in hunting season actually. Hadn't thought about that. God I hope nobody mistakes us for game out there. I shake my head, focus on the well-stocked shelves of Fox Creek's Freson's supermarket. They tried to make a go of it in Amiskwaciy, but the market was already crowded with grocery chains and Freson's didn't last more than about a year in the city.

Freson's are big where they're needed, out in the little country towns. And nowadays, they're a power themselves as the little towns rebuild, and Freson's is cool. They smell of fenugreek and cardamon, of turmeric and fennel and they smell of local foods brought in.

Except not so much in Fox Creek.

It's bush. Not a lot of really local food beyond game and berries. I shake my head. Blink.

It's George.

Right there in front of the cooler, in this very Freson's, bold as brass in the middle of the day. I've run him to earth when I wasn't even looking.

Shit. What do I do now?

Chills run down my spine, and I spin around quick and quiet and beat it out the door, around the corner, duck behind a pickup truck, whip out my phone.

'He's here.'

'Where?'

'In Freson's. What do we do?'

***

We follow him, that's what we do. Shanaya drives over, I get in her car undetected, and we follow George like we're some kind of detectives in an American show.

He appears to be staying in a bungalow on a street of bungalows, up on the hill where the real town of Fox Creek sits. I write down the house number in my notebook, because I am too shaky to take a photo discreetly.

It's adrenaline and rage, not fear, but it's just as bad as being terrified. It's all I can do to write.

Shan discreetly says nothing. She's good that way, she knows I don't want coddling or sympathetic noises. In fact, I can hear her growling under her breath as we swing around a corner and head back down the hill.

'Hazel?' She says in a quizzical tone, and I realize it's me who's growling. Ridiculous.

'Didn't you hear me?' I say, 'I said RRRRRR.'

And we are still laughing when we get to our room to find Édith watching *Law & Order* on TV. I swear, when society falls, there will remain some eternal hotel somewhere with *Law & Order* streaming on the half-cracked screen in the apocalyptic corner.

She looks up at us laughing and smiles, willing to join the joke. I feel tears prick my eyes, and push past into the bathroom, as if I have to pee. This little stranger. The past we share.

So bite me. I need a few minutes to pull myself together.

I pull my pants down, sit down for the authenticity of it, press against the cold reality of the cheap plastic toilet seat.

Why do we so easily fall into thinking we can possess others? Thinking that 'belonging with' means 'belonging to' and that the height of romance is to be possessed by someone? We have at least come some distance toward understanding that the person who supposes they possess another might have an unhealthy perspective. We just never think that person's us.

I don't know if I ever loved George. I know I was young and impressionable and impressed. I know that my mother warned me against him, and my father did too. But Dad was so sad about my mom's passing that I saw his warnings as springing from grief. He lost her, now he was trying to cling on to me. But I wanted my own life. So, George. So, my babies. So, a wild ride that felt like it must be important because it was so all-consuming.

It was mine, all mine. I was an adult.

And to be fair to me, when the time came to get out for the sake of my girls, I made the adult decision, packed up and left. And Frank helped me, though I told him not to; I know he took a couple of friends and went and told George in no uncertain terms not to bother me and my girls. Not that George would have. No, I'd already been saved from his possessive attentions, although I didn't see it that way. To me it was a painful loss.

Tell me, why are we so illogical? I wanted out. But I wanted it to be my power that got me out. And instead, it happened because he threw me over for The Embryo. Eighteen years old, *barely legal* as they say. He started carrying on with her even while he kept on pushing me around, treating me like his possession.

My rage at her helped me to get free of him. But I certainly never thought to thank her for that. Even though I knew what she was getting, I didn't care. I see it now–I let myself see her as the catalyst for our break up, when it was me all along. But life is like that, it's all call and response. And we may think we're making the call, but how often are we just responding? Or we may think we're responding to a situation, and not see that, from another perspective, it is us making the call.

We blame each other.

We think we can pick and choose what we take responsibility for; and we're right, but we're also very wrong about that. So me, I decided to blame The Embryo for breaking up my marriage, even though at the very same time, I thought of it as my call.

I'll say this for me. When people would bleat on earnestly about how brave I was to leave him, at least I'd shrug that off and it wasn't self-deprecation, but bone-honest truth. I was selfish, if you want to know. I saw myself dying if I stayed there. Blaming the Embryo for forcing his hand was my ticket out. I had to hate her to let that happen to her, never to warn her.

I knew I was leaving a vulnerable person in a bad situation. I'd been there.

And here we are, and she's watching *Law & Order*, and she still looks eighteen.

DEVIN: ASHES

Devin sits on a chair in the reverberating morning, just breathing; beside him, the little oxygen tank, in his hand the mask. He doesn't need it now.

He watches Reg Sawitsky stamping about as the paramedics load Akasha into the ambulance and leave. Another ambulance has come with more paramedics, and they load Leandro.

Sawitsky points at Devin: 'What about him?'

'He should probably come in to get checked,' says a paramedic.

'I'm okay,' says Devin.

Sawitsky rushes over, pulls Devin up, hugs him and slaps his back.

'You damned young fool!' she bawls, her voice shaky. 'Go with him.'

Devin starts to reply, but she cuts him off.

'I will keep care of Roy. And I will call your auntie.'

'Oh god,' groans Devin.

'You shut up,' says Sawitsky and shoves him toward the paramedic.

'Hey,' says a voice behind him, 'just a minute. I want to talk to you before you go.'

Devin turns and meets the cool, level gaze of Kjell Kristiansen.

'You know this guy?' Sawitsky says. Devin nods.

'Officer Kjell Kristiansen,' says Kjell Kristiansen, and he briefly shakes Sawitsky's blunt hand, then turns his attention back to Devin.

'Listen. What you did today was exceptionally brave–'

Sawitsky makes some sort of noise, turns her head away.

'–and incredibly foolish. You could as easily have died in there.'

Devin shrugs, looking down. 'I didn't.'

'No,' says Kristiansen, 'you didn't. And you maybe got us to those others a few seconds faster. But,' he pauses, and Devin looks up to meet his eyes, 'you could as easily have become one more casualty.'

Devin feels a sudden surge of rage. He spins and starts to stride away.

'Devin Buck!' bawls Sawitsky. 'Get back here!'

He doesn't know what to do. He will not be called to heel like a dog. But he turns and glares at them both.

Kjell Kristiansen growls, 'Look. I'm not saying you weren't brave. But we can't–'

'When you are here,' Sawitsky hollers, 'You are my responsibility! We have protocols and muster points and procedures and I cannot have everyone just running around like headless fucking chickens in a panic!'

Her eyes are running over with tears, her face red.

'What if you had died in there too?!'

Devin drops his head, humiliated by Sawitsky's righteous rage.

'S-s-sorry,' he says. 'I di-didn't think.'

Sawitsky stomps over and grabs him in a crushing hug.

'You are a *hero*, Devin Buck,' she says, glaring over his shoulder at the fireman. 'Now. Let's go to the hospital.'

HAZEL: STARFISH

So what's our plan now that we know George is here?

Priority one, keep Édith safe from him. When we tell her he's here, she goes all still and far away, and God do I recognize that look. Édith's not too bright, her eyes are a little close-set for my liking, and I've spent years overcoming the irrational hatred a woman feels when someone steals her man.

See, I was told, and my logical mind says it's true: nobody can steal anyone. Nobody owns anyone. A person is with a person. If they want to go with another person, they will. If it means breaking a vow, that's on them. I know all that, and I try to live by it, and I mostly find it a very peaceful and empowered place to occupy. But this skinny little bitch got my hackles up from the outset, and my sense of sisterhood with her is still a bit shaky at times.

But when I see her like this, gaze turned inward, I know all too well what she's thinking. I've been there. And I want to beat the man who put her there. Who put me there.

Me, I escaped. Ironically, that's thanks to this woman catching his wandering eye.

But who got the shitty end of the stick there? Her.

Both of us were eighteen when he scooped us up. But I had kids pretty much right away, and they saved me. I simply could not let them grow up watching their parents and thinking this was normal, this was what it meant to be a woman, this was the destiny in store for them.

And finding that strength for them meant remembering my own power.

For stakes high enough, most people given the chance can find their power.

I learned to swear. I learned to smoke. I pulled my riding boots out of the corner of the barn we'd designated the 'tack shed' when we had ponies, put on those boots and walked out of there like a Nancy Sinatra song, like the boots were in charge and walking all over George.

Now his other wife sits there hunched and shaking, and I want to put on my boots and kick George to death. I see her clear. She was just a kid. She didn't know any better. And for her, things got so much worse than they ever did for me.

Shanaya shoots a look at me.

'You're growling again,' she murmurs.

'No, I'm not, that's you.'

She shakes her head and we both look again. It's Édith, moaning and growling and shaking. Suddenly, she shoots to her feet, her arms flung up and out like wings.

'I want to kill him,' she rasps, her voice high and deadly. She pulls her arms in tight around herself again and prowls around the room, panting. I stare at her feet, how she steps toes first, how she almost seems to bob, how she darts here, now there, now seizes a mug from the kitchenette countertop and flings it at the door. It shatters, cheap ceramic shards falling like smashed egg shells to rock on the floor.

Shanaya is beside her, arms around her.

'Hey now, hey now,' she says. 'Easy girl. Ady, it's okay.'

'It's not okay.' Édith pushes her away and spins around, big eyes flashing around the room.

I catch her gaze.

'No,' I say in my best crisis voice, 'you are right, it is not okay. It's shocking and dangerous and real. But you have to get a grip now, Édith.'

'You—' she shakes her head, but she stands, her eyes black hollows going down so deep. I hold her gaze and let her see my own eyes, let some of the memories well up into my gaze.

'I know,' I say simply, 'Believe me. I *know*.'

'Hazel, I'm so sorry,' she starts to cry, standing there in that utterly generic room. And she flings herself down on a bed, full on wailing into the pillows.

I'm rooted in place. Shanaya has seized the broom and stands rooted too.

'No,' I say, and damned if I'm not crying too. '*I'm* sorry. *I'm* fine. I left. I should have warned you about the bargain you thought you were getting.'

I don't know if she's even heard me, but she pushes herself up on her elbows, turns and slides 'til she's leaning on the headboard. She lifts her tear streaked face and raises a ghastly smile.

'I wouldn't have listened,' she says, and the little bitch laughs.

And I shake my head, laughing too, and sit down on a chair and we feel the wave of grief and rage wash away.

Shanaya clears her throat. She looks suspiciously bright eyed, on the verge of sympathetic waterworks. *Women*. What are we like anyhow?

'As your lawyer, may I say that we should hope that Mr. Jones survives, given that I've just heard a death threat, and some might construe this little conversation as a conspiracy to murder.'

She's trying for humour, but it sobers us up right quick.

Priority one, keep Édith safe. One-A, keep her from killing George. I probably won't kill him, since I haven't done it yet. Shan? She's good as long as she's channeling her tiger rage into lawyer thought.

'We have to figure out how,' Shan says, 'to find out where he and The Harvestmen are keeping their prisoners. How many there are, we don't know. Nor do we know who they are, where they're from, how they got scooped up into this.'

She paces as she talks, thumping the broom down in time with each step, the bristles dulling the thump, her hair crackling with energy in the stuffy little room.

'We understand it in general terms: the revitalization of Canada's agricultural sector, the repopulating of the smaller rural centres, the acceptance of five million displaced persons.'

She gestures with her right hand, little whip crack moves of emphasis.

'–the inevitable bureaucratic fuck-ups, the myriad ways for people to fall through the cracks either by intent or by official sloppiness; the eternal vulnerability of young, inexperienced people just looking for a way to make a life for themselves in a world that has given them a grudging welcome from the moment they appeared, one more mouth to feed. One more voice in the chorus, but they're clamouring to be fed, to be clothed, to find a place and a purpose, and maybe they don't want to work the fields like peasants in this time when media makes it appear that everyone else is living some sort of high-tech paradise gangster life.'

I get a chill, not for the first time.

'These Harvestmen,' Shan concludes, 'Whoever they turn out to be, they are not alone.'

'Law of supply and demand,' I murmur randomly. They stare. I sigh and take the broom from Shanaya, start sweeping up the shattered cup.

'I was just thinking about how many young women there always are, vulnerable to mean, controlling men. How many boys grow up with injustice, or bad parenting, or whatever the fuck situations make them twist.'

I lean on the broom and sigh again.

'This is a fool's errand, girls. A drop in the ocean. We might be able to save these kids. But we'll never stop the whole messed-up reality that guarantees that more like them are being born every minute, somewhere.'

'Yes,' says Shanaya, 'but it's like starfish.'

'What?!'

She nods, eyes glinting with ironic pride and humour.

'It's on our bathroom wall.'

'Exactly,' says Édith, chuckling grimly.

'Oh come on!' I drop the broom and step into the bathroom and look. Sure enough, there's a cheesy bit of plasticized wall art in there. A beach scene and the smarmy text about the kid walking along throwing stranded starfish into the waves. And the cynic comes along and points out he can't possibly throw them all back in before they die. Therefore why bother? What difference does his puny effort make? And the kid hits the punchline as he throws, *It makes a difference to that one.*

'I hate this fucking poster,' I say, flicking my hand at it. I shut the bathroom door against its banality.

'Diya gave me a copy when I turned 13,' says Shanaya. 'Made me put it up beside my *'hang in there'* kitten.' She shakes her mane of glorious hair.

'It's rubbish of course,' she says, mimicking her mother's slight accent, 'but not without truth, unfortunately.'

I shake my head.

'Listen,' I say, 'I had a friend at university, Minkah, who wrote a pretty good essay about how that Starfish poster was part of the whole White Saviour/Social Justice Warrior cult; not entirely useless, but dangerous if unexamined, pre-supposing as it does that the starfish have no agency, and that it is obviously wrong for them to be on the beach, anytime anywhere.'

Édith gets up, picks up the broom and puts it away.

'Every little starfish matters,' she says.

DEVIN: CARE

Sawitsky comes to the hospital too, and brings Sandra, and Roy in the back, and drives them all home.

'Devin,' says Sandra, 'you sure you don't want to come home with me?'

'I'm okay,' says Devin, frowning a bit. He sees the hurt look on her face. But he can't bear to be near her or anyone tonight. He looks at her, gives her a little forced smile.

'It'll be okay, Auntie,' he says, 'I've got Roy for company.'

'At least stay for dinner?'

'I'd love to Auntie, but,' he shrugs, 'I'm not really hungry.'

'Let me send you something for later.'

Sawitsky glares at him. He nods acquiescence.

Back at the apartment, he puts the care package in the fridge, pours himself a tall glass of water, and sits down on the sofa. Just sits. Roy, beside him on the rug, starts nudging Devin's knee and peeking at him from under his brows questioningly.

'Yeah, okay,'

And the big pup leaps up on the sofa, curls up against Devin.

'Frankie's gonna kill me, letting you up here,' mutters Devin, burying his face in Roy's heavy ruff. Roy sighs contentedly and lets out a fart, the events of the day too much for his digestion.

***

Later that evening, the phone rings, insistently.

He goes to turn it off. Sees the name and hesitates. Roy nudges his hand as it rings again. And he answers.

'Hey,' says Kjell Kristiansen, 'I'm calling to see how you're doing.'

'Fine,' says Devin, startled.

'Listen, Devin,' says Kjell. 'No bullshit, okay? What you did today was brave, but it was also reckless.'

'I don't need–'

'No. *Listen*,' says the fireman, talking fast and hard, 'just listen. You are either a natural born hero, or a young man who is hurting enough that you didn't care whether you lived or died when you ran into that building. And I have been doing this work long enough to know that you could be the first, and still be the second, and I don't want to be wrong about you, and not follow up, and find out you went in there because you have a death wish.'

'Who do you think you are?' snaps Devin.

'I'm a fireman,' says Kjell Kristiansen. 'I'm a man who gets paid to go into danger for others. I'm trained to know how to do that.'

'Hooray for you,' Devin says. 'But–'

'*No. Listen*,' says Kjell, and the urgency in his voice stops Devin from cutting off the call.

'I'd leave you alone–'

'Not alone. Roy is here.'

'–leave you with your dog, except that Reg Sawitsky beat down the firehouse door insisting that someone go follow up. Some madwoman she says is your auntie was with her.'

'How is this your business?'

'I was there.' Kjell lets the silence hang. 'And now I am here. Calling to see if you need to talk to anyone. Calling to tell you those women love you and they're out of their minds with worry.'

'Oh great,' snarls Devin. 'I suppose they told you what? That my best friend died this spring? And my parents are dead? And they think today might've been one thing too many?'

'Yes,' replies Kjell, and his quiet affirmation once again slows Devin's anger. He doesn't quite know what to say.

'I don't know what to say.'

'Say that you'll get a good night's rest, and meet me for coffee tomorrow at the Mill Creek Cafe. Say ten o'clock.'

Devin stares into the darkness, leans against Roy's warm body. An eternity ticks past. His thumb hovers over the red button. He stares at that.

'Devin?' He hears Kjell Kristiansen's voice from a long way away.

'Yeah. Okay. See you.'

HAZEL: TRACKING

So what we do is, we go back that night, and we hide Édith's cell phone in his truck.

'Are you sure?'

'Yes,' she says, 'it's the obvious choice. Even if he finds it, he'll just think I lost it.'

'Won't he notice it's fully charged despite you being gone so long now?'

'I doubt he'll think about it one way or the other.'

There is that about having someone under your thumb for a long time. The longer they stay down, the easier it gets to underestimate them.

It's a fancy truck. Electronic locks, alphanumeric code. Of course Édith knows the code. Of course George never changed it. Why would he? For all he knows, Édith is dead, and if she's not, he sure as hell doesn't suspect she'd come hunting for him. That would be as ridiculous as…a sparrow hunting a merlin comes to mind, thinking about my neighbourhood birds. But George is not a merlin. Nothing so cool. Okay. A vulture. Sorry vultures, that might not be fair to you.

The truck is parked in the darkest part of the street. The nearest streetlight isn't functioning. Huh. Almost like the vulture disabled it for the sake of privacy.

Édith keys in the code, opens the door, and the cab light blares out. Shit. But she jumps in like she owns the truck, reaches up and switches off the light.

Nothing stirs. We stand by, across the street in the shadow of a hedge, holding our breath for an eternity. Then she opens the door as quietly as possible, slips out, and comes soft-footing across the street to us. Her hair in the dim glow of the distant streetlight bobs up like a crown of feathers. I'm grinning in the dark, I know it, should be scared but now that we're doing this, *I feel my mojo rising*, like the old song says.

We go back to the car, drive back to the hotel, but none of us wants to go in.

We should sleep. We know we won't.

So, we stay there. Shan and I tip back our seats, Édith curls down in the back and we wait for something to happen.

It's still half-dark when the GPS phone-finder pings. Don't ask me how they do that. I am too creeped out by the surveillance society to want to know. But the dashboard screen lights up and we see the little blue-green dot that represents Édith's phone begin to move.

We drive up the hill, not too fast, and follow the dot as it heads for the north edge of town.

We're not stupid. We don't follow past the pavement. We just watch where it turns off, press save on the GPS tracker and then we go back down the hill, slink into our room and grab our maps.

I love a physical map.

I am so grateful that Diya does, too, and that she sent us with these printouts, unwieldy though they might seem to the digital-age folks. We know they might not show every possible hiding place, but they do show the majority of the work camps in the area, and we plot our course.

We're not supposed to, but Shan and I huddle by the window and blow smoke out into the cold morning air. Surveillance society though it is, nobody is likely to be watching the fourth floor window on the backside of a crew hotel on the edge of Fox Creek to see if someone up there is smoking. We drop our butts in a pop can like teenagers at a bush party, and sit there just sagging a little.

We have a plan.

Back in Amiskwaciy, Diya was able to rent a small bus-like thing from some business here in Fox Creek supplying work camps, and it is waiting for us to pick it up in the morning. We just have to act like we know what we're doing. I'll go in and pick it up. I'm the driver they're expecting and they have a scanned copy of my license and I'll just pick up our getaway bus, pick up my co-conspirators and drive out in the daylight like we belong there.

There's a big hole in this plan, of course. We don't know who might be guarding the victims, nor precisely how many will be there. Édith thinks they ship them in groups of about a dozen, big enough to be profitable, not so big as to attract too much attention. They will fit, for instance, into a crew bus.

But I don't like not knowing what danger we might face.

'I don't know about you,' Shanaya says, 'but I am going to take a nap now.' And she moves over to a bed and flops down and falls instantly asleep. Édith and I exchange glances. I beat her to the sofa. She gingerly subsides onto the other bed.

'You sure?'

'Yeah yeah,' I say, 'I'm not going to sleep anyhow.'

But of course I do, too, once the air is full of their womanly snoring.

DEVIN: TESTIMONY

Devin sits up, aware that he is cramped. Roy snores half on top of him, belly rolled upward, entirely at ease, his ears sprawled like wings to the sides of his lolling head. Devin's hair stands out from his head, and he scratches a hand through it, stretches slowly, gingerly. He extricates himself from beneath Roy, who simply wriggles more luxuriously into the sofa, taking up all available room.

Devin leans a moment against the coffee table while the pins and needles run down his legs. Then he slowly gets up and goes over to stand before the corner shelf. He stands in stillness, then looks around, as if checking to be sure he's not watched.

Then he picks up the lighter laid to one side and lights the fat white candle.

He moves the candle holder to the kitchen table and goes to stand behind it, facing the window. He clears his throat, folds his hands, unfolds them, squares his shoulders.

He doesn't know why but he needs to speak.

'This is the life,' he intones, 'of LeWayne Ducharme. Hear my witness. LeWayne was born in Amiskwaciy, in the Royal Alexandra Hospital, to Adeline Ducharme and a father unknown. He grew up moving from one shit hole apartment to another...he-he loved s-soccer and the s-stars...h-h-he was a good friend...' Devin muffles a small sob, 'and he once said he wanted to study astronomy. He...died because I couldn't stop him.'

Devin bows his head and falls silent, crying in the dark apartment, dashing the tears away.

Then he whirls away and paces through the galley kitchen. *Where did he put it?*

He paces back though the living room, where Roy snores on. In the same little corner shelf, he recalls now, there is his little round tin with the curl of sweetgrass, the small wand of a sage bundle.

He carries the tin back to the kitchen, takes down the tiny cast iron pan hanging among the others. He prepares the smudge and bathes himself in it, using his hands to scoop smoke so it feathers over his head, against his heart, around his limbs and body.

'I am sorry,' he whispers into the rising smoke. 'LeWayne, I'm sorry I wasn't a better brother to you. I tried.'

Thoughts intrude. *What about LeWayne's own family? Why didn't they teach him better?* He stares at the candle flame, his inner eye scanning images and flickers of knowledge. If it was a balance, he was never going to be enough to tip it. His hand on one side. Everything else pushing down on the other.

Angrily, he snuffs the candle and curls down onto the floor, nobody to see him hug himself.

The morning sun reveals him sprawled asleep, dressed in sweatpants and an orange t-shirt declaring Every Child Matters.

A magpie settles beadily on the balcony. Tipping his head from side to side, he considers the lumpish human snoring on the kitchen floor, the big blonde dog curled tight against his side.

HAZEL: MUSKEG

How does it come to this?

I find I have time, lying in the damp and fragrant moss (redolent of piss and other mysteries), to cast my memory back and see the spooled line of circumstance that unwound me to this moment.

I blame my family.

If my mother hadn't died.

If my father hadn't doubled down on his efforts to make us so unbearably proud that we would be bulletproof in a world of guns.

If my stupid sister hadn't come to live with George and me and help us out.

If I hadn't believed the poison tongues who wagged about that.

If Dad hadn't left that place to both of us.

If George hadn't bamboozled my stupid sister and stupider me into letting him claim that place, anything to get away clean–

If Big Frankie, my stupid brother, hadn't gone and died so soon after his wife died, so much sudden death that I ceased to have the energy to care about what I might have lost in letting George claim my land. At least I can say it's good that my stupid sister took over raising Frank's boy.

If only both being single parents of a sort had proved to be a bond between Sandra and me rather than some stupid competition.

Some would lay that at my door, but Sandra could always get away with looking so innocent. What did she sacrifice to raise Devin? A life of spinsterdom, that's what. And then to blame me for losing the land. And to talk so piously about forgiving me.

Her? Forgiving me?! Pfft.

So imagine my surprise, when my stupid sister came to me asking for help getting the land back, because of Devin having a breakdown...she needs that holy place because her garden isn't big enough for the trouble he's having.

I guess she thinks I'm somehow responsible too, because Devin had gotten all wound up in what was supposed to be my investigation of Nell August's murder, and Devin's bone stupid friends had gone off half-cocked and tried to 'capture' the person who'd been killing the people who killed Nell...not that they understood the whole situation, fucking stupid kids. They got half the information...they...I don't actually know what they were thinking going after Rabbit...what kind of an idiot goes after a teenage string of a girl with a knife in his hand, and doesn't expect her to fight for her life?

LeWayne Ducharme, that's the sort of idiot. And Rabbit killed him stone cold dead. And Devin couldn't get there fast enough to stop LeWayne. And now he thinks he's to blame for all of it.

Teenagers! They're so self-centred, and not in that good way we're supposed to be when we are authentically present in our lives, or whatever fucking bullshit Sandra's espousing these days. God, but I hate her naked spirituality. Can't deal with me dressing to show off the body I maintain, but she'll flash her spiritual underpants all over town, that one, working on ecumenical projects and urban garden reclamation, and cross-cultural reconciliation (the post-TRC kind) and fuck knows what other -*ations* she finds occasion to fill up her days with.

***

And I am lying in the muskeg and I realize I'm thrumming. I mean of course right now, but also always. I'm always a little bit tightly wound, always vigilant. I probably have high blood pressure, and it's probably only the smoking that keeps me from having a big gut the way so many middle-aged Indigenous women do. Okay, I know, lots of kinds of women get that menopausal gut, not that I'm quite there yet, but probably peri-menopausal, if I know anything about bodies, and I think I do, having lived in this one all my life and having Sandra for a sister with her unsolicited wholistic advice out the yingyang...

The point is, nature is meant to make us whole again, and I do feel that way, but I don't like these crowded trees. I'm thrumming and it feels like these weird wild trees are thrumming too.

I've never told anyone, but when I first arrived in Amiskwaciy, when I was trying to find my feet and get used to it, I'd go to parks whenever I could; not the wild river valley bits, but the little neighbourhood parks where the trees were tame and well-spaced and full of light, and I'd just absorb those trees. And by and by I came to feel like trees in parks are more comforting than wild trees.

I know, I'm an asshole to think this way. And it's not like I think this way all the time. I know better than that–*how you think, that's how you are.* And how I am is, I'm lying here in the dirt in the middle of nowhere, in the middle of a rescue operation that I did not plan on, did not see coming, and I have next to zero idea whether this craziness ends with me getting out of it alive, let alone whether at the end of this madness we can get our land back.

I'm not stupid. I know the land matters. I get how Sandra hopes it might be a sanctuary for us. I know how much Sandra loved living there, loved taking care of garden and fruit trees and chickens and goats, how she thrived on it. I'm not sure how she managed to look past the darker parts of our history there and make it sanctuary. For me, it was as much struggle as it was home. But then again, I'm not sure how I manage to live in Amiskwaciy some days.

It's an interesting city, but honestly, there are a lot of ugly things about it. I'm not going to beat my chest or write a song about how much I love my city... I start mentally listing songs about cities...

I Love Paris in the Springtime
New York New York
Chicago is My Kind of Town

I left my heart in San Francisco–huh. They're all American. Does Canada not make songs about our cities? Toronto? Nope. Vancouver? Nope. For sure I've never heard a song for Amiskwaciy, much less Edmonton, its old name–you know, after it was Amiskwaciy for the first time... Anyhow, my point is there are no songs... oh! *Hank Snow.* The original *I've Been Everywhere* was all Canadian places. And Stompin' Tom had that doofus song about Pilsenburg, which I've always hated vicariously because I know nothing about Pilsenburg except his complaints...but Americans? They write city songs in all the genres.

Street of Laredo

Abilene... I remember Dad teaching Big Frank when he was just little Frankie, how to use a butter knife handle like a slide to make bar chords up the neck and sing *Abilene... slide slide slide... Abilene... slide slide slide.. prettiest town that I ever seen...*

I tried it but my hands were way too small. Frank could barely make it work, but he sure was proud of himself, and I can still hear his boy treble singing about how *Folks down there don't treat you mean in Abilene, my Abilene.*

Years later, Frank and I heard that song somewhere, and they were singing *Women there don't treat you mean.* We both heard it. Looked at each other, laughed and shook our heads. Didn't have to say what we were both thinking, how typical of Dad to change women to *folks* and teach it without the sexual innuendo, because it's gross for little kids to sing about adult situations.

Mind you, we sang Streets of Laredo and he didn't feel we needed protecting from the dead cowboy in that one. Mind you, what's one more dead cowboy in the grand scheme of things?

Typical Americans, typical Dad, so much about death, so much about guns.

I remember *Galveston!* That one takes me back, riding in the back of the grain truck down to the post office to get our report cards, and singing Glen Campbell's hit...and wondering why the singer figured he had no choice but to *Clean my gun, and dream of Galveston.*

Well, Glen, I'd like to see you write one about lying in the bush outside Fox Creek, waiting for some kind of a signal so I'll know it's the right time to go in and try to rescue a bunch of kidnapped migrant farm workers. Me, I do not have a gun.

I do have a tiger, currently a lawyer who is in there helping Édith talk to the victims, calm them down and break them out of their camp prison and out to the bus I stole. Why am I not in that bus, waiting?

I know, it's Plan B, and I'm the one who suggested it, that one of us goes out to the road and hides in the bush and watches for bad guys coming down the road. If we can't get to the bus and gone, we'll pull back into the bush and hide and wait 'til the bad guys leave to try again. Or if they come in a vehicle that has room for a group, we break the kids out and hide them in the bush.

Standing here, that seems like a stupid fallback. I mean, I know how to lie quiet in the bush, learned it as a kid and you don't forget. But these people we're here to rescue? God alone knows how they'd manage if it comes to duck and hide.

I mean, I know how to do this, and I hate it. Can't help thinking it would be more comfortable in the bus.

Probably for the best. I'd be tempted to try to play the radio–do they even have radios in the buses these days? We're far enough out in the bush that cell phones don't work, and there's no radio signal either, but in the bus I'd be tempted to see if I could turn up something. Better to wait quiet, here in the undergrowth, wait for the sign.

I almost miss it, in the event, listening to Glen in my head dreaming of Galveston.

But there, Shanaya emerges for just a moment, cuts one sharp wave. They are ready. I pick myself up, step out to the edge and flick my red handkerchief so she'll see it, then ghost foot through the tangled brush back to the bus.

Shanaya is there before me, a tiger now, pacing back and forth in front of the bus.

'Why not get on the bus and come back, and we all go together?'

She mutters a purring something, shakes her massive head.

'Plan A,' I say, 'on track.'

She utters another purring phrase and bounds away. I watch her go for a second. Shake my head. *Don't watch her go. She will meet us at the pavement.*

'You sure?' I'd asked her before we started.

'Yes,' she'd replied blandly. 'You two can handle the bus and the passengers, and I can prowl ahead and distract anyone who looks like they are looking for you.'

'It seems kind of…unrealistic,' I say.

'Got a better idea?'

I have to admit I don't. But I hate the idea of her charging around in tiger form. Sure, that would distract any pursuers, but it's reckless, especially if they're armed. Tigers aren't bulletproof.

What I say is, 'What if you get lost?'

'Tigers,' she'd replied a little smugly, 'don't get lost. I will be there in time to change.'

I climb into the bus and start it up. I'm not the praying kind.

Unless *'this better work'* is a prayer. Sandra would say it is. Me, I just focus, one thing at a time, the way Dad taught me–as much as he taught me to drive before Mom intervened. Funny, that, her not wanting her girls to drive–*focus. Here and now.*

Here and now, I ease the crew bus down the rutted, empty road. Trees, fireweed, dry grass, deadwood. Empty road, for how much longer? It seems an eternity before I turn into the site.

I drive past the empty Security trailer, skin crawling, and circle the bus in front of 'our' portable, so Édith can see me out the window. She instantly opens the door, and I pull around so that they have the shortest possible run from the door to the bus.

DEVIN: GETHSEMANE REPRISE

A bear at his door. He opens the door. The bear snatches his hand in its teeth. Sinks its teeth in, past the pain. Pulls him along. They step into a garden, with olive trees–how does he know they were olive trees?–rustling in spring dark. Through a window come voices, and the bear throws Devin against the wall, forces him to watch through the window.

The Last Supper. The plush wallhanging reproduction of the Leonardo DaVinci painting that his mother had treasured, but come to life. There. The bear slaps his shoulder. Look. Listen.

They've had their dinner, now they're eating croissants. Devin sees Jesus's face close up, his eyes a little wild. Hears Jesus haranguing the rest of the table, going on about how he knew he couldn't count on them, how he's sure they will betray him. Simon Peter rants back, 'Not me, man!' pounding the table with his calloused fist, fish spraying out like mist and disappearing, plastic cups tumbling.

And then The Disciple Jesus Loved leans on him lovingly and says, 'Surely you can't believe it would be me who'd betray you? I love you, man.' That is one thing too much, and Jesus pushes his friend away, fleeing past Devin into the garden of Gethsemane. The bear grunts.

And the whole gang of apostles follows. Devin sees their faces flick past him, reads their love and fear as they search the dark garden until they find Jesus. The garden echoes with their calls. Devin hears Jesus first, praying about how he'd rather not be sacrificed. At the moment he asks 'Take this cup from me,' but before he can intone 'Nev-

ertheless, not my will but Yours be done,' the apostles come bumbling
out of the dark and shouting. 'Yeshua! Shut your caterwauling! You
want out? We'll get you out. But we have to move NOW!'

Peter and The Disciple Jesus Loved step out of the dark, dragging
Judas Iscariot between them, Judas with his eyes swollen from the Fist
of the Fisherman, his purloined silver swinging like a cudgel in the
hand of The Disciple Jesus Loved.

'Everyone's got to die sometime, Love,' says that Disciple, 'but not
on our watch.'

A low rumbling begins then, shaking the olive trees.

'But...' begins Jesus.

'But NOTHING!' roars Peter the Rock, his face transforming to a
bear's face from the teeth outward. 'Judas made his choice, and we're
making ours,' and they smash Iscariot flat upon the ground, sink their
teeth into the hands of Yeshua Ben-Joseph, and pull him, still struggling and protesting, toward the back gate into the dawning light.

HAZEL: EYES

I don't know what I expected. I've lived in central Amiskwaciy for long years now, in the old part of the city, so I've seen street people. Seen what meth does, seen what opioids do.

Right away, it's pretty obvious which way these poor zombies have been drugged.

How are we going to get them out? I look at Édith wading in and my eyes glaze with tears. She followed George. She stole these kids from him one time, hid them in a…what was it? Freight car? Granary? I don't remember. She stole them. And she got caught. And they beat her to within an inch of her life and stole the kids back and she fled through the night.

Where were they that first night? I shake my head. It doesn't matter. They are here, now.

I count fifteen of them, mostly girls, mostly dark-haired, dark-skinned and young. Their eyes are glazed with drugs and fear and they barely look at us, staring around wildly. God knows how long they've been here, but this place smells like penned animals, so it's been a while. And for all that time, I can bet nothing good has come through the door for them.

I don't know what to say.

Thankfully, I don't have to say anything, just witness.

'Hey,' says Édith ever so softly, 'I'm back.' Their dumb eyes swing to her, and a couple of them start crying. She turns to us, her eyes huge. 'Those girls…' those are the two she stole in the first place. I get it. George caught those two. Who knows who captured the rest. What was done to them along the way. How long they were held before they were brought together here.

'Shh,' she says, 'It's okay now. I'm back. This is Shanaya, and this is Hazel, and we're going to get you out of here, take you someplace safe.'

I nod and lift a hand in a kind of feeble wave. Not my place to invade further. I step back to the door and keep an eye out. Édith cradles each of those girls in turn, briefly, then moves among the rest of them, touching a shoulder here, pressing hands there.

'Believe me,' she says, her raspy little voice piercing. 'I know what you've been through. But it's over. You've just got to gather yourselves now, and we'll go.'

'I am ready,' says a voice from the back of the room, and I look. A slim young man, one of maybe three–it's hard to be absolutely sure of their genders in this dimmish room, huddled and crouched as they are–but this boy stands up, pushes back a mop of ridiculous dark hair, and flashes a grin.

'What do we do now?' He asks. I just stare.

He catches my eye, quirks a brow in response, and there is something grim and fierce under the jaunty exterior. Of course there is. He's here but he's not drugged, somehow. He is the only one with clear eyes. No time to wonder why right now.

I take a deep breath. Now, we just have to get these terrified little zombies to go with us and get on the bus. Simple. But these people look inert, except Bright Eyes Big Hair.

'Help us,' Édith says to him, 'yes? Please.'

He moves to her side, speaks to each huddled prisoner. I force myself not to jitter as he calls each by name and Édith repeats the names, coaxes each one to come, move now, you will be safe. Once they begin to move, it's like watching a slow stream carrying chips of wood, they seem to float without intent in the wake of Édith and the girls who each hold one of her hands like the lifeline it is.

Bright Eyes Big Hair brings up the rear, talking to Shanaya.

'They come late afternoons. Make us walk outside for ten min-

utes…check us…' he sounds hollow and I feel my stomach clench-
ing. I can feel Shanaya's fierce anger radiating.

'How long have you been here?'

'Ten days the longest ones. Some for a week. I…arrived later.
I heard them talking. They plan to move us in the next four days.
Two week turn-around, they said.'

Late afternoon they come.

We have time. We have time. I tell myself this and my spine
keeps right on crawling.

Their transit to the bus seems to take a century, but they climb
on board one by one with a minimum of talk and fuss.

'One per seat and duck,' calls Édith softly. She stands in the aisle
at the back, a hand on the shoulder of each of her two, now in rear
seats each side of the aisle.

Almost eerie, how quiet they are as they trudge shakily past me
and take their seats, all eyes on Édith.

'Duck,' she repeats as they stare at her. 'Get down.'

The mop-haired boy demonstrates, bobbing up and disappearing below the seat back, calling 'Duck, duck, duck,' until they finally
follow his lead and disappear. My skin has not stopped crawling
and my heart is throbbing like the diesel engine of this bus. I feel it
through my hands on the wheel, but we've got them.

I take a deep breath.

'I need to go back,' says Édith, and she whirls and runs for the
trailer door just as I hear it, a vehicle approaching.

Fuck.

Shanaya has changed and her tiger self comes leaping.

Thank God the prisoners are all down.

'Stay down,' I hiss loudly for good measure.

Édith calls,' Go now! We'll meet you,' and she runs. *We?!*

Shanaya roars. I can't see her but I know what she means. *Go!*

One head shoots up.

'Down!' I shout. There is a pickup hurtling down the driveway
toward me.

I floor it and haul ass up around the other side of the Security trailer–God bless the circular drive concept–and gun it as hard as I dare, the pickup churning dust as it spins and follows me. *Just go.*

I check my rearview–it is George driving. Funny how you know a person even after years, the shape of a head, the psychotic eyes. He's got shades on but I can feel his eyes burn with rage.

He's glaring at me and my busload of terrified kids, so he doesn't see a tiger with a human on her back, bounding into the thick bush. Why did Édith go back?

The little talisman of Durga on her tiger swings on the mirror. I shake my head.

I have to turn all my attention to driving this bus.

DEVIN: AWAKENING

Devin wakes up and it's already after nine. He pushes himself up to sitting, stiff from sleeping on the floor.

'Hey, pal. Thanks for keeping me warm,' he says, running a hand down Roy's back.

Roy says nothing in reply, just cocks his head and grins.

Devin rises from the floor, gets a drink of water, then pads over to the bathroom for a shower. When he comes out, Roy is lying just outside the bathroom door, nose on toes, watching.

Devin pats his head, pulls one silky ear gently. Feeds the dog. Sets an egg on to boil. Pads into the living room and picks up the guitar. He sits on the sofa in his towel and strums, and Roy curls on the rug beside him, one paw over Devin's foot.

Devin eats, dresses, checks the time.

'Time to go,' he says to Roy, and Roy leaps up, ready.

Devin shakes his head.

The number is in his phone memory. He calls Kjell Kristiansen, who picks up right away. In the background, café noises tell Devin the fireman is already waiting.

'Listen,' says Devin, 'do you mind a change of plan?'

Kjell clears his throat, and before he can say more, Devin goes on.

'Roy wants to come. After yesterday, he needs a good walk. Could we just go down through the ravine?'

'Oh. Okay,' says Kjell, relief in his tone, 'sure. Sure. You want to meet me here and go down together?'

'Okay. We'll be there in ten minutes.'

'Coffee?'

'Tea,' says Devin, 'if that's okay?'

'Sure. Sure. What kind?'

'Chamomile?'

'Can do.'

Devin walks, and Roy trots alongside, brimming with evident joy.

And with every step, Devin reviews the things he's always known, the things he's never examined. He thinks about the way his friends grew up. Their homes, with that smell of dirty despair. Mattress on the floor, grey and lumpy pillows without cases. The flotsam of cheap toys bought to compensate for the jetsam of empty bottles, needles, butts and roaches. The cupboards full of sugared conveniences, the shelving units full of mental junk food–plotless action flicks, first person shooter games, porn the boys snickered over when they showed it to him.

His own home, never pristine, but full of what he'd have to call *comfortable* smells–home cooking, coffee, rosin. He thinks about his father and mother, how they delighted in reading and discussion, in probing conversations about the official and the hidden histories. How his mother loved creating both artwork and artistic harmony in the home. How his father sneered at pop culture and ranted about the narcissism of the music industry. How he claimed that as his right, being a musician himself.

The best nights were the gatherings where music flowed.

How the child Devin wanted to be part of that music. How his father excitedly showed him a chord progression, then snarked reflexively when the boy's small hands blurred notes or moved slowly. His mother sent him into the circle one night with his toy guitar, urging him just to play along. So he did, thumping and blurring and inaccurate. And the rest of the circle cheered him. But his father snapped, *Don't praise him for playing wrong.* And he'd pulled the boy aside and added, *Any idiot can thrash around. That's not musicianship. And it's nothing to be smug about. Unless that's all you want to be.*

And he'd turned away from the round soft face of his son, embarrassment and humiliation radiating through the last resonances of the night's songs.

How to reconcile that with the hard knowledge that, compared to his friends, Devin was a child of privilege?

How to account for his Auntie Sandra, quietly teaching him in the garden, singing songs with him, mysterious songs in Mi'gmaq? Sandra with her unspectacular voice nevertheless earnestly teaching him the songs, phrase by phrase without critique, and telling him stories of how she herself had learned these songs from Elder Gilbert Sewell, from Elder Maggie Paul.

He smiles, remembering Sandra sharing what the Elder Gilbert had told her, *It's okay if you sing it a little different. Sing it how you hear it.*

His eyes sting with sudden tears when he recalls Sandra's sudden flash of fierceness as she passed on the Elder Maggie's words.

'She told me, *Never let anyone tell you not to sing.*'

He blinks, coming around the corner. Kjell Kristiansen comes out the cafe door, lifts a to-go cup in greeting, and they set off toward the ravine, with Roy trotting along grinning beside them.

HAZEL: UNREALISTIC

Yeah, so here we are. A car chase is happening. I am driving a bus, which realistically I do not know how to drive, a bus full of frightened shrieking strangers, while behind us a madman caroms over the gravel shooting at us out the window as if this is some unrealistic American movie.

George has a hand gun and he's driving and shooting. *Unrealistic.* That's all I can think. I want to scream back at him. *Stop that now! It's unrealistic!*

It's unrealistic when he hits the driver's mirror and it doesn't break. Unrealistic when something shatters the window and my arm begins to burn. Unrealistic that there doesn't seem to be any way out of this for me.

Where are my people? Where is Shanaya? And Édith?

Are they dead? Are they running, too? How am I driving with one eye behind me?

Suddenly I see a tiger charging head-on at me, past me, a banshee madwoman clinging to her back like an avenging goddess.

I see the madman swerve, the tiger leap so high.

The truck's wheels catch in the ruts, it bucks and twists and drops back into the dust.

I jam the brakes. The passengers scream but I'm screaming louder.

Shanaya!

The bus shudders to a halt, somehow still upright.

Stay here! I holler to the passengers, and I don't even wait to see if they understand.

I kick through the door, leave a smear of blood–*I'm bleeding? Unrealistic*–and stumble clear.

The road roils with dust.

Out of the dust comes the pickup truck.

From the side, the tiger leaps again, twisting in mid air.

And I see a woman diving, golden hair streaming unrealistically behind her, and it's Édith and her face is a mask of concentrated fury as she dives straight at George in his pickup.

It's unrealistic, how the truck leaps through the ruts as if it's another charging tiger. Unrealistic the roar and bang, the shattering of trees as the whole tumbling mass veers into the muskeg.

Fire, and a flock of small birds fly up in the smoke of it, spiral into the roaring air. That's unrealistic, too.

It can't be.

DEVIN: BACK TO THE FOREST

Kjell says, 'I am what my father made me. And my mother, by her tacit acceptance and support for all he was. They set the path.'

Devin nods, eyes on the ground.

'But I chose to walk it. And I choose every day. And some days, I think I'd choose otherwise if I weren't just tired from the grind.'

Kjell rubs his hand across his bristling short hair, then stops still, with his hand before his face. He holds out the hand, and Devin can see in the dappling light that it is thick with use and marked with scars.

Kjell addresses the hand as much as the young man at his side:

'But then I look to my own scars, and I remember. This is *my* pledge. *My* service. *My* work.'

The big man heaves a sigh.

'And on the nights when I can't remember that, I come out here. I set a little fire. I force myself to sit with it and admit its beauty, its utility, its actual nature. Fire does not care for our notions of good and evil. Fire is simple and clear. It burns what will burn. I sit with it until I am clear again, and then I put it out.'

The fireman resumes walking. Sun stripes the meadow ahead of them.

'You save people,' says Devin.

Kjell nods.

'I watched a friend run to his death.' Devin stops walking, looks away across the meadow. Kjell says nothing, only murmurs a tiny wordless affirmation.

Devin gathers himself and keeps walking, keeps talking.

'I had–have–these friends. Have known them all my life. And from early days–y'know…you can tell…stuff would happen…they were bound for trouble, one way or another. So…'

'You tried to stop them.'

'No,' says Devin softly. 'I didn't suppose I had any such power. I never even tried. I just stayed out of it. And they let me.'

He keeps his gaze fixed across the little meadow. Kjell glances at him, looks off to the distance as well.

'But you knew,' says the fireman, 'and you figure if you'd done something about it, that friend would have turned aside from his path. Not died.'

Devin breathes, 'Yeah. But…'

He remembers the night in Giovanni Caboto, the northern sky rimed with luminescence, LeWayne and Cody and Tomlin and him; the girl Rabbit. The boys shouting incoherently about how she was the one killing people… *Killer! Kill her!* The boys milling around him. LeWayne breaking from the pack of them, running after the slim figure of the girl. Around the corner of the Boys & Girls Club into the black.

The ravine is busy, and other walkers pause to exclaim over Roy, but Kjell leads onward, not talking to anyone, and Roy, for a miracle, focuses on the path and begins to ignore the other walkers and they pass from light to shade to light and into shade untroubled by random dog-park friendliness.

Kjell crosses a bridge, turns left, leads the way down a tiny path to a slight hollow, away from the breeze, out of sight of the trail. He sits down on a stump, waves a hand at a fallen log for Devin. And they sit, Roy quiet between them, and finish their drinks.

'I became a firefighter because my dad was one. But I swore I'd do it better than him. He'd bring it home, you know? The bad ones. He'd drink and he'd cry and if anyone tried to comfort him…well, at first it worked, he'd hold onto us and cry, pull himself together. But it got worse. And he hit my brothers. And then my mother, when she told him to stop. And then he left. She told him to leave. And he remarried. Twice.'

Kjell looks over at Devin.

'He's still alive, probably. I wouldn't know. Last I heard, he was living in some little town in BC, Winfield or something down in the Interior. Raising horses.'

'You're not in touch, eh?'

'My brother Sten lets me know. But he doesn't call much either. So I guess there's nothing much changing.'

'Where are the rest of your family?'

'Mom's dead. A house fire.' He shakes his head. 'Can you beat that? She went to visit some distant relatives in the States. Burned the house down.'

Devin nods.

'And my brothers? Well, Johnny died. Killed himself. They said it was an accidental overdose but Sten and me, we knew better.'

'And Sten?'

'Sten doesn't talk to me unless he has to. He hates that I became a fireman. The one and only time we talked about it, he said I might as well just kill myself and be done with it. Then Johnny went and did that.'

The big man looks down in silence for a while. He looks up and a galaxy of pain shines from his eyes.

'The thing is, Devin, you can save people from burning buildings, if you're strong and well-taught and lucky. Or even if you're just lucky.'

Devin scruffs a toe in the leaves.

'You can save them from fires. But you can't save people from themselves. From their fates.'

Devin looks up.

'That's what I believe. If a person is intent on dying, you can't stop them.'

He holds up a scarred hand.

'I tried to pull Johnny out of the trailer. He was on heroin, living in a little shitty trailer, passed out with a burner on. They tried to stop me, but I reached in and pulled him out. He was already dead, you know. But he was my brother.'

They sit in silence for a while, listening to Mill Creek rustle as it bends around them and back toward the main valley.

'I needed to know,' says Kjell, 'that you didn't go in there to hurt yourself, rather than to help someone else.'

Devin nods owlishly.

'I sing,' says Devin. 'The songs I sing are Mi'gmaq songs. I don't know how old they are. One of them at least, the Honour Song, was written in the 1970s. Given in a dream, in a ceremony. I sing to try to give the songs back to my ancestors who never learned them. My Auntie Sandra went on a quest, met relatives down East, got given some songs, and tried to share them with my dad and mom. But... Dad didn't like to listen to her. Especially about music. He didn't want to admit she could know something meaningful that he didn't know. I don't know why. But my Auntie, after Mom died, she started bringing me to her garden and teaching me the songs. And when Dad died...I sang with her at his funeral.'

'He would've been proud.'

Devin considers this. Then he stands up, stretches and replies.

'No. He probably would have told me all the notes I missed, critiqued my timing. He didn't even know those songs,' laughs Devin, a shaky laugh, 'but he'd have told me how I was doing them wrong.'

The big fireman stands up too, stares off toward the creek bank.

'Well. My dad? He told me, last time we talked, that I should've saved Johnny. That if *he'd* been on the job that night, Johnny would still be alive.'

They shake their heads, each in his own vision for a moment. Then Roy barks, and the spell breaks. They look at each other and nod their heads in mutual respect and understanding.

Fire and water, two men descend through the trees. The tiny wilderness in all its inner vastness murmurs around them, buzzing and humming with its own eternal secrets. Mill Creek Park welcomes another day and Amiskwaciy rumbles all around it, unaware as a body of the blood's passage.

HAZEL: POETRY APPRECIATION

In scenarios like this, somehow you expect to hear sirens. But out here it falls quiet, except for the burning of the twisted vehicle, and ragged breathing, someone groaning. It might be me.

I squeeze shut my eyes, ground and centre, *what was it–ground and centre, or centre and ground?* I am not the only sound.

I slowly turn back toward the bus, aware that my arm is throbbing and burning. Okay, I've been hit, either by a bullet or by glass. I don't want to look. It will do no good. I cradle that arm tight, and that seems to help. I can't be bleeding much, or I wouldn't be standing.

Hard to think, but I force myself. There are people on that bus. They are watching me, their faces drawn and terrified, some past terror into a kind of numb shock. That's the thing about disaster, there is a place you can go, inside, to get through it. Fall apart later, if you must, but in the middle of it you have to find your footing and do what needs doing.

So, what needs doing?

We need to get out of here.

The people on the bus are moving around. Someone is going to come out here. They'll look into the car crash.

They shouldn't have to see that. I didn't want to see it myself, but it's clear to me. George is dead.

That's the thought that finally gets my feet going, and I climb back into the bus, just in time. One of the young men is opening the door to come out.

'Hey,' I say.

He looks at my arm, wild-eyed.

'I'm okay,' I say. 'Okay.'

I hold his gaze. '*Okay*. You understand, right?'

He nods. He swallows. He holds my gaze 'Yes. I speak English.'

'What's your name?'

'Robin.'

Robin? I think of birds, bite my lip. The bus feels electrified, all that fear and shock.

'Robin, can you drive this thing?'

He holds my gaze, his voice a tiny breath, 'I think so.'

Then he nods, speaks full voice, 'Yes. I can drive.'

'I need you to drive us out of here, as if everything is okay.'

'But–' he gestures toward the smoking ruin in the middle of the road. I shake my head.

'They're gone.'

He nods.

'We're safe for now; but someone else will come, and we need to be gone.'

'Right,' he says, and bobs his head. A thick swathe of black hair falls into his eyes, and he shakes it back. He grabs a little mini-broom–*who so thoughtfully equipped this bus with a mini-broom just when I was going to get shot through the window?* –brushes away greenish cubes of shattered glass, climbs into the driver's seat.

I turn to the rest of them, brace my feet and take a deep breath. They are murmuring and staring.

'Robin,' I say, as if in casual conversation, 'is going to drive us out of here.'

They are a sea of goggling eyes.

'I didn't have a chance to say so earlier, but I'm Hazel. And I need you to–'

Robin interrupts me, his voice strong and calm. He speaks in another tongue, repeats himself in English, reminding them of what their friend Aditi told them.

'Aditi?' I murmur... *Édith...anyhow...* Robin sorts them out, as I sink into a seat behind him.

Someone brings me some water.

Someone binds my arm.

Someone puts a cap on Robin's ridiculous hair, and we roll out. I stare out the window.

'Hazel,' says Robin, still casually, 'tell me where to turn, yes?'

***

So, Robin drives us out of the bush. The rest of the gang are just stunned. They aren't stupid, though. They stay low, and they stay quiet.

Too quiet, really. I wish they'd say something.

Too bad I'm not the singing type, or I could lead a singalong. I may be getting delirious.

I focus on Robin's hat. It's ugly. But it keeps his hair in place. And the window is shot out, so the wind is blowing in. I am beginning to notice that this road is bumpy. Painfully bumpy. And this bus has crappy suspension. My head is ringing.

I close my eyes.

'Madam,' says Robin with controlled urgency, 'do not fall asleep on me.'

'Tell me something good, then, Robin,' I say. 'Like...why did your parents name you Robin?'

It sounds stupid to me as a question. But he seizes on it.

'Oh, this is a very interesting question. I am named for a very important writer. Do you happen to know Rabindranath Tagore?'

'Heard of him. Poet, right?'

'Among other things. He was a poet, a playwright, a musician. He painted. He wrote about politics and society. Tagore was a genius.'

'Huh.' I focus. 'So, your name is Rabindranath?'

'Yes. Robin for short.'

'Makes sense.' I look out the window.

'Shall I recite some of Tagore's poetry?'

'What, in English? Or in the original Bengali?'

He shoots me a grin in the mirror.

'So, you do know who he was.'

'Nope. Just a dilettante, me. I know a bit about a lot of things, not too much about any one in particular. But what about you, Rabindranath? Are you a poet?'

He smiles and winks.

'I hope so. One day. But for now, here is a poem of Tagore's.'

He starts to speak, in a mellifluous voice, and I have no idea what he's saying–do I speak Bengali? –but it sounds beautiful. I'd clap, if my arm was any use.

My head must be lolling.

Robin says sharply, 'Want to hear the English?'

'Okay, sure,' I nod. I suddenly remember driving with my dad. I was sixteen. We were coming back from a meeting with some people who wanted to build houses. We were coming down the big hill at Dunvegan, a big truck rumbled by, and Dad's head snapped upright, and my blood ran cold. He was falling asleep. He shook his head. He knew I couldn't drive.

'Did I ever tell you, my girl,' he asked, 'how to properly gear down on a hill like this?'

And all through the valley and up the other side and through the rest of the dark road home, he lectured me on transmissions, while I scrambled to keep questions coming, to respond, to keep him talking and awake. So we survived, and I'm also a pretty good driver, really.

'Robin,' I say, 'why don't you teach it to me?'

And we work through the poem line by line, call and response style:

'*Suddenly, I heard in the evening sky*'

'*The sound of thunders in the open expanse.*'

'*Darting into the distance, a flock of geese flying by.*'

I look out the window. Birds. Flying. Not possible.

'Hazel,' Robin says urgently, 'repeat: *A flock of geese flying by.*'

I get it this time, and he goes on:

'*Intoxicated by the storm, your wings flapped in gales of delight*–
no actions, please, Hazel,' he says, winking. I manage a sick little
smirk in response.

'*Arousing waves of wonder across the sky.*'

How far is the highway, I wonder. And how long before somebody catches us?

'*O wandering wings!*'

Focus, Hazel.

'*O wandering wings.*'

'*Your message fluttered*'

'*In the soul of the universe that day:*'

'*Not here, not here, but somewhere far away.*'

His voice has grown quiet. Damn it. I give him a look. He's been
working so hard to keep me going. I can't let him down.

'Robin,' I say, 'that's not half bad. One more time.'

And we go through it again, line by line.

'Now let me see if I've got it.' And I get halfway through before
he has to prompt me.

The third time through, I've got it.

'Amazing!' He cries. It's not, really. I've always been good at
memorizing things. But it's keeping us both afloat.

'Good old Tagore,' I say. 'Let's do it together.'

'Yes. A duet,' he says, his knuckles gleaming on the wheel. I'm
sweating like a pig, never mind the geese. But here we go down the
endless road, reciting Tagore in the bush outside Fox Creek, running for our lives and why not do it in poetry?

We get to that last line, and my head jerks around. I know I
heard another voice whispering,

'*Not here, not here, but somewhere far away.*'

Where the fuck is the highway? Where is Shanaya? I cannot
think of Édith, her hair like a crown of feathers, her mouth drawn
open, her eyes wild. I didn't physically hear it, but I know she was
screaming like Lzzy Hale, and I saw the birds swirl up in the smoke.

'One more time, Robin,' I say, and we go again, and I hear chanting in my ears, I hear another voice whispering.

'Your message fluttered in the soul of the universe that day
Not here, not here, but somewhere far away.'

And we drive out of the bush, me and a crew bus full of shell-shocked, fear-crazed victims. No, I correct myself, me and a crew bus full of survivors. I squeeze my eyes shut.

'Robin,' I say as quietly as possible, 'pay attention as we go, because you and I are going to have to come back here, once we get these people to safety.'

'Okay, Hazel,' is all he says.

The bush rolls past us.

The world is echoing silence.

I am leaving my best friend and my former nemesis, leaving my sisters, in the bush with my dead ex-husband, and I do not know whether they are dead or alive, don't know what state they're in.

I push down the panic knotting in my chest.

There is nothing else I can do but this. I cannot search for them, with all these people on the edge of utter panic. I cannot mention what happened.

I cannot say to them, 'Yes, you saw a tiger.'

Maybe they didn't see her. Maybe they didn't see a flock of sparrows whirling up. Maybe I'm crazy and my friends are dead and I am alone–

'Hazel,' Robin interrupts me, his voice controlled and barely wavering, 'this time you do the English, I'll do the Bengali, call and response, okay?'

Call and response.

Not here, not here, but somewhere far away.

DEVIN: RECKONING

'Let me do this for you?'

He waves the money, puts it on the table. She pushes it back to him.

'Kid,' says Sandra, 'you've always helped out plenty around here.'

He scuffs his toes and hunches his shoulders, blows out a breath.

'Yeah, well.' He says finally, 'I'm not a kid anymore.' He scowls, not at her, but out the window. 'And I'm not a bum.'

He remembers his father's voice, speaking as always in over-emphatic absolutes:

Don't be a bum. People might not say anything at first, but they'll come to resent you, even if they start by saying 'no, no, it's okay.' You pay your own way, and you'll always be able to look anyone in the eye.

'Devin!' Sandra's tone cuts through and he stares, shocked.

'You,' she says, her face grim and red, 'have never, ever been a bum, nor a burden. *Never. Never say that.*'

His gentle, slow-moving auntie startles him further by shooting out of her chair and stomping out of the room. He hears the back door bang and sits there stunned.

After a few minutes, he rises and slowly follows, out the door into the back garden. He sees her on her knees among the squash, and walks over, hauling up short when he sees she is crying.

She puts up her hand toward him.

'Aw, kid,' she says, her voice gruff, 'I'm sorry.'

He just stands there.

She sighs, shakes her head, wipes her eyes with the backs of her hands.

'You remind me so much of your dad, sometimes.'

She gives him a wry smile.

'He was so concerned about that–not being a bum. Not that that's a bad thing to avoid. It's just...it's something our dad, your grandpa, would go on about. *Don't be a bum*...but he'd add, *unless you plan to be the best fucking bum in the world.*'

Devin feels the shock of the rough language. His Auntie Sandra doesn't swear. Aunt Hazel, yes. '*Talks like a trooper, that one,*' he hears his mother's voice chiding.

Sandra heaves a huge sigh.

'Devin, I know you're having a hard time right now. And no surprise. But this is your home, and I've got the money aspects covered. And what I want for you is to...'

She stares around her, as if she has suddenly forgotten how to read from her garden the wisdom she has always found there. Then she sits back on her heels and pulls a stalk of onion loose.

'Devin. I know he hit you.'

Devin stares, begins to rock.

'Devin–Dev, I'm so sorry... I hate myself for it...'

Sandra shreds the onion stalk, gets up and steps closer to him.

'I knew. But I just didn't...know what to do about it. How to stop him. How to help.'

Devin takes a big ragged breath.

'Yeah. Well. You were his kid sister.'

She spins, stares at him. His face is red, his shoulders turtled in.

'He wouldn't have listened to you.'

'But I was an adult. Old enough to say something.'

Devin shakes his head.

'I mean...mom didn't know how to stop him. How could you? And it's not like that's all he did, either. He was a good dad, better than lots. He hit me when he didn't know what else to do.'

He sinks down on the patio bench, starts rocking back and forth.

'Aw, my boy,' says Sandra. She knows better than to crowd him;

she hates the way he flinches aside when she settles too near to him. She feels rage boiling up.

'I hate him.'

'Don't,' says Devin quietly. 'He was just a person. Just living with whatever made him who he was. He tried.'

She gazes at him then at the ground, grinds the broken onion stalk under her heel.

'I'm sorry I brought it up, okay? I mean–'

'It's okay. Really, it's okay,' he says.

She knows it's not healed or over, but she lets it lie.

HAZEL: DECIDER

So, we make the pavement, and I ask Robin to wait, there at the stop sign. He shakes his head. Guess I don't look too good.

'Robin,' I say, as firmly and clearly as I can, 'just for five minutes, okay? Come on!'

'No,' he says. I look at the heads popping up from the seats.

'Get down,' says Robin, gesturing broadly with his arm. They get down.

They might not handle five more minutes.

I look around.

Shanaya is not here.

Tigers don't get lost, I hear her mocking voice. Cry later.

'Never mind, Robin. Get us to town,' I say, even as he stamps down on the gas and we surge forward. People thump and shriek behind us.

'Sorry 'bout that,' he calls.

I'd say something smart in response, but I'm using all my energy to think about where the hospital is. I know I've seen it.

Robin turns confidently up a street.

'How do you know—?'

He flicks his thumb out the window at the 'H' sign as we pass it.

When we pull up at the hospital, I don't even get a chance to talk.

'Now listen,' says Robin, addressing the passengers. 'You must all stay quiet for just five more minutes, please. Hazel and I are going to get help.'

I try to protest, but he just grabs my good arm and pulls me toward the door.

'Now,' he says, under his breath, fiercely.

He exits first, half supporting me, then shoves the door closed behind us.

My head is buzzing. How long has it been?

The nurse or receptionist or whoever takes one look at us and runs. And returns in five seconds with a wheelchair and I drop into it.

I hear Robin talking to her. I hear her voice.

I will not pass out, not now.

And I don't.

But neither do they let me stagger to my feet and barge back out the door like the guy in the movie would do. *Whassname? Dick Francis is books... Bruce Willis. Jason Statham. Idris Elba. Whatever.*

Whatever they gave me for the pain and shock eats a few minutes and I return to clarity in a hospital bed, hooked up to an IV drip bag on a pole. Robin is there, and so are a couple of medical sorts in scrubs. The one that appears to be in charge introduces herself.

'I'm Alva,' she says. 'Got yourself shot, eh? Who told you you could do a convincing impersonation of a moose?'

I blink. Alva and Robin laugh.

'Just checking that you're fully alert,' says Alva, and she winks one twinkling black eye. Brown, chubby, mid-forties, with the accent of the northern bush communities. She shakes her head.

'Now, Hazel,' she says, 'how do you feel?'

'Not too bad,' I say, having considered the situation.

'Good,' she says. 'This is Amelia,' she wags her chin at the other nurse. 'Amelia and Robin here have got nine really frightened, badly abused people huddled up in a room meant for four, just down the hall. Before some idiot with a gun comes looking to finish what they started on you, how about you tell me your version of what the hell is going on here?'

She speaks as if it's all normal, in that way people do when they've seen a lot.

I look at Robin.

He stares back at me. Just for a few seconds.

Long enough.

I nod at him.

'Thanks, Robin,' I say. Neither of us needs the whole conversation that I might have imagined when I set out to rescue these people. Robin had taken matters into his own hands. And why wouldn't he?

He cracks a smile, reaches over and pats my foot. Then he and Amelia–a slightly shorter, thinner copy of Alva–turn around and leave us there.

We look each other over, Alva and me. I sigh. That's the thing. Life is not a Dick Francis hero story. Not James Bond or whoever. I am not a Hollywood actor. I'm a middle-aged, reasonably competent, adequately brave woman; a brownish woman who is a survivor, with survival as my main inheritance. Alva stands there with her arms crossed as I read her. I know she didn't waste any time reading me, she knew that 'moose impersonation' crack would land well.

'Alva,' I say, 'I'd talk a whole lot more easily if you could take me outside to wherever people smoke around here.'

DEVIN: GROWN

Devin looks around his auntie's garden and realizes this is no longer his sanctuary. It shocks him. This has always been a place he could come, in any weather, since before he became an orphan and simply moved in. Living with his Auntie Sandra had been so easy. She'd shown him the glory of getting your hands in the dirt, of paying attention to the living world of it, of approaching the garden as a living co-creator. Auntie Sandra's garden might look random to a professional designer, but all the parts flowed together. In the shambling, rambunctious brawl of perennial and annual there was a sense of certainty and order, and the boy had grown well here. So many times he's come to this place and found his auntie at work, and fallen in beside her, waiting for her to ask him what was on his mind.

But now?

Now he needs something else, some other place.

He can't be at peace here.

He's full grown.

He follows Sandra back into the house, at a loss for the right words.

She's standing at the kitchen sink. She is a mid-sized, broad-beamed woman, but he is well over six feet tall. She looks tiny to him now.

He realizes he doesn't need words. Devin pads quietly across to her, and gathers his little Auntie into his arms.

HAZEL: CLARITY

So.

Alva is the head nurse of this hospital. Since the government wised up and dismantled the health super-boards, regional hospitals have run their own shows. Mind you, Alva would have run this place anyway. She's that kind of woman. Thank God she's a smoker, too, or no way would I be allowed to be out here. As it is, she stuck me in a wheelchair and rolled me out herself.

We smoke, and I tell her what I know about The Harvestmen. Which is scarily little.

'Do I know exactly how those kids got captured by The Harvestmen? No.'

'Do I need to know particulars?' says Alva. 'No. I understand, it is bigger than you or me, it's systemic, same as any kind of violence done to any identifiable group of people.'

She takes a drag and I note the tattoo on her forearm, calligraphy reading *'Every Child Matters.'*

'I mean,' she continues, 'somebody is going to have to sort out the particulars of how and why. But me, here, I've just got to make sure my team treats whatever physically ails them, and keep them safe until someone–'

Someone.

'Alva,' I gasp, 'I need a phone. Now.'

She just fishes her cell out of her smock pocket and hands it over. I don't know Diya's number. *Stupid twenty-first century. It's in my phone's memory, not mine.*

'I don't know the number. I need my phone.'

'Stay calm, hang on,' she says, takes her phone back and taps a quick text. She lights another smoke, and a tiny orderly comes trotting out and hands me my phone and trots away, not without a pointed look at our cigarettes. Whatever.

I call Diya.

She answers right away. We had arranged code words for trouble, but I can't remember any of them.

'Diya,' I choke out, and she doesn't waste any time. She doesn't have to ask *Where is Shanaya? Why isn't she the one calling?*

'We're on our way,' she says, her voice over-controlled. 'Ramesh will drive me. Where are you? Fox Creek?'

'Yes. At the hospital.'

'Did you get them out?'

'We did.'

'Beti–' she whispers, and I know that feeling. She doesn't want to say Shanaya's name, doesn't want to give voice to the dread every mother knows.

And I don't know what to tell her. She's out in the bush. *She attacked a truck. I don't know if she survived.* I nod, foolishly, as if she can see me.

'I...don't know... But I believe...'

I can't lie to Diya. I take a deep breath...and she disconnects. I stare at the phone. I'd call back and tell her *No, no, don't worry*, but I can't lie to her.

I pick up my cigarette, take one last drag and grind it out, blinking hard.

'Hey,' says Alva, 'you okay?'

I nod.

'Yup. Our...our legal advisors...are coming out from Amiskwaciy. They'll be here in a couple hours.'

'And I've notified our local police,' she says, 'they'll be here in a couple minutes.'

She shakes her head, holds up a hand before I can protest.

'No. No need to worry. They're clean. They'd better be, their wives work here and we'd kill them if they were part of something like this.'

'Still, you don't sound surprised.'

'No.' She smokes. 'I'm not. Like I said, human trafficking is systemic and everybody knows it happens. We just pretend it doesn't happen exactly here. But, you know...' she taps her fingers on her tattoo, 'people like you and me, we can't forget that it happens, the worst happens right here. To our families. To people we know.'

We smoke a little more.

'And it goes on because mostly, we can't pin down the pattern, pin down all the arms of it. At best, we catch one person. And that person is not enough help, because they don't have a global view of what's happened to them. It's done to a group, but each individual experiences it alone.'

She smiles at me, the sad little smile of the frontline people. I nod. She knows.

In the midst of trauma, we don't tend to think first of how this must be happening to someone else too. We feel it happening to us first of all. And if we make it through the bloody immediate, then we know in our very bones or our soul or something that we can't survive it alone, and that's when we make community of those who wear the same mark, who vibrate with the same trauma, however you want to put it.

We speak at the same time.

'They're like magnets,' I say.

'They're like coyotes,' Alva says.

We share a bitter little laugh.

'So, picture kids coming across the world to a land completely unlike their own. They search for some landmark, something familiar, and more than that, for family,' I say.

'They need connection of some kind,' says Alva. 'So nobody has to *steal* them, they only have to be kind, to offer kindness and connection and shelter. *Come with me*, says the coyote, and the solitary pup follows the dancing coyote and then–too late–he looks around and sees he's surrounded by hungry predators who've lured him out into their territory and now he's dinner.'

'Like coyotes,' I agree.

'Magnetic coyotes,' Alva says. I like this Alva.

'They call themselves The Harvestmen,' I say, a little lightheaded, 'but you know, Harvestmen are a kind of invertebrate also known as Opilliones, and they hunt alone, and they're not really spiders at all.'

'Hazel,' says Alva firmly, 'you're done. I've kept you out here way too long. Put that out,' she flicks her chin at my newest smoke and when I hesitate, she grabs it from me.

'Here I was starting to like you, Alva,' I say.

She scoffs, takes the handles and wheels me back inside.

Someone wants to put me in a bed, but I figure I'm okay.

'Look,' I say, 'good as new.' And I pull on my boots and do a stupid twirl. Nobody who knows me would be convinced by that, fyi–I do not twirl–but I twirl and smile and promise to keep my shot arm in its sling.

Alva bustles in.

'Sit down,' she says. I sit. She conjures an orderly with a tray bearing a covered plastic bowl of something, and two cups of coffee.

'Chicken soup. Eat it.'

I'm surprised how good it tastes.

Alva looks around meaningfully and everyone is suddenly very busy.

'Now look,' she says, 'those kids are going to be okay, okay? I mean, they'll make it out of here. Your pal Robin is helping the police take statements. Good man, that.'

I just nod. What can I say? Robin and his namesake saved my life.

'Where do they get taken?' I muse to Alva. 'Is there a world of nasty brothels all around us, alongside us, where these victims are all warehoused?

'Maybe,' she says and drains her coffee.

'But maybe not. Maybe they're passed here and there one at a time. Say, one goes to a family who pays a fee for a live-in servant. And that family doesn't think they're human traffickers. They think they have made an arrangement with a legitimate broker of immigrant labourers. They think, our country and their country made a deal, and so we get to hold their passports and control their lives and movement and we're not doing anything wrong. We don't have slaves. We don't whip them. They look around at their lives and they can see that they are not a Southern States plantation with darkies in the fields; they don't have barefoot chattel in rags, they have a girl, or a couple of girls, who help them, and if they didn't give those girls a place and decent work, where would those girls be?'

'On welfare,' I reply to her rhetorical question. 'So they tell themselves, or on the streets, and so these theoretical people are not a force of social ill, they are the antidote, they are lifting these naturally lower people into a better life than they could get for themselves. Isn't it proof enough that they are here, all the way around the world, by themselves? They don't speak the language, or not properly. They are stupid or at least ignorant, and even if they are not strictly illegal, the are helpless. Stuck.'

'And yes,' she says, rising from her brief respite, 'there are some who are forced to be whores at the work camps. We try to stop that. We don't always manage. Sometimes we just find a body in the muskeg, by the road back to town.'

She's a bush woman. A small town stalwart. The daughter of Nehiyaw and Beaver people who have survived all manner of outrageous history—pass laws, road allowances, residential schools, enforced poverty, internalized festering abuses—she is one of the ones who never wavered. She found a good road and stuck to it. Here, she's head nurse. Head Nurse, or whatever her official title is, is just the modern version of what women like her have always been. I'm not surprised to hear that Amelia is her little sister.

'She's seven of nine,' says Alva. 'Like in the old Star Trek.'

'TNG' I say, nodding. The Next Generation. Alva and me, we are middle-aged. Amelia and Robin, they are that next generation.

And they have triaged those kids, taken statements and fed

them, and Amelia has rounded up a couple of stout lads who sit outside the door of the big room. Like that scene in the original Godfather, I think inconsequentially, except that these boys look sharp. They will not be distracted. They don't work for the bad guys.

Whoever the bad guys are. George would know, but George is dead.

And now Robin and Amelia have brought their own coffee and food, and we're all sitting at the picnic table out back. Alva and me smoking, Amelia and Robin drinking their coffee and refraining from saying we shouldn't be smoking. We stand downwind and socially distant, we're not total assholes.

I realize we still don't know the scope of this Harvestmen trafficking ring. But what matters, I think, smoking another one of Alva's cigarettes, is that it *is* we. It is me. And Robin, who was smart enough to evade the worst of the abuse by feigning simplemindedness before his captors, by pretending he was already high when they came with dope to tranquillize the captives.

'Showed them tablets in my hand, grinned like an idiot,' he says, as if it were no great thing. 'They looked at the prescription bottle I showed them and believed what it said. Thought it made me easy to manage. I let them think so.'

He looks away from us, and I study his profile. So much about this young man astonishes me. But then again, isn't that humanity–full of surprises…

It strikes me that I am exceptionally lucky.

Look at all the people I know, the fucking astonishingly brave and resourceful and perfectly normal people around me. Alva and Amelia fit right in with that same pattern that's been my fortune since I took fate in my hands and came to Amiskwaciy.

***

'Hazel,' says Robin, 'are you alright? Do you need to sleep? Or maybe more poetry?'

I open my eyes, answer his little smirk with my own.

'What,' I ask, 'would you have done if we hadn't come for you?'

His smile fades.

'I don't know,' he says seriously, 'but thankfully, I didn't have to figure that out.'

And I sigh and smile at all of them. Thankfully, I don't have to figure out what to do with and for the room full of trafficking victims. I've done what I can for them. Their situation is far bigger than one woman can sort out. Far bigger than three women, even if one of them is a tiger with a mother of world-moving energy and drive.

Diya's an academic; but she's also been in this with both hands from the second Shanaya called her about Édith. Shanaya called knowing Diya would be there. Diya will come with Ramesh, who knows immigration law and has resources, connections to put to work unravelling the hideous web that caught these young strangers. I do not even know their names, except for Robin.

The ones *I* know are out in the bush.

Now I just have to summon my strength and go back.

'Robin,' I say, 'why don't you walk me back to my room?'

'Tell me,' I say when we're safely inside and private, 'why didn't you tell Alva and Amelia about Édith and Shanaya?'

He starts shaking.

'Sit down,' I say. I pass him the half-full glass of water from the bedside table.

'I gather you saw–?'

'A tiger,' he whispers, 'and…'

He stares at me, shaking. I nod, shrug.

'I don't know what that thing was either. But yes, you did see a tiger.'

He gulps down all the water, and raises a weak half-smile.

'Well, obviously, Hazel, that is not something I'm going to tell to strangers. I mean, I suppose I could. They might just think it was the drugs we were all supposed to be on. Or stress. Mania. Madness. But they also might have insisted on coming with us to look.'

'Us?'

'Us.'

We have one of those stare downs people have when they don't know what to say.

I crack first.

'Look, Robin,' I say, 'That tiger is my friend. But I've never seen her in such a rage. And you, she doesn't know. I don't want you to get hurt.'

'Hazel,' he replies, 'you already are hurt. You are not fit to drive.'

'And you are?' Yeah, I'm an asshole. But he laughs.

'Well, I got us here.'

'Well, I'm not going back in that fucking bus.'

'Nor me. But Amelia has given me her keys and the okay to take you back to your hotel. For some reason, they trust that I will do just that.'

I do not know this young man, but for some reason I nod, and shrug and agree to let him drive me back to the scene of the crime.

DEVIN: DISCONNECT

The phone rings.

Devin pulls it out from his pocket, looks at the number, blows air from his mouth and sets the phone down on the kitchen counter.

'Hey, Roy,' he says, 'you want a snack? That was a pretty good walk, eh?'

He looks at the dog, still damp and a little muddy from their journey with Kjell.

'Maybe you need a bath first. Come on.'

The big pup willingly pads down the hall and at a gesture from Devin, hop-clambers into the bathtub.

He emerges clean and laughing. Devin chases him down the hall, waving a big towel.

'Roy! No, stop! Wait!' *Not the sofa.*

The big dog, as if hearing his unspoken plea, turns into the kitchen and beelines for his bowl.

Devin lays out the towel under the table and gestures at it.

'First, you sit to get dry. Then you get a snack.'

He takes the bowl from Roy's mouth and the pup sinks cheerfully onto the towel, content to wait for whatever treat comes his way.

'How about a couple of weenies?'

Devin breaks up the last of a package, drops them in the bowl, and shrugs off the thought that this is not health food for man or beast. Roy does not care.

The phone rings again.

Devin glances at it in passing, ignores it, picks up his guitar.

He plays for a while, working on the Gethsemane Breakdown, singing it thoughtfully, thinking about fathers and struggle and failures.

On the third call, he answers.

'Father E,' he uses the old familiar neighbourhood nickname, but his voice stands back.

'Devin,' says the priest. 'How are you?'

Devin lets it hang a minute before answering.

'I'm fine, thanks.'

'That's good. Good.'

The silence stretches. Devin knows this trick. He can picture the priest leaning against a countertop, patiently waiting for Devin to say what's on his mind. *Not this time,* thinks Devin. He's angry, and he can't even say why.

'Devin,' says the priest, breaking first, 'Your Auntie told me about the fire. I just…just wanted to call, see if you are okay.'

'I'm fine,' says Devin coldly.

'Devin,' the priest tries again, 'would you be open to a visit? You could come here? Or I could come to you?'

Devin holds his voice very tightly.

'I'm pretty busy just at present. Thanks, though. Got to go now.'

And he hangs up, then drops the phone back on the counter. He goes back to the sofa, sits down and curls into a ball, crying.

Roy comes out from his cave, and without asking, hops up beside the boy.

'I don't know what I'm supposed to say to him,' says Devin to the dog, to the air in general. 'How can I ever have talked to somebody like him? Servant of the Church. The Fucking Church that broke our people's spirits, and has gotten fat for generations, living off the carcass.'

The solitary hero sacrificed. Fine for the Son of God, but a hell of a finish for LeWayne.

Roy nestles closer.

'Dude,' says Devin into the big pup's ruff, 'you are still damp. Frankie is going to kill me.'

HAZEL: EX MACHINA

It's not too many miles back out to that place. But there will never be enough time to explain anything to Robin.

And yet, here he is, sitting beside me, real as the daylight, a young man driving grimly and firmly and well–it has to be said, the kid can drive–back down the road to the hell where we met. So, I owe him something. The best explanation I've got, which isn't much.

But Robin starts talking as soon as we're rolling.

'Hazel, let me tell you about my family. I want you to know why I'm here.'

He doesn't give me a chance to protest.

'My mother was my father's second wife. He was a lot older than her, okay?'

'This back in India?'

'No. Montréal.' I boggle. His accent strikes me anew. How didn't I hear the Québécois?

'I know,' he says, quirking his near brow at me. 'People out here often don't hear the Québécois, they see my face and think of India.'

He shrugs a very Gallic shrug.

'So you're French?'

'No. Canadian. Born in Ottawa, grew up there 'til I was ten, moved with my mom to Montréal when my folks split.'

'Oh.'

'She got tired of loving a man who was still in love with his first wife.'

'Uh-huh.'

He sighs, runs a hand through his boisterous hair.

'I remember it too. It was tedious. All he talked about, Diya this, Diya that. Diya was so brilliant. Such a phenomenal mother. On and on....'

'Diya?!' I look at him. It can't be.

'Diya Bhattacharya.' He says it high, angry, his voice pitched like a woman's. 'My poor mother said her name like a curse. And finally she told him she'd had enough of being compared to his precious Diya. If she was the light of his life, he should go find her and tell her all about it. She threw him out, no messing.'

I sit in stunned silence.

'She took me with her to Montréal, and we lived a pretty good life there. Mom is a professor of Comparative Literature.'

'Of course,' I sputter, grasping for sanity. 'Hence Rabindranath.'

'Yes. Tagore was her favourite poet. Father said he was over-rated. Talked about how Diya had criticized Tagore's politics and his writing as facile.'

I look at him. Look away. Don't know where to look.

'Robin,' I say, 'are you trying to tell me...?'

He turns off onto the gravel, shoots me a wild glance.

'How many Diya Bhattacharyas do you know of?'

'But it's impossible!'

'No.' He cracks an impish grin, slowing down and letting the engine quieten, easing down the road. 'It's improbable. But not *impossible*. Shanaya Bhattacharya is my half-sister.'

'But–!'

'But she's a tiger, you're going to say.'

I gape at him.

'How–?'

He lets the truck roll to a stop, throws it in park.

'Look, Hazel. Here's the thing. My mother hated Diya Bhattacharya because my father was obsessed with her. Me, I hated her too, because she made my mother so unhappy. But a boy grows up, and begins to question things he's heard.'

'How old are you?' I break in. He looks not a day over sixteen.

'I'm free, brown and twenty one,' he quips.

'Wow.'

He shrugs. 'Anyhow, I heard them fighting:

Why don't you go back to her? My mother cried.

Because she is a tiger! yelled my father.

And so is her daughter!

And he slammed a kitchen cabinet door.

Actual tigers! Fur! Stripes! Fangs! Bang!

Impossible! raged my mother. *You're drunk!*

Yes, I'm drunk, but I am telling you, that woman turned into a tiger before my very eyes! And what could I do? I ran away. Because she had turned my daughter into a tiger too. Witch! Witch! Monster!

And my father stomped out of the apartment like that, waving his arms and shouting, *Witch!*'

I shake my head. Maybe I'm still weak from blood loss, but I start to laugh.

'How is this funny?' cries Robin.

'Because,' I gasp, 'you do not know how many times Shanaya and I talked about how would she ever tell her mother about this peculiar affliction of being a shape-shifting tiger.'

Tears run down my face and I lean my head on my window, laughing weakly.

Robin sighs, and I subside.

'I did not know,' he says. 'I had no idea what I would find. I was in Calgary for a conference, and I thought, should I go up to Edmonton? Should I go find this Diya Bhattacharya? Maybe find my half-sister? See for myself this woman who had so messed up my dad's head that he was convinced she was a tiger, an actual shape-shifting tiger. You can imagine how unlikely that seems.'

'I can.'

'And I was nervous about it, too. So, I thought I'd just take a weekend, relax. Do like my father would do, go up to the mountains. But my father was a mountain climber. Me, I am an urban boy. I booked a last minute room at the Fairmont.'

'No,' I say weakly, my head lolling.

But of course I know it's true.

'I had no idea,' he says, shaking his unruly mop of hair. 'I was sitting in the hot tub, minding my own business, thinking about my father, and I overheard you two talking.'

'No no no,' I murmur, chuckling again. It's too absurd.

'Yes. You were there again at breakfast, and I heard her tell you who she was.'

He holds up a hand to forestall my obvious interjection.

'But why not introduce myself there and then? Because I am crazy.'

I just stare limply at him.

'I am the crazy son of a crazy soldier.' His voice drops into serious tone. 'My mother…this thing about his first wife being a tiger? That wasn't the only crazy thing my father said. He'd tell me stories sometimes. Some were crazy. He saw, he said, the actual Abominable Snowman.'

Robin huffs and shakes his head.

'But he also told me about things he'd done, as a soldier on classified missions, things he shouldn't have told me. The evil men do. And my mother overheard him telling me these things, and she pulled me away and sent me to bed, and that night she didn't shout. I heard him crying, though.'

'So?' I am as lost as a tiger in muskeg now.

'So,' he says, 'I joined the army. Not the regular service. Like my dad, I signed on for work that nobody is supposed to know is happening. For instance, I investigate human trafficking.'

Of course he does.

'Of course you do.'

When will people stop surprising me?

'So, that's why Édith told us about a boy in the first group.' Now he looks puzzled. I explain that Édith had actually told us, there was a boy in the group she escaped from who was there looking for his sister.

'How did you manage–?'

'To stay when they shipped off one group and brought in another?' He laughs mirthlessly.

'Neat trick. I really was sick. I couldn't stop them from beating her. Beating Aditi.'

'Why do you call her *Aditi?*'

'Aditi is a Hindu goddess. She is the personification of the boundless infinite. She is motherhood. Édith…she was as kind as a mother to us, when she came. When she was pretending to them that she was there to support her husband. There to help. It didn't last, of course. They were not long fooled. But now…' his voice trails off and we both just sit there in the quietly idling truck.

'Goddess of the Infinite. Aditi,' Robin whispers, looking out into the endless muskeg.

'Or Durga on her Tiger,' I whisper back.

And there they are, it seems. Or is it a trick of the light? Something is moving among the bristling density of spindly trees. And then it grows still.

'Let me go alone,' I say.

'No.'

'But yes. She does not know you. She might kill you.'

'But your arm.'

'It's clean. No blood to smell. And she knows me. Knows I'm looking for her.'

I open the door, step out into the grassy verge as slowly and smoothly as I can. I can still discern an eye, watching me, though stillness has rendered the creature nearly invisible. The eye looks wide and wild. I feel fear. But I move toward it.

It moves slowly back into the muskeg.

I don't look away. I follow, slowly, breathing all the calm I can muster, beaming with all my heart, *It's me. Shanaya. It's me.* Beaming love, beaming family.

I follow it, and it lets me, so long as I move slowly, it stays just beyond clear sight.

And then, it steps into a clearing, and I fall slowly to my knees.

It strikes me that I have no idea how the world works, how we move in this world of wonders and horrors. The evil men do. The petty things all assholes do.

The cosmic threads that bind us all somehow.

It's all so very unlikely. But it is real.

I am here now, spider webs on the half naked rose bushes, galls on the ends of little branches, the last thorns and abrasions of the summer all turned to hoar-frost artistry. All that, and a deer light-footing into the clearing, head up, eyes dark fathomless mysteries full of galaxies of love and meaning.

He turns and looks full at me, then fades back into the tree-line and I understand the compact then, between lives and kinds of living–*He has done this for you, come in answer to your incoherent prayers; and the cost is that you will never again eat deer meat. Not become a vegan, nothing like that. You eat from the land, ducks and eggs and moose and cattle and you don't scruple about your relationships with the domesticated ones, but just deer just now, because he looks at you in the grey and silver morning, and he looks to the other side of the clearing, and he raises his antlered head and huffs and fades back into the dark and you understand he is telling you where to go, showing you what you seek, and now you owe him not just a life but your reverence, and you will honour that in every bit of you from now on. You won't necessarily wear it in tattoos or regalia or anything that shows to anyone else, you'll wear it in your heart, that one morning moment of clarity in the mist. That is all that matters now.*

***

I step further into the clearing. A tiger lies in the grass. She cradles a broken tapestry, a little woman whose hair bristles like feathers. She nuzzles the body. The crumpled little woman does not move.

'Shanaya' I whisper.

She looks at me with her great sad golden eyes, and she shakes her head.

I see that she is wounded, blood beaded down one shoulder,

across her face.

'Can you walk?' *Can you hear me? Can you understand? Are you in there?*

The tiger struggles to her feet, but her head hangs low, her muzzle touching the limp body on the ground.

I approach, slowly, carefully.

She lets me get close enough to reach out. Reach down, slowly.

Suddenly, her great head thrusts up, her jaws open wide. I close my eyes. Who wouldn't?

There is a gust of hot wind. Then darkness.

***

'Hazel, open your eyes,' says Shanaya. She is crouched among the hummocks of grass and Labrador tea bushes, pulling tattered clothes around herself. She stands up.

Édith's body looks so peaceful, curved against the mossy, leaf-littered ground.

We just gaze at her without speaking. My father's voice rises in my memory.

Muskeg means medicine, my girl, he'd said, showing me the way to identify Labrador Tea leaves, telling me how they used to use sphagnum moss for wounds.

There isn't enough moss, I think inconsequentially, as Shan and I step closer, weep together leaning on each other.

And then a sparrow barges past, dodges at us and away.

'Oh!' I gasp.

'Another!' Shanaya whispers. And we step back from the body, startled, watching as three more sparrows fly into the clearing. The birds rise together, twisting against the sky. Six. Seven. Sparrows. Les Piafs. Namesakes of Édith Piaf, who is the namesake of Édith Serifa Pomeroy. They swoop and swing in arcs around us, diving and plucking, dropping down moss on the broken birdlike body of Édith. The cold air fills with a smell of muskeg. The sparrows begin to land, to push under the moss, or maybe my tear-filled eyes only make it seem so. Because I don't know how to fix this broken little woman, I want to believe in these birds.

How do you save somebody?

Sometimes you just stand aside for the Mystery, the little voices threading together a tiny ribbon of sound that fills the air as if it is the personification of the Infinite, of All Song.

DEVIN: WHAT NOW?

Devin walks into the room and Missy notices that everything subtly shifts, making way for him. It's not that he's big. He's been big for a long time. The difference, she supposes watching him walk toward her, is that he's stopped trying not to take up space.

He walks like a big bear rolling through the woods, his woods, and with that same calm aplomb of the bear who need fear no other, and need not fear himself either.

He knows himself.

The Bear Who Knows Himself pulls out a chair and sits down.

'Hey,' he says.

'Hey, Devin,' she replies. The waitress comes gliding, smiling and nearly bowing.

'What can I bring you, sir?' she asks.

'Chamomile tea, if you've got it,' says Devin. She hustles off to check.

'So...' Missy finds herself momentarily at a loss, watching the Bear, who until the night that Jim died had just been her younger cousin. She twists her silver ring, clears her throat.

'So, how are you, Devin?'

A slow smile lifts the corners of his mouth, and he tips his head to one side.

'I'm okay.'

His round eyes flash over her shoulder, out the window, then he meets her gaze again and nods.

'Yes, I think I'm pretty okay now, Miranda.'

He uses her real name, and somehow it feels vice-regal.

The waitress returns, triumphantly bearing a ridiculous little teapot and a sensible mug for Devin. Missy lifts her empty coffee mug. 'A refill, if you would?'

'Oh. Of course. Yes, yes,' The waitress departs The Presence.

Missy squints at Devin. He makes no sign that he's aware of his effect on the waitress. *Okay*, she thinks, *so maybe the Bear Who Doesn't Quite Know Himself, then.*

He pours some tea. The waitress brings more coffee, checks that all is well, withdraws from the Presence.

'Miranda,' Devin says, 'I need some advice.'

He blushes, just a little. The boy he'd been wouldn't have even asked.

'Anything,' she says.

He stalls, and she almost asks 'but why me?' As if he's heard her thought, he continues.

'You know I'd usually ask Auntie Sandra? Or,' and he bobs his head in the old, shy way,' or Father Efren. But...' and a frown creases his brow, 'they're, well, pretty wrapped up in each other, you know?'

'Yeah, you'd said,' Missy says.

'Seriously,' says Devin. 'I think...I think he's planning to leave the priesthood.'

Missy stares.

But it makes sense, really. Sandra has always had a kind of spiritual bent, which Missy supposes is part of what drove a wedge between Sandra and her sister Hazel, Missy's mother. No, not supposes. She knows it. All the times Hazel muttered and bitched about Sandra and her 'woo woo ways,' and actively pushed away the soft, slow-spoken Auntie. Missy blinks back a sudden tear, shakes her head. She and Devin might have grown up awkwardly anyway, with the age gap between them. *Why* doesn't matter. What matters is they have become good friends now.

'So, he's serious about Auntie Sandra?'

Devin nods. 'And she's serious about him, too. I've never seen

anything so…serious.' Disconcertingly, he laughs. Missy stares, and
then she laughs, too.

'Wow,' she says when they've composed themselves, 'so Auntie
and the Priest eh?'

'Well, I mean,' he says, 'it makes sense, right? She's always been
pretty holy.'

He says the word without embarrassment, admiringly.

'And he… well, you know,' he sips his tea, 'when I come to think
about it, he's always been kind of…missing a piece. And I think,
when I see them together, that it was her, or someone like her, all
along.'

'So, you're okay with that? With him? With them?'

Devin shrugs.

'No.'

He drinks his tea.

'I fucking hate the Church, Missy. And I can't take Father E seriously anymore. And I have no idea what Auntie thinks she's doing.'

Missy looks away, thinking about Devin's father. About how
alike Big Frankie and Father Efren were in some ways.

She studies her cousin, sees the traces of their teaching in him.
But something else, too. Something untouchable, something that is
purely him.

'So,' she says, 'you made any decisions about your path and that?'

He looks at her, looks away.

'I suppose you heard about the fire?'

'Devin,' she says, shaking her head, 'everyone heard about the
fire.'

'Thanks, by the way,' he says. 'You and Maengan both. Thanks
for not coming crowding me afterwards.'

'We texted.' She frowns. 'To tell the truth, I didn't think it was
enough.'

'It was enough,' he says decisively. 'Thanks for respecting me.'

She swallows, doesn't tell him that she would have come, had she
felt better. He doesn't need her excuses.

She shakes her head.

'Well, we're proud of you, you know.' She waits a bit, but he says nothing. 'So, you thinking about going in for fireman?'

He smiles.

'I dunno. Maybe. It's good work.' He drinks. 'I got to know one of the firemen on that call, you know. Pretty weird guy. I think you'd like him.'

'Why don't you invite him to join you at our house sometime?'

'Well,' says Devin slowly, 'I might. But I was thinking…do you think Frankie would mind if I had…had…a few people over to her place?'

'Come on,' says Missy. 'You know she'd love that. She'd be thrilled.'

It sounds stupid, and they laugh together, but they both know it's true.

I've been working on some songs, he thinks, but for now, Devin stays quiet, drinking his tea.

HAZEL: URBANE

Robin helps us into the truck, helps us lift in the limp form of Édith, helps Shanaya clamber in after her. I heave myself into the front and I fall against the seat. I know just looking at him that he's not about to say anything, not just now.

He drives us back to town, smooth, calm, quiet.

People are waiting there to help us. I look out the window at the infinite pattern of skinny trees. Some say they are all one creature, a being that is more a community than the simple sum of the individual bodies in it.

Some say so are we.

I don't know.

I don't know what mycelium of light connects families, what can draw a father to hunt for his unknown daughter, a son to seek his sister? Why do we love who we love? What does it mean to be bonded by love of the same person, or hate for them?

***

The lights of Fox Creek come upon us. Human. Urban. Lighting Robin's face. Displacing the mystical. No, I think, illuminating the human truth. We can't handle a steady diet of mystical darkness. We need solid ground. The hearth. The beaten path. The helpers. I don't have to know what to do next, because I'm not alone. I'm part of a community. I belong to Amiskwaciy, and to a network of people there, some of whom have come out here to help me help the people here who need help and healing.

'We're like muskeg,' I whisper.

'Hmm?' Says Robin.

'Nothing. Just thinking.'

Robin drives like he was born in this town.

'Robin?'

'Hmm?'

'How did you know you could trust Alva and Amelia?'

'I didn't.'

We turn in at the hospital.

Shanaya's eyes are closed and she might be asleep, and I should probably wake her up to keep her from succumbing to shock. But first one more thing.

'Robin?'

'Hmm.'

'What's your last name?'

'It is my father's name.'

'Robin Bacon?'

'Don't laugh.' But I glance across at him, and he's got the beginnings of a grin rising, and he winks as he tosses his unruly dark hair.

"What?!"

'Shit. She's awake.' I say to Robin. 'You're awake.'

'What did you say?' Shanaya repeats.

'Hi,' says Robin, utterly failing to look unterrified that his tiger sister is sitting behind him with one hand gripping the back of his headrest.

'Shanaya,' I say firmly, channeling Diya. 'Not here. Not right now. First things first.'

'Édith. Right,' she says, gulping a huge breath to steady herself.

'Édith. And you.'

Robin taps on the horn, and they open the ambulance bay door as if they're expecting him, and we drive inside. I'm barely breathing, trying to hear Édith. *Be alive.*

They bundle Shanaya into a wheelchair, strap her arm and

shoulder. She keeps her wild golden eyes fixed on Robin, as if she might devour him

'Where's Amelia?' asks Robin as they wheel a gurney over.

'Here,' says Amelia, striding into the scene and taking charge.

'What's this?' asks one puzzled EMT as they ease Édith out onto the gurney.

'Muskeg,' says Amelia in quelling tones. 'They packed her wounds with it. Good job.'

SHANAYA: FOUND

And Robin walks beside Shanaya's chair and just keeps quiet while they settle her into a bed. He sits down in a chair at the foot of the bed. To the attendant nurse, he says simply 'I'm her brother.' Nobody questions that. She keeps her eyes half-closed, observes him through her lashes. His face is nothing like Diya's but she finds lines she recognizes, and images flash through her mind:

Her father, bouncing her on his knee, singing some silly song. His father.

Her father shouting 'Monster! Witch! Monster!' Blood red light. Running toward them. Roaring. A blow. Pain. Terror. Hiding in the library among the potted palm trees. Her mother's voice rising into a bottomless roar. An engine in the night.

A mother tiger lifts her cub in tender jaws, carries her to a human bed. A human hand smooths her hair. 'It will be alright Beti. Life is life. It will work out. Beti. My daughter.'

'Your father, Beti? He fell off a mountain.'

But no memory of a ceremony. Just the roaring night and then the silence. Diya furiously cleaning her house. Diya some nights on the phone after Shanaya was meant to be asleep, her voice indistinct but bitter. Diya throwing all her fire into her work, pushing her daughter to work, to study, to make something of herself.

'We must never think ourselves lonely, Beti, so long as we choose to work diligently, there is all the opportunity we need to make a place for ourselves here.'

When the nurses are gone, Shanaya opens her eyes fully, looks full into the eyes of her brother. She can't decide whether he is predator or prey.

'Hi,' he says again.

HAZEL: EVERY ONE

Diya and Ramesh arrive.

Diya hugs me.

'Where is she?!'

'Wait,' I say.

'NO. Where is my daughter!?'

'Ma'am,' says Alva, swiftly there. 'She's sleeping. She's okay. Just sleeping.'

I think Diya's going to blow right past her but Alva stops her.

'She's with her brother.'

The unthinkable happens and Diya reaches out for me, grabs my arm for support, speechless with shock. Ramesh steps in and slips an arm around her, guides her to a chair and settles her. Alva has conjured an orderly with a tray.

'Orange juice. Drink,' she orders. And for a miracle, Diya obeys. I see her hand shaking, though, see her fingernails seem to twitch, see the light stripe for a moment across the back of her hand. I take the glass from her as she surges out of the chair, revived, and pull her close, ignoring the clamour of my shot arm in its sling pressed against her.

'It is alright,' I murmur in her ear. 'Durga mama, your Beti is safe. And he knows about her.'

'He knows?' she pulls back and stares at me wild-eyed, for a moment revealing the depths of a mother's anguish and fear.

'He knows who she is. Knows about your family.'

'How?'

'Come with me,' I say gently, 'she'll be so happy to see you. And she can introduce you to her half-brother.'

Ramesh looks like he wants to come along, but Diya puts a hand on his arm and shakes her head.

'She is really okay?' Ramesh asks me.

'Really.' I study him a moment. Opaque. No idea what to make of this guy. But Diya trusts him, and he seems to care for them both.

'Thanks for bringing Diya,' I say to him. 'And…for everything.' I sigh. So much for Shiva Daycare and the safe house idea. The kidnapped are in the hands of the Fox Creek authorities and we have nobody left to hide, so to speak. I wonder what Ramesh must think of us. He holds my gaze in a measuring stare for a long moment, and I'm no wiser. But, he's here, he brought Diya, he appears to have a firm grasp on when to listen and how to hear subtext.

I decide I like him.

I don't quite know if it's mutual, but Ramesh nods briskly and just as briskly turns to Alva. I hear him introduce himself and begin to ask questions as I tuck my good arm under Diya's elbow and walk a slightly shaky old academic down the hall. By the time we reach Shanaya's door, Diya Bhattacharya, legendary tiger mother, is in full control of herself again, and she pats my hand, winks, and opens the door with her elegant nose high, a slight and queenly smile on her lips.

Through the window, I see Rabindranath Bacon spring from his chair, turn his bright eyes to meet her gaze a moment, and step back as she sweeps to her daughter's bedside. He watches them, respectful, quiet, but unafraid, and then joins me in the hall.

'What now?' I ask.

'Now I wait a few minutes, and then when Shanaya texts me, I go back in and she introduces me to Diya Bhattacharya.'

He's come too far to back down, say his up-tilted chin and squared shoulders, but for a moment I wonder whether he'd like a handy mountain to fall off just now.

'It'll be okay, Hazel,' he says, as if I'm the one who should be worried.

It's a long evening. I stay out of the family discussion in Shanaya's room.

Instead, I sit down with Alva and Ramesh and one of the policemen—his name eludes me, he looks like a Ben—and we go over what we know about the fourteen migrant survivors, who are currently taking up four multi-bed rooms, a whole wing of this little hospital.

I can't stand it for long.

'Alva,' I say, 'you've got this. I need to go check on Édith.'

Alva purses her lips, nods permission, and I stand. She fishes her smokes and beaded lighter out of her smock pocket and pushes them wordlessly toward me.

'Thanks.'

'Mmm.'

***

Édith's just lying there looking pretty much as awful as she did that night at the cabin, but they tell me she's alive. As if she knows I'm there and can hear me willing her to move, Édith raises her skinny arm, splays her hand out. Is she having a spasm, a stroke, what?

Then she closes her fist, then slowly spreads her fingers open again, hand high, and gently lowers her hand. What's wrong with her?

Car accident, is what we tell the good people, but it's not that. Not as simple as that.

She's bruised all over, but they say there's no other damage. She looks so small, so helpless there.

Her eyes open. She looks over at me.

She whispers, *'One more,'* and falls asleep again.

I can't stand looking at her, so I go out for a smoke.

The wind is cold, and a beady eyed sparrow hunches on the window sill, staring at me.

Suddenly, I look again in the last of the short day's light. There is a shadow on the glass, the pathetic shape of wings.

Why do birds fly into windows?

Because they don't see the glass.

Or because they're trying to get in.

In the muskeg, the sparrows spun and flew and dropped moss and Shanaya roared and I fell and then they birds were gone. Gone where? Édith. Le Piaf. Sparrows. *Les piafs. A cloud of sparrows flies together, battered by the storm. They share one soul and that soul homes on a hearth where she knows there is safety. Landing, she becomes her human self, knocking on the door. I open the door...*

I stub out my smoke and take a deep breath, slow myself... I walk toward the sparrow. The sparrow eyes me sourly. I wonder if it's as simple as this? Maybe I'll just reach out my hand and the sparrow will hop across...

No. The sparrow's having none of it. She lifts off. She's exhausted, can't get height, comes to rest on a concrete parking berm. Her beak is slightly open.

Sparrows are tough. But any bird can die of shock and thirst and I stop staring and run around the building, run inside, burst into Édith's room. The windows, the windows.

The windows don't open.

Stand back then. I wrap my hand and I hammer on the glass, punch with all my power. One. Two. Three blows and the glass cracks, but it won't break, though I use my whole good arm like a battering ram and smash at the window.

It's no good. Safety glass. Fucking safety glass. My shot arm throbs, my good arm too.

Stop, Hazel. Think.

If Sandra were here, she could pull off that *calm your breathing, open your heart* thing. But I smell of blood and fear and I can't change that fast enough to coax the missing part of Édith, that last sparrow of her soul that's sitting panting on a parking berm. Birds die so easily.

Use your head, Hazel. There isn't time for mystical connection here. I think of Sandra and her chickens, back in the farm days.

Édith does it again, lifts her arm, flutters her fingers, her arm falls. I smell of blood. But on the chair, tattered but folded, lie Édith's clothes. I paw through the pile, pull out a camisole–it's got a heart on it, sewn in sequins that catch the light ridiculously.

I rush back outside, thanking all the deities attendant that nobody heard me whacking the window. They're looking at me. I lift my chin in as casual a nod as I can manage, stride as purposefully as possible out the door with Édith's camisole tucked under my shot arm, head around the back.

The little bird droops on the concrete berm. I edge as close as I dare, hardly breathing. Improbably, I hear my brother Frank's voice in my head, laughing at me as he pelts me with snowballs and I run. *You throw like a girl! I throw the snow, the ball comes apart in midair, becomes a million sparkling useless sequins of light falling on his laughing face.*

I throw like a girl–which is to say, with all my heart and mind focused on the target. The camisole floats up, drops down on the sparrow. She struggles weakly for a moment but I'm there, I've got her. I cradle her against me as I run, both my arms throbbing, both our hearts hammering, back into the hospital. People turn, move toward me, I shoulder Édith's door open, stagger to her bedside. How does this work? Birds in the muskeg, nestling under moss. I open the camisole, hands shaking, tuck the panting bird into Édith's limp hand, drop the camisole over it. As I'm falling, my hammering heart and the thumping of approaching feet roar in my ears. My eyes swim closed, but I swear I see a bird, one sparrow–one more– become a shimmer in the air above Édith's bed.

I wake up in a hospital bed beside Édith Serifa Pomeroy, and I look across at her. She's awake too, and looking whole again, bird-bright eyes and her spiky hair, her shoulders hunched a bit like wings. She sees I'm awake.

'Hazel.'

'Yeah.'

'Thanks.'

'Don't mention it,' I say, surveying my two bandaged arms.

She sounds weak, but she won't shut up.

'Hazel.'

'Yeah?'

'How did you know … to bring her in…'

'You told me. The first time we met. Your name. Édith. Like Piaf. The Little Sparrow.'

The pain meds make me sleepy, but there are things that need saying.

'Édith.'

'Yes?'

'That first day?'

'Yes?'

'I should've just punched you in the face.'

'Probably,' she giggles, a bit raggedly.

I drift away, thinking of the first time ever I saw her face. She was eighteen and beautiful and I opened the door of my house and she was there, in my kitchen, and she turned when the door opened, and I cocked my fist and snarled '*Hello there Edith*' and she corrected me, '*Édith, like Piaf, the Little Sparrow. The French Singer. She is my inspiration.*' And in that moment of suspended time I knew I could choose: fight this ridiculous creature for a man I hated, or grab my girls, put on my boots made for walking, and spring myself from the trap.

If I had hit her? The fight would not have been over. She thought she won that day, but I chose.

I chose. She chose. George chose.

You can't save people from themselves.

Even the starfish have agency. If they want to be on the beach, even if it kills them, that is their right. But if you see a starfish where you know it's in peril, then you have to decide, did it choose this, or was it thrown upon this shore by powers beyond its own?

And you do have a responsibility, if you discern that maybe it needs to get back to the ocean, to use your arms, to lend a hand and send it home. But if it wants to be there, let it lie.

And if a bird needs to get in a window, let it in.

And maybe you can't tell what a starfish wants. What a bird really needs.

But as for humans, maybe that's what we're here to find out, how we shape each other for better and for worse, and just where is the line between a punch in the face and letting go.

The little bitch is humming again. I know the song now. Édith Piaf. The Little Sparrow. Careening through her own tragicomic, epic life and singing with all her might:

Non, rien de rien

Non, je ne regrette rien

I regret nothing? I can't say that's true. But as I start to drift back to sleep I can admit that I'm glad I took that bird in my hand...

'A bird in the hand is worth two in the bush,' I murmur groggily and it makes me laugh.

'What?' Édith asks.

'Rien,' I say, 'Rien de rien.'

THE END

ACKNOWLEDGEMENTS

This story is a work of fiction.

It's not meant to define the experience of any identifiable group of people, though I do hope that the experiences of the characters herein find some resonance with the lived experience of readers of diverse backgrounds and life experiences. Once again, I offer thanks to the many good people I know who embody the best of the characters in *Urbane*, and I ask forgiveness for any sense of judgement or exposure anyone might feel if a character looks, sounds or thinks a bit too close for comfort.

Urbane is a sequel. So it would never have happened with *Humane*, so again thanks to all the folks who made *Humane* possible, who read and enjoyed it and let me know. In particular, thanks to my dauntless publisher, Netta Johnson of Stonehouse Publishing, for her impeccable sense of what I need as a writer in terms of space, encouragement and patience. Likewise, thanks to my miraculously patient little family who endured and supported my ridiculous process, and my larger family who keep me grounded in the real world.

Anna Marie Sewell
Amiskwaciy Waskahikan/Edmonton, Alberta, Canada

ABOUT THE AUTHOR

Anna Marie Sewell is a multi-genre writer and artist. After an undistinguished career in theatre and reasonable success in poetry, she launched her first novel, *Humane*, in 2020, also with Stonehousepublishing.ca. *Urbane* is Ms. Sewell's second novel. While writing it, she also saw her first works as a choral lyricist published: Journey Song (cypresschoral.com, 2022) and At First Light (hinshawmusic.com, 2023).

Anna Marie Sewell lives in Edmonton, close correlate of *Urbane*'s Amiskwaciy, capital of Alberta, Canada. Find more of her work via prairiepomes.com